TREASURY OF LITERATURE—READTEXT SERIES

ENCHANTED ISLES

Selected and Edited by
ELEANOR M. JOHNSON
Editor-in-Chief
My Weekly Reader
and
LELAND B. JACOBS
Professor of Education
Teachers College, Columbia University
Specialist in Children's Literature

CHARLES E. MERRILL BOOKS
Columbus, Ohio

TREASURY OF
Readtext Series
LITERATURE

The books in this series are:

TREAT SHOP
• • •

MAGIC CARPET
• • • •

ENCHANTED ISLES
• • • • •

ADVENTURE LANDS
• • • • • •

CHARLES E. MERRILL BOOKS
Columbus, Ohio

Dallas   San Francisco   New York

A CHARLES E. MERRILL BOOK. Copyright, 1954, by Wesleyan University and Artists and Writers Guild, Inc. Printed in the U.S.A. by Western Printing and Lithographing Company. Published simultaneously in Canada by Thomas Nelson & Sons (Canada) Limited.

CONTENTS

CONTENTS

CONTENTS

CONTENTS

VII — REAL PEOPLE

Illustrated by Robert Magnusen

VIII — JUST AROUND THE CORNER

Illustrated by William De J. Rutherfoord

Animals
Wild and Tame

Be gentle and kind
To the Auk and the Hind;
Be good to the gallant Gnu:
For animals all—
Both tremendous and small—
Have feelings, exactly like you.

—*Dorothy Hall*

Little Georgie Sings a Song

Robert Lawson

*New folks were coming to the old house on Rabbit Hill!
All the animals were very excited. The right folks would
mean a good garden, good days to come.*

*Little Georgie, one of the big rabbit tribe, was sent by
his family to get Uncle Analdas, who lived several miles
away. They all thought Uncle Analdas would enjoy watching things happen at the Hill.*

It was barely daylight when Little Georgie started his
journey. In spite of her worrying, Mother had managed
to put up a small but nourishing lunch. This, along with
a letter to Uncle Analdas, was packed in a little knapsack
and slung over his shoulder.

Father went along as far as the Twin Bridges. As they
stepped briskly down the Hill, the whole valley was a
lake of mist on which rounded treetops swam like floating
islands. From old orchards rose a mounting chorus as the
birds greeted the new day.

The houses were all asleep. Even the dogs of the Fat-Man-at-the-Crossroads were quiet, but the Little Animals were up and about. They met the Gray Fox returning from a night up Weston way. He looked footsore and sleepy, and a few chicken feathers still clung to his ruff. The Red Buck trotted daintily across the Black Road to wish them good luck and good morning. But Father, for once, had no time for long social conversation. This was Business, and no rabbit in the county knew his business any better than Father—few as well.

"Now, Son," he said firmly, "your Mother is in a very nervous state. You are not to add to her worries by taking unnecessary risks or by carelessness. No dawdling and no foolishness. Keep close to the road, but well off it. Watch your bridges and your crossings. What do you do when you come to a bridge?"

"I hide well," answered Georgie, "and wait a good long time. I look all around for dogs. I look up the road for cars and down the road for cars. When everything's clear I run across—fast. I hide again and look around to be sure I've not been seen. Then I go on. The same thing for crossings."

"Good," said Father. "Now recite your dogs."

Little Georgie closed his eyes and dutifully recited: "Fat-Man-at-the-Crossroads — two Mongrels. Good Hill Road—Dalmatian. House on Long Hill—Collie, noisy, no wind. Norfield Church corner—Police Dog, stupid, no nose. On the High Ridge, red farmhouse—Bulldog and

Setter, both fat, don't bother. Farmhouse with the big barns — Old Hound, very dangerous —'' and so on he recited every dog on the route, clear up to Danbury way.

"Excellent," said Father. "Now, do you remember your checks and doublings?" Little Georgie closed his eyes again and rattled off, quite fast, "Sharp right and double left, double left and double right, dead stop and back flip, right jump, left jump, false trip and briar dive."

"Splendid," said Father. "Now attend carefully. Size up your dog; don't waste speed on a plodder—you may need it later. If he's a rusher, check, double, and freeze. Your freeze, by the way, is still rather bad. You have a tendency to flick your left ear; you must watch that. The High Ridge is very open country, so keep in the shadow of the stone walls. Porkey has lots of relatives along there and if you are pressed hard, any of them will gladly take you in. After a chase, hide up and take at least ten minutes' rest. And if you have to *really* run, tighten that knapsack strap, lace back your ears, and *run!*

"Get along with you now, and mind—no foolishness. We shall expect you and Uncle Analdas by tomorrow evening at the latest."

It was gray and misty as Little Georgie crossed Good Hill Road. The Dalmatian still slept. So, apparently, did the Collie up the road, for all was quiet as he plodded up Long Hill. People were beginning to stir as he approached Norfield Church corner. Little plumes of blue smoke were rising from kitchen chimneys, and the air was pleasant with the smell of frying bacon.

As he expected, the Police Dog rushed him there. Loping along with tantalizing slowness until they were almost on an old fallen apple tree buried in briars, he executed a dead stop, a right jump, and a freeze. The bellowing brute overran him, and plunged headlong into the thorny tangle. His howls were sweet music to Little Georgie as he hopped sedately along toward the High Ridge. He wished Father had been there to note that during the freeze his left ear hadn't flickered once.

The sun was well up when he emerged on the High Ridge. On the porch of the Red Farmhouse, the fat Bulldog and the Setter slept soundly, soaking up its warmth. On any other occasion, Little Georgie would have been tempted to wake them, but he kept dutifully on his way.

The High Ridge was a long and open strip of country, very uninteresting to Little Georgie. The view was beautiful, but he didn't care especially about views. The brilliant blue sky and the bright little cream-puff clouds were beautiful, too. They made him feel good; but frankly, he was becoming slightly bored. So, to ease his boredom, he began to make a little song.

The words had been rattling around in his head for some days now. The music was there, too, but he couldn't quite get them fitted together. So he hummed and he sang and he whistled. He tried the words this way and that way, he stopped and started and changed the notes around. Finally, he got the first line of the song so that it suited him.

The Leap at Deadman's Brook

It must have been his song that made Little Georgie careless and almost led to his undoing. He scarcely noticed that he had passed the house with the big barns. And he was just starting to sing his first line for the forty-seventh time when there came the roaring rush of the Old Hound right on his heels.

Instinctively, Little Georgie made several wild springs that carried him temporarily out of harm's way. He paused a fraction of a second to tighten the knapsack strap, and then set off at a good steady pace. "Don't waste speed on a plodder" was Father's rule. He tried a few checks and doubles and circlings, although he knew they were pretty useless. The great fields were too bare, and the Old Hound knew all the tricks. Georgie looked for woodchuck burrows, but there were none in sight. "Well, I guess I'll have to run it out," said Little Georgie.

He pulled the knapsack strap tighter, laced back his ears, and *ran*. And *how* he ran!

The warm sun had loosened his muscles, the air was invigorating, Little Georgie's leaps grew longer and longer. Never had he felt so young and strong. His legs were like coiled springs of steel. He was hardly conscious of any effort, only of his hind feet pounding the ground. Each time they hit, those wonderful springs shot him through the air. Why, this was almost like flying!

He glanced back at the Old Hound, far behind now, but still coming along at his plodding gallop. He was old and must be tiring. Why didn't the old fellow give up and go home?

And then, as Georgie shot over the brow of a slight rise, he suddenly knew. *He had forgotten Deadman's Brook!* There it lay before him, broad and deep, curving out in a great silvery loop. Whether he turned to right or left, the loop of the creek hemmed him in and the Old

Hound could easily cut him off. There was nothing for it but to jump!

This sickening realization had not reduced Little Georgie's speed; now he redoubled it. The wind whistled through his laced-back ears. Still he kept his head. He picked a spot where the bank was high and firm. He spaced his jumps so they would come out exactly right.

The take-off was perfect. He put every ounce of leg muscle into that final kick and sailed out into space. Below him, he could see the cream-puff clouds mirrored in the dark water. He could see the pebbles on the bottom and the silver flash of frightened minnows. Then, with a breath-taking thump he landed, turned seven somersaults, and came up sitting in a clump of soft grass.

He froze, motionless except for heaving sides, and watched the Old Hound come thundering down the slope, slide to a stop, and take his way slowly homeward.

Little Georgie did not need to remember Father's rule for a ten-minute rest after a good run. He was blown and he knew it, but he did remember his lunch. So he unstrapped the little knapsack and combined lunch and rest. As his wind came back and his lunch went down, his spirits came up.

Father would be angry, and rightly, for Georgie had made two very stupid mistakes. He had let himself be surprised, and he had run right into a dangerous trap. But that leap! Never had any rabbit jumped Deadman's Brook, not even Father. Georgie marked the exact spot and calculated the width of the stream there—at least eighteen feet! And with his rising spirits, the words and the notes of his song suddenly tumbled into place.

Little Georgie lay back in the warm grass and sang his song—

> *New Folks coming, Oh my!*
> *New Folks coming, Oh my!*
> *New Folks coming, Oh my!*
> *Oh my! Oh my!*

Frosty's Surprise

Lavinia R. Davis

Terry was spending the summer with her cousins, the Wades, at Hobby Horse Hill. For the first time, she had learned to care—really care—for horses. Now she was to ride in the local horse show. Her horse was Frosty, a former cow pony.

When the day of the horse show came, Uncle Herbert took them all over to the show grounds in the station wagon. They had ridden the horses over the day before.

Kate led the way to the ring, and Terry and Rod followed. The boxes were still bare and empty, but there was a cluster of people around the ring to watch a saddle-horse class.

Terry looked the saddle horses over carefully. They were almost like pieces of machinery, with their high action and their small, arched necks. Pretty, but sort of useless and silly, Terry thought. Not one of them sturdy and dependable like Frosty. Terry had almost decided that a small bay mare was going to win. Then the announcer called the winners into the center and a flashy chestnut came out again with the blue rosette fluttering from his bridle.

"Whose horse is that?" Terry asked.

"Belongs to Mr. Anthony Brett," Kate said. "Its name's White Socks."

There was a sudden sharp, shivery blast from the announcer's bugle as the first jumping class began. In a little while, the jumping was over. There was another sharp call on the bugle, and the announcer shouted through his megaphone: "Get ready for Class 45. Local saddle horses next."

Terry looked at Kate. For the first time in weeks, the old shiver of fear went up and down her back. Why did her class have to come so soon?

Terry had barely time to get into the saddle and ride into the ring. She caught sight of Pam Anderson mounted on the Bretts' White Socks, and she forgot all about being frightened. For the first time, she was on the defensive about Frosty. She patted his little neck. He might not be as showy as White Socks, but he was a better local saddle horse.

They started in with a walk, trot, walk, and canter. Frosty's trot was still too slow and his canter too fast. Terry patted him reassuringly. He'd cantered on the right foot, and he'd done his best.

Then the announcer signaled them into the middle of the ring, and called to them through his megaphone. There were so many good horses in the class that it was hard to pick out the best. Would they please trot by twos past the jumps of the outside course so that he could see which hack had the best road gait?

The announcer arranged them in twos, and Terry found herself paired with Pam Anderson. Terry bit her lip as White Socks pawed the ground and arched his neck disdainfully. White Socks made Frosty look smaller and humbler and less like a show horse than ever.

They watched the first pair, and the second, trot around the course. In the third pair, one horse had a swift, splendid trot, and the other lagged hopelessly behind. Pam giggled. "That's the way we'll look," she said, and then apologized for being rude.

The announcer hurried them forward, and they started

to trot. With the first step, Terry's heart sank. White Socks was outdoing himself. His free, showy trot carried him yards ahead of Frosty. Frosty joggled along as best he could, but he wasn't in the same class.

They got down the short straight stretch of the course and to the corner. White Socks was way ahead, and Terry was scared that Frosty would break into a canter to catch up. "Easy, pet, easy, pet," she said. It was bad to trot slowly, but to break into a canter was a disgrace.

Terry rounded the corner and saw White Socks change his gait. She looked again, and saw him break into a fast, unmistakable gallop.

Terry stared, and then she understood! A small white terrier had run out across the road. White Socks wasn't used to surprises. He had dashed off before Pam could stop him.

Terry expected to see Pam pull White Socks down into a trot. White Socks kept right on going. The dirt came up in clumps from his flying feet, and his head was down. White Socks was running away!

Pam tried to give and take on the reins, but it didn't do any good. Once the great chestnut horse had made up his mind to go, the light show bridle was useless.

Terry hesitated for a moment. Frosty was going along at his own safe pace. The dog barked at him, but he only cocked his ears forward and went on. Terry looked ahead. White Socks was off the dirt road now, and running wildly across a field to the concrete highway.

Terry didn't wait another second. "Step on it, Frosty," she urged. "We've got to stop him."

The small pony flattened out into a gallop. Terry could hardly feel the rise and fall of his back as they raced along. This was what Frosty had learned as a foal in the West, and it was still his best act.

Riding Herd

White Socks made awkward work of the field, and they gained rapidly. But there wasn't a second to lose. Terry saw a truck roaring southward on the state highway. The driver didn't see them, and there wasn't one chance in ten that Pam could swerve White Socks away from that road.

"Hurry, Frosty!" Terry urged. "Hurry!"

The little pony drew up to the horse just as he reached the road. Terry had one arm out for the reins, but Frosty had ideas of his own. With his whole weight, he shoved into White Socks!

For a minute, Terry's leg was crushed into White Socks' soft side. She felt Pam's hair in her mouth and heard the shriek of brakes. In another minute, Frosty had forced White Socks into a turn. They began to gallop back almost the way they had come.

Terry gasped for breath as she straightened herself in the saddle. Frosty had come into his own. He had ridden herd over White Socks!

In no time, Frosty had herded White Socks back to the show grounds. A groom ran out and swung on White Socks' bridle. The horse dragged him for a few feet. The creature's nostrils dilated, its sides heaved, its eyes rolled wildly. But at last it stood still. At the same moment, Frosty stopped in his tracks.

Terry patted his wet sides. "Good boy," she whispered. "Good boy!"

She rode slowly over to the side of the ring, and then she heard the applause. "Good work!" somebody called. She looked around and saw Uncle Herbert shouting like a school boy. "Good work, Terry! Oh, good work!"

Terry felt dazed. At first, she had been embarrassed for Frosty among all these show horses. Now he was a hero. Terry watched the announcer give out ribbons to four big, handsome horses. She started to go toward the gate, and her heart was singing. Frosty might not be a show horse, but he was a clever cow pony, and everybody there knew it. He didn't need a ribbon to show he was good!

Terry dismounted almost into the arms of the Wade family. "Oh, Terry, that was great!" "Gee, Terry, how did you do it?"

"That was some surprise!" Kate said.

Terry patted Frosty's white, speckled nose. "It wasn't my surprise," she said. "It was Frosty's."

Papa Takes Over

Rutherford Montgomery

Jerome Kildee, a retired stone-carver, lived in the California hills in a house built against a giant redwood tree. With Jerome lived two raccoons—Old Grouch and his wife Charmine—and their babies, and Mama and Papa Skunk and their family.

Then Charmine was killed by Strong Heart, Donald Cabot's dog. Emma Lou, who lived near-by, hated Donald and his dog as much as she liked Jerome; and she was determined to revenge Charmine's death. Jerome had begun to carve a headstone for Charmine.

Jerome opened his eyes and sat up. Sunshine was coming in through the big window. Old Grouch was sitting by the window in the sun.

Jerome sighed deeply. As he expected, the young raccoons had not returned. He felt sad. The place would be pretty quiet with only Old Grouch around.

"Just a couple of old bachelors," he said.

Old Grouch grumbled an answer. He was hungry and wanted his breakfast.

Jerome laced his boots. Then he washed his face. Old Grouch marched around the room grumbling and scolding. Jerome fried a strip of bacon and an egg for himself, and a strip of bacon and an egg for Old Grouch. As he ate, he studied the figure he was chiseling out of the cream-colored stone.

He hurriedly finished breakfast and washed up the dishes. Then he set to work upon the figure again. He worked steadily into the afternoon. He was now adding the fine touches, a chip off there, a sliver here. He had caught the coy look Mrs. Grouch always lifted to him. He worked awhile on the lower lip. Then he got up and stepped back. Yes, there was the little lady peeping over the edge of her box at him.

Old Grouch came wandering across the meadow. His face wore a discouraged frown instead of the scowl which was usually there. He had searched far for his wife, but had failed to find any of her tracks except very cold ones. He marched into the cabin and began demanding lunch. Jerome gave him some canned meat, and then made himself a sandwich.

Jerome got the sheet of paper Emma Lou had written the inscription on. He was busily figuring a layout for the wording when a shadow darkened the doorway. He looked up and saw Donald Roger Cabot standing there.

Donald Roger stepped into the cabin. In spite of an

attempt to appear bored, he showed quite a little interest as he looked around.

"You ought not to come here," Jerome said.

"I came up to pay you for the raccoon my dog killed," Donald said stiffly. He reached into his hip pocket and pulled out a billfold.

Jerome looked quickly toward the door. Donald Roger smiled coldly. "I tied Strong Heart to a tree down the hill," he said.

Jerome's cheeks began to flush. The boy's manner and his offer to pay for the death of Mrs. Grouch stirred anger in him. "You can't pay for a thing like that," Jerome said sharply. "And you better go before Emma Lou shows up."

Donald shrugged his shoulders. He looked around the cabin. "Nice fireplace," he said.

Jerome stirred impatiently. Donald was looking at the figure on the table. He bent forward. "Not bad at all," he said. Then he added, "It's good."

In spite of his worry and dislike, Jerome was pleased. "It's not finished yet," he said.

"A raccoon looking over a wall watching you," Donald said. "What is it for?"

"It's a headstone," Jerome said.

Donald turned and looked at Jerome. Then he turned back to the figure. "I'll get some red stone and you can do a dog's head for me. I'd like to have it for my room."

"I'm not doing any work for anybody," Jerome said.

"You're doing this for that redhead, aren't you?" Donald asked.

"It goes on a grave," Jerome said.

Donald looked at Jerome again. The man was as odd as his house.

Jerome was looking through the window. Suddenly his mouth closed into a tight line. Emma Lou was coming across the meadow. "There she comes now," Jerome said.

Donald turned and glanced out through the window. His air of bored laziness left him. "Golly," he said. "I can't let her catch me here."

"No way for you to get out." Jerome stepped to the door. Perhaps he could get Emma Lou away from the house long enough for Donald to escape.

"Hello!" Emma Lou greeted him. "Did you get it finished?" She was looking down at the rock chips scattered on the doorstone.

"Not yet," Jerome said, without moving out of the doorway. "Thought you might take a look in the woods. The young raccoons went off and haven't come back." As he spoke, Jerome stepped out on the doorstone and looked down the slope. He expected Emma Lou to follow him.

"Soon as I have a peek at the lovely lady." She stepped past him quickly.

Jerome jumped, but he could not stop her. So he followed her into the house. Looking over her shoulder, he was relieved to see that Donald had vanished. He did not have to make more than one guess as to where he was. Jerome was certain Donald was under the bed.

Emma Lou drew in her breath as she looked upon the figure. She clasped her hands. "Oh! Oh! It's beautiful! Why, she's smiling up at us!"

Jerome beamed proudly. Emma Lou moved about, looking at the statue from different angles. "I'll bet no raccoon ever had such a fine headstone," she said.

"Lucky I had a nice piece of stone left," Jerome said. Then he heard a noise under the bed. He glanced quickly at Emma Lou. She hadn't heard the noise.

Papa Enters the Scene

At that moment, Papa Skunk appeared at the door. He had heard Emma Lou's voice and had roused himself to see if she had brought anything for him. He walked over to her, waving his tail and churring a warm welcome. Emma Lou reached down and scratched his head. Papa looked up at her. She hadn't brought anything. He cocked his head and listened. He had heard a faint sound under the bed, and sounds from there meant mice. With a swish of his tail, he skipped across the floor and ducked under the bed.

Emma Lou laughed. "He'll be out in a minute with a mouse," she said. "He's a fast worker."

Jerome had an idea things were going to start happening.

"Say!" Emma Lou burst out suddenly. "I forgot all about the little raccoons. When did they leave?"

"They left last night right after supper. Haven't been back since," Jerome said. Out of the corners of his eyes,

Jerome was watching the blanket hanging over the edge of the bed. It was waving gently.

Emma Lou's lips tightened. "All the more reason for my bagging that Cabot dog."

"I don't think he'll bother up this way," Jerome said. He was beginning to squirm. His ears were strained for the sound of small feet stamping angrily. Unless young Cabot had iron nerves and sense enough to play dead, there would be an explosion.

At that moment, they heard a dog barking outside. The yelps and barks were rapidly coming closer. Emma Lou jumped to her feet. "That dog!" she shouted.

A black form darted across the floor. Papa had heard the dog and was on his way to defend his family. Jerome caught Emma Lou's arm. "Wait," he said.

Emma Lou struggled to get away from him. She could see Strong Heart through the doorway. He was bounding up the path. Then she saw Papa marching down the path to meet the dog.

Strong Heart was a society dog. The black and white animal walking toward him looked somewhat like a cat. In fact, he was certain it was a cat. It would turn and flee, but it had used poor judgment. It would never be able to get to a tree before he nabbed it.

Jerome pulled Emma Lou back a few feet. "Let Papa handle this," he said.

Emma Lou stopped pulling and started to grin. Papa had started stamping his feet and churring savagely. Then he did his handstand. Strong Heart let out a wild and eager yelp. This would be the easiest cat kill he had ever made. His mouth opened wide.

Papa's hind feet hit the path, and like a cowboy facing a badman, he fanned his gun and fired. Strong Heart's wild yelp changed to a stifled gurgle, which was followed by a wheezing gulp. He hit the path with all four feet planted and digging frantically. He lunged away toward the woods.

Emma Lou and Jerome dived out into the open as a
wave of highly scented air rolled into the house. When
they were in the clear, they stood and held their sides and
laughed. Strong Heart had looked so foolish.

Finally Emma Lou said, "You'll have to move out for
a while."

Jerome nodded. "If Papa could have taken him on down
the hill a little way." Then he chuckled. He was thinking
about Donald under the bed.

Emma Lou started off down the hill. "If I hurry, I may
get that dog," she said.

Jerome didn't think she'd catch even a glimpse of Strong
Heart. The dog had been traveling fast when he entered
the woods. But he was glad Emma Lou was leaving for a
little while.

Jerome turned toward his house. Donald burst forth,
holding his nose. "Phooey!" he burst out. "Do you keep
skunks too?"

"I have seven," Jerome told him, with a pleased grin.

"Seven?" Donald Roger looked startled. "I saw only one. The darned thing licked the end of my nose."

"Your dog trailed you here and tried to kill it." Jerome was still grinning. "I don't think your dog will ever bother another skunk."

"When he gets back from the dry cleaner's, he'll be locked up, I know that." Donald started away. "I don't smell so good myself."

Jerome walked to his house. There really wasn't any damage done. Papa was standing beside the doorstone, waiting. He beamed up at Jerome. Papa did not seem to have a bit of scent on himself. It was easy to see he was all puffed up over his victory.

After a while, Emma Lou came back.

"See him?" Jerome asked.

"No, he ran like a deer. I guess Papa did a better job than I could have done," Emma Lou said.

Duff Strikes Back

William Marshall Rush

When he was only a year old, Duff, the black bear, had wrecked the Doone cabin in search of food. Danny Doone and his uncle, Web Doone, had been hunting Duff ever since. Danny hunted Duff fairly, with a rifle. But Web Doone used an illegal set-gun—a shotgun that would go off if an animal touched a string tied to its trigger.

Insects had begun to be troublesome. Duff batted at the big horseflies that buzzed around his head. They even lighted on his nose and bored through the skin to suck his blood. Hitting at them with his paws rid Duff of the pests for a moment, but a fresh swarm came right back.

When evening came the horseflies left, but droves of small buffalo gnats crawled into his fur. The high, singing whine of mosquitoes added to his unhappiness.

He hunted a creek and crawled into a deep pool. That helped for a while. Flies, gnats, and mosquitoes did not like a wet bear. But as soon as his fur dried, they came down upon him with renewed strength. He loped off along a bear trail. But he could not outrun the pests.

The trail ended at some mineral springs in a big, grassy park. Duff caught sight of a pool of blackish mud in the middle of a clump of bushes. He splashed out to it, and sank down until only his eyes and nose were exposed. He brushed a muddy paw across his face so that even it would be covered with mud. When he crawled out, he let the mud stick to his coat until it dried, making an armor that neither mosquitoes nor horseflies could get through.

Duff climbed a tree and settled down for his first peaceful nap since warm weather came. Of course, the dried clay crumbled and brushed off as soon as he began his nightly travels. But insects did not bother so much at night. He went back to the wallow at the salt lick whenever they became troublesome in the daytime.

One very hot day, he had put off his mud bath longer than usual. Horseflies drove him in a fast lope toward the wallow. Fifty feet from the wallow, Duff lengthened his stride and galloped his best.

Suddenly, there was a deafening roar and the bitter smell of lightning. Red-hot pain burned his hip. He was thrown clear off his feet by the impact. He had run squarely into an almost invisible cord stretched across the bear trail, pulling the trigger of Web Doone's set-gun. If the bear had been traveling at his usual leisurely pace, the charge of buckshot would have hit him just behind the shoulder and killed him instantly.

As it was, he was still alive. He bawled loudly in pain and rage, tried to stagger to his feet, but fell again. Slowly, painfully, he got up and stood on three legs. He gave one more loud bawl. Then he shut his lips tightly together and without another sound crawled back along the bear trail, stopping to lie without moving for five, ten, fifteen minutes at a time to gather strength to go on. Within a mile, he came to a small creek. He lay for a while in its cooling water.

He was so weak he could hardly drag himself forward. At last, he crawled out of the creek and into a spruce swamp. He floundered out to where the mud was soft and lay there, while Web Doone hunted the forest looking for him. The blood trail was plain as far as the creek. There, the man lost all trace of the bear.

Web gave up. "Critter will die, anyway," he muttered. "No use for me to be wearing myself out looking for it."

For three days, Duff lay in the wallow—three days of absolute quiet. Mud stopped the flow of blood. It drew some of the soreness from his shattered hip. He needed something more, however, than mud and rest. He needed medicine.

On the evening of the third day, he eased himself out of the swamp, an inch at a time, and hobbled into the pine forest. Oregon grape was in bloom. Its roots were both blood purifier and tonic. Duff lay down to scratch them from the soil. He went on to a spring for a cooling drink. Anemones grew near by, and he dug some of the roots.

Duff lay for hours in the sun, ignoring flies and mosquitoes, while the herbs hastened his recovery. In a week, he could touch the foot of his hurt leg to the ground. In two weeks, he could bear some weight on it. It was stiff and very sore. But he would soon be able to travel the bear trails again.

The first day Duff was able to go along the trails for any

distance, he found Web Doone's camp. The horses were picketed in the meadow near the tent. Duff stole back into the forest to wait until darkness fell. Then, as silently as a mountain cat, he crept upwind toward the clearing.

Duff Watches His Chance

The man sat beside a campfire in front of his tent. Duff crept close. Web stared into the flames, not moving except when he got up to stretch his arms and add new fuel to the blaze.

Duff had no fear of fire. He had been near lightning fires in the forest, and he loved the smell of wood smoke. So he lay there, nose stretched out, watching the man who had tried to kill him.

Suddenly Web Doone moved uneasily, got up, and turned to peer into the darkness toward the bear. Duff did not move. His beady eyes did not shine in the light as the big ones of a cat would have done. Web stared for a moment, turned, and sat down. Duff eased forward until he was only thirty feet from the man. A swift rush, one blow of a front paw, the bear's powerful jaws could close on the man's neck—and Web Doone would never aim another set-gun. Duff opened his mouth and licked his chops with a red tongue. His great shoulders tightened.

One of the horses stamped restlessly. The other snorted as if displeased at some small sound, some drifting smell. Web peered toward them. These were signs that a good woodsman did not ignore. He stood up, picked up his rifle, and went off grumbling to see what was wrong with the animals.

Duff heard the sound of his boots on the soft ground. The bear could see him dimly as he walked through the darkness. He was gone for a long time. Duff did not move. When the man came back, he tossed the ends of his fire together. It blazed up brightly. He went inside his tent. Duff heard the rasp of canvas as tent flaps were tied shut. The man grunted as he pulled off his boots. Finally, there was the sound of heavy breathing. The man was asleep.

Duff stole back a hundred yards from camp. He could hear the horses greedily cropping grass. He had been afraid to attack Web Doone at the campfire. Web was too dangerous. But horses were different.

A foot at a time, the bear crept ahead, upwind, into a fresh breeze out of the southwest. Crunch—crunch—the horses did not sense that anything was wrong. Duff was only fifty feet away when one of them jerked up his head with a snort.

"Woof! Woof! Woof!" The bear exploded into sound and action at the same instant. He threw himself toward the horses, a thing of terror out of the quiet night. "Woof!"

The nearest horse reared, the picket pin pulled out, and the animal raced down the trail. The other horse's rope broke, and it was scarcely ten yards behind. Duff did not chase them far. There was no need. They would run for miles before they stopped. Duff limped off to a bear trail and vanished.

At daybreak, Web Doone bent over a plain track in the soft earth beside the creek. It was a bear track, but it was unlike an ordinary bear. On the right side, the hind footprint was ahead of the front footprint, as it should be, like that of a deer. On the left side, however, a lame hind leg shortened the stride a little. The hind footprint was squarely on top of the front one, more like the track of a wolf or coyote. The man would know that track, next time he saw it.

That afternoon, as Web went wearily after the runaways, fifteen miles from camp with halters over his arm, Duff came back to the tent. Once before, he had made a mess of men's belongings in a spirit of curiosity and play. This time, seeking revenge, he was more thorough. He ripped the white tent to ribbons with his sharp claws, banged the stove about until he had smashed it flat, smashed the water pail by sitting on it, tramped on pots and pans, and chewed the saddles.

He ripped open packages of food, squashed cans, threw sacks of flour and sugar against the trees until the sacks burst. He scattered what oats were left among bushes along the creek. He even dragged Web Doone's blankets to the creek, wrinkling his nose in disgust at the strong man smell, and left them to float away.

He went back to see what was left, discovered a hunk of bacon and a kettle of dried stewed fruit, and ate his fill. Then he hobbled off into the forest, sure that nothing was left of that camp that could possibly be of use to any man.

And everywhere he left a plain track, the unmistakable track of a bear with a lame hind leg.

He traveled without stopping, day after day, away from the land where he had been so cruelly hurt. Fifty miles away, across the mountains, he came to a new land. Here were many black bears, a world of good food—and no men. Duff grew as fat as a cub and went into winter quarters, alone, under the roots of a giant spruce tree.

The Cat
and the Bear

"Who are *you?*" asked the cat of the bear.
"I am a child of the wood,
I am strong with rain-shedding hair,
I hunt without fear for my food,
The others behold me and quail."
Said the cat, "You are lacking a tail."

"What can you *do?*" asked the cat.
"I can climb for the honey I crave.
In the fall when I'm merry and fat
I seek out a suitable cave
And sleep till I feel the spring light."
Said the cat, "Can you see in the night?"

Said the cat, "*I* sit by man's fire,
But I am much wilder than you.
I do the thing I desire
And do nothing I don't want to do.
I am small, but then, what is that?
My spirit is great," said the cat.
                    —*Elizabeth Coatsworth*

Troubles With a Penguin

Richard and Florence Atwater

When Admiral Drake sent Mr. Popper a real live penguin from the South Pole, the Poppers were rather pleased. They named their new pet Captain Cook, and decided that he should live in the refrigerator.

The day after the penguin's arrival was quite eventful at the Poppers'. First, there was the service man, and then the policeman, and then the trouble about the license.

Captain Cook was in the children's room, watching Janie and Bill put together a jigsaw puzzle. He was very good about not disturbing the pieces after Bill had spanked him for eating one. He did not hear the refrigerator service man come to the back door.

Mrs. Popper had gone marketing for canned shrimps for the penguin, so that Mr. Popper was alone in the kitchen to explain to the service man what he wanted done to the refrigerator. The service man put his tool bag down on the kitchen floor, looked at the refrigerator, and then at Mr. Popper, who, to tell the truth, had not shaved yet and was not very tidy.

"Mister," he said, "you don't need no ventilating holes in that there door."

"It's my icebox, and I want some holes bored in the door," said Mr. Popper.

They argued about it for quite a while. Mr. Popper knew that to get the service man to do what he wanted, all he had to do was to explain that he was going to keep a live penguin in the icebox, and that he wanted his pet to have plenty of fresh air. He felt a little stubborn about explaining, however. He didn't want to discuss Captain Cook with this unsympathetic service man, who was already staring at Mr. Popper as if he thought Mr. Popper was not quite right in his head.

"Come on. Do what I said," said Mr. Popper. "I'm paying you for it."

"With what?" asked the service man.

Mr. Popper gave him a five-dollar bill. It made him a little sad to think how many beans it would have bought for Mrs. Popper and the children.

The service man examined the bill carefully, as if he didn't trust Mr. Popper too much. But at last he put it in his pocket, took a drill from his tool bag, and made five small holes in a neat pattern on the refrigerator door.

"Now," said Mr. Popper, "don't get up. Wait a minute. There is one more thing."

"Now what?" said the service man. "I suppose now you want me to take the door off its hinges to let in a little more air. Or do you want me to make a radio set out of your icebox?"

"Don't get funny," said Mr. Popper indignantly. "That is no way to talk. Believe it or not, I know what I'm doing. I mean, having you do. I want you to fix a handle on the inside of that box so it can be opened from the inside."

"That," said the service man, "is a fine idea. You want an extra handle on the inside. Sure, sure." He picked up his tool bag.

"Aren't you going to do it?" asked Mr. Popper.

"Oh, sure, sure," said the service man, edging toward the back door.

Mr. Popper saw that for all his words of agreement, the service man had no intention of putting on an inside handle. "I thought you were a service man," he said.

"I am. That's the first sensible thing you've said."

"You're a fine kind of service man if you don't even know how to put an extra handle on the inside of an icebox door."

"Oh, I don't, don't I? Don't think I don't know how. I've even got a spare handle in my tool bag, and plenty of screws."

Mr. Popper silently reached into his pocket and gave the service man his last five-dollar bill. He was pretty sure that Mrs. Popper would be annoyed at him for spending all that money. But it could not be helped.

"Mister," said the service man, "you win. I'll fix your extra handle. And while I am doing it, you sit down on that chair over there, where I can keep an eye on you."

"Fair enough," said Mr. Popper, sitting down.

The service man was still on the floor, putting in the final screws that held the new handle in place, when the penguin came out to the kitchen on his silent pink feet. Surprised at seeing a strange man sitting on the floor, Captain Cook quietly walked over and began to peck him curiously. But the service man was even more surprised.

"*Ork,*" said the penguin. Or perhaps it was the service man. Mr. Popper was not sure just what had happened when he picked up himself and his chair a moment later. There had been a shower of flying tools, a slamming of the door. And the service man was gone.

These sudden noises, of course, brought the children running. Mr. Popper showed them how the refrigerator was now all remodeled for the penguin. He showed Captain Cook, too, by shutting him inside it. The penguin at once noticed the shiny new inside handle and bit it with his usual curiosity. The door opened, and Captain Cook jumped out.

Mr. Popper promptly put Captain Cook back inside and shut the door again, to be sure that the penguin learned his lesson. Before long, Captain Cook became quite skillful at getting out. He was ready to be taught how to get inside when the door was shut. By the time the policeman came to the back door, Captain Cook was going in and out the refrigerator as easily as if he had lived in one all his life.

Captain Cook and the Law

The children were the first to notice the policeman.

"Look, Papa," said Bill. "There's a policeman at the back door. Is he going to arrest you?"

"*Gook,*" said Captain Cook, walking with dignity to the door.

"Is this 432 Proudfoot Avenue?"

"It is," answered Mr. Popper.

"Well, I guess this is the place all right," said the

policeman. He pointed to Captain Cook. "Is that yours?"

"Yes, it is," said Mr. Popper, proudly.

"And what do you do for a living?" asked the policeman sternly.

"Papa is an artist," said Janie.

"I'm a house painter, a decorator," said Mr. Popper. "Won't you come in?"

"I won't," said the policeman, "unless I have to."

"Ha, ha!" said Bill. "The policeman is afraid of Captain Cook."

"*Gaw!*" said the penguin, opening his red beak wide, as if he wanted to laugh at the policeman.

"Can it talk?" asked the policeman. "What is it?"

"It's a penguin," said Janie. "We keep it for a pet."

"Well, if it's only a bird . . ." said the policeman, lifting his cap to scratch his head in a puzzled sort of way. "From the way that fellow with a tool bag yelled at me outside, I thought there was a lion loose in here."

"Mamma says Papa's hair looks like a lion's sometimes," said Bill.

"Keep still, Bill," said Janie. "The policeman doesn't care how Papa's hair looks."

The policeman now scratched his chin. "If it's only a bird, I suppose it will be O.K. if you keep it in a cage."

"We keep him in the icebox," said Bill.

"You can put it in the icebox, for all I care," said the policeman. "What kind of a bird did you say it was?"

"A penguin," answered Mr. Popper. "And by the way, I might want to take him walking with me. Would it be all right, if I kept him on a leash?"

"I tell you," said the policeman, "honestly I don't know what the municipal ordinance about penguins is, with or without a leash, on the public streets. I'll ask my sergeant."

"Maybe I ought to get a license for him," suggested Mr. Popper.

"It's certainly big enough for a license," said the policeman. "I tell you what to do. You call up the City Hall. Ask them what the ruling about penguins is. And good luck to you. He's kind of a cute little fellow, at that. Looks almost human. Good day to you. Good day to you, Mr. Penguin."

When Mr. Popper telephoned the City Hall, he found it was not so easy to learn whether or not he must get a license for his strange pet. Every time he would explain, he would be told to wait a minute. Much later, a new voice would ask him what he wanted. This went on for considerable time. At last, a new voice seemed to take a little more interest in the case. Pleased with this friendly voice, Mr. Popper began again to tell about Captain Cook.

"Is he an army captain, a police captain, or a navy captain?"

"He is not," said Mr. Popper. "He's a penguin."

"Will you repeat that, please?" said the voice.

Mr. Popper repeated it. The voice suggested that perhaps he had better spell it.

"P-e-n-g-u-i-n," said Mr. Popper. "Penguin."

"Oh!" said the voice. "You mean that Captain Cook's first name is Benjamin?"

"Not Benjamin. Penguin. It's a bird," said Mr. Popper.

"Do you mean," said the phone in his ear, "that Captain Cook wishes a license to shoot birds? I am sorry. The bird-hunting season does not open until November. And please try to speak a little more distinctly, Mr.—Topper, did you say your name is?"

"My name is Popper, not Topper," shouted Mr. Popper.

"Yes, Mr. Potter. Now I can hear you quite clearly."

"Then listen," roared Mr. Popper, now completely outraged. "If you folks at the City Hall don't even know what penguins are, I guess you haven't any rule saying they have to be licensed. I will do without a license for Captain Cook."

"Just a minute, Mr. Popwell. Our own Mr. Treadbottom of the Bureau of Navigation of Lakes, Rivers, Ponds, and Streams has just come in. I will let you speak to him personally. Perhaps he knows this Benjamin Cook of yours."

In a moment, a new voice was speaking to Mr. Popper.

"Good morning. This is the Automobile License Bureau. Did you have this same car last year, and if so, what was the license number?" Mr. Popper had been switched over to the County Building.

He decided to hang up.

Not Necessarily So

Is there gold at the foot of the rainbow?
  Not necessarily so—
And yet there are riches in rainbows,
  As every wise man should know.

Laughter and wonder and beauty
  And even wisdom may glow
Through many a quaint old story
  Not necessarily so.

—Dorothy Hall

The Old Woman and the Tiger

Retold by Mary Hemingway

In the village of Gwai-lin-di, between the curve of the Yellow River and the Great Wall of China, there lived a poor old widow woman. Every day, her only son went up into the mountains behind the village and gathered faggots and brought them home to his mother. She would exchange some of the faggots with her neighbors for a few handfuls of millet to cook in the pot. So from day to day they just got by.

But one day, while her son was up in the mountains gathering faggots, an enormous tiger leaped out of the bushes and ate him up. Some other boys from the village who were gathering faggots near by ran back to the village and knocked on the door of his mother's house. "Old woman, old woman, a terrible tiger has eaten up your son!"

The old woman was very indignant. Now that she had no son to gather faggots for her, how could she get along from day to day? She would have no millet to cook in the pot, and no faggots to burn under it. So she determined to see that justice was done.

Seizing her stick in her hand, she hobbled straight to the headman of the village. She shook her stick under his nose and cried angrily, "A tiger from the mountains has eaten up my only son. Now how can I get along from day to day? There will be no millet to cook in the pot, and no faggots to burn under it. I demand that you capture this tiger and punish him, so that justice may be done!"

But the headman of the village replied, "The tiger ate up your son in the mountains behind the village. I have no authority outside the village. There is nothing I can do about it. So, old woman, I would advise you to go quietly home."

But the old woman did not go quietly home. She took her stick in her hand, and she hobbled along the dusty road until she came to the city of Funjo. There she went to the house of the magistrate of the city. She shook her stick under the magistrate's nose and cried angrily, "A tiger from the mountains behind the village of Gwai-lin-di has eaten up my only son. Now how can I get along from day to day? There will be no millet to cook in the pot, and no faggots to burn under it. I demand that you capture this tiger and punish him, so that justice may be done!"

The magistrate of the city of Funjo replied, "The tiger ate up your son outside of the city limits of Funjo. I have no authority over him. There is nothing I can do about it. So, old woman, I would advise you to go quietly home."

But the old woman did not go quietly home. She took her stick in her hand, and she hobbled along the dusty road until she came to the capital of the province of Shansi.

There she went to the palace of the governor of the province. But the gates were shut. No one would let the old woman in. So she banged on the gates with her stick. She shouted and scolded so long and so loudly that finally the governor inside the palace heard the noise. He sent his servants running to find out what was making such a terrible racket. They returned with the little old woman.

She shook her stick under the governor's nose and cried angrily, "A tiger from the mountains outside the village of Gwai-lin-di has eaten up my only son. Now how can I get along from day to day? There will be no millet to cook in the pot, and no faggots to burn under it. I demand that you capture this tiger and punish him, so that justice may be done!"

Now the governor of Shansi at that time was a kind and a just man. He replied, "Venerable old woman, this seems to me to be a very reasonable request. Certainly, if justice is to be maintained in my province, this tiger must be punished."

The Case of the Dutiful Tiger

So he sent a score of his best hunters into the mountains behind the village of Gwai-lin-di. They captured the tiger, and bound him heavily with ropes, and loaded him onto a cart. Then they dragged him to the Court of Justice. A great crowd of people followed behind to see the tiger brought to justice.

The governor was dressed in his finest purple silk robes. When the tiger had been brought before him, the governor stepped forward and said:

"Tiger, it has been proved by many witnesses that you ate up the only son of this poor old widow woman while he was in the mountains gathering faggots for his mother. Now she is left alone in the world to starve. The punishment for murder is death. Therefore, Tiger, I sentence you to be dragged to the East Gate of the city, there to have the head chopped from your shoulders with a sharp

ax. You have heard the sentence, Tiger. Have you anything to say?"

"Only this," replied the tiger. "I am sorry now that I
ate this woman's son. If I had known that he was the
only son of his mother, and she a poor widow, I would
certainly never have done it. Nevertheless, I do not see
that justice will be served by beheading me. It will not
bring back the old woman's son. It will not leave her any
better off than she was before. And of course *I* will not
like it at all. I have a better suggestion. If you will spare
my life, I myself will be a son to her, for as long as she
shall live. Every day, I will bring faggots to her. Every
day I will bring her deer, or a rabbit, or a fat pheasant
for the pot. I will be indeed a dutiful son to her, a truly
filial tiger."

"This suggestion sounds to me like a very reasonable
one," said the governor. "However, the old woman must
agree to it. Venerable old woman, if this tiger will promise
to be a dutiful son to you, for as long as you shall live, will
you consent to adopt him?"

"He looks to me like a very honest tiger," replied the
old woman. "If he will swear by the souls of his ancestors
that he will do all that he has promised, I shall be content
to adopt him for my son."

"Do you swear by the souls of your ancestors to do all
that you have promised, and to be a good and dutiful son
to this old woman, for as long as she shall live?" asked
the governor.

The tiger raised his right paw, and replied solemnly, "I do."

So the governor ordered the tiger unbound, and the little old woman took her stick in her hand, and led the tiger back to the village of Gwai-lin-di. And all the villagers came out of their houses, and went down the road to meet them. The old woman introduced them all to the tiger by name, and they all said that they were very glad to meet him—in a social way.

Then the tiger bounded up into the mountains. He returned with a perfectly enormous bundle of faggots, which he dumped by the old woman's door. Then he went hunting, and returned with a freshly killed deer. The old woman invited all her neighbors in, and there was a great feast in honor of the dutiful tiger.

And every day after that, the tiger brought plenty of faggots and fresh meat for the old woman. And the old woman lived in plenty and happiness for much longer than anyone would have thought possible.

Then one morning, the tiger bounded up to the old woman's door, and heard a great sound of weeping and wailing inside the house. And the neighbor woman came to the door and said, "Tiger, tiger, your mother is dead." The tiger gave a great howl of sorrow and grief.

On the day of the old woman's funeral, the tiger walked in the front of the procession with a white mourning band around his head. After the funeral, he lay down beside the old woman's grave with his head on his paws. For three whole days and nights, he neither ate nor drank nor slept. At the end of that time, he arose and ran around the grave three times.

Then, with a tremendous roar, he bounded off into the mountains. And he was never again seen by anyone in the village of Gwai-lin-di.

Knute, the Giant Bullsnake

Glen Rounds

Knute was no ordinary snake. He was never content to be just an ordinary snake. He wanted to be the greatest snake that ever was. From the time he was just a little fellow, he was all the time taking stretching exercises to develop his muscles. So he grew very fast, and it is said that when he was three years old he was able, with his bare tail, to lasso and hogtie a full-grown buffalo bull. And that is something that most snakes cannot do even when they are much older.

When he was full grown, he was so long that, when he was taking a drink out of one of the Great Lakes, his tail, likely as not, was scaring the daylights out of homesteaders out by where McCook, Nebraska, now is. What we call the Great Plains was once his bed ground. Tossing in his sleep over the course of some centuries, he wore down the trees to sage brush and smoothed off the hills as we know them now.

During the Indian wars, Knute joined up with Custer's army, where a missionary taught him to talk. He was quite a pet with the men because of the tall tales he could spin of the things he'd seen here and there. But he scared the Indians so bad that the soldiers never could catch them, and he was so big that the General was afraid he'd accidentally squash a bunch of men some day. So the General asked him please to leave, which was all right with Knute, he being very accommodating. Anyway, he was a little tired of army life.

So Knute went off up into the Bad Lands in South Dakota, where no one much was living at that time. For a while, he was quite happy there, game being plentiful, so he had plenty of time to think. Not that he had anything special to think about, but he just liked to think.

However, one day when he was prowling around near Laramie, Wyoming, he came across a railroad track, the first one he'd ever seen. He thought it was some kind of a varmint trail. So he sat himself down to wait for the varmint. Directly, along came a freight train a mile and a quarter long, with two engines—and he swallowed the whole thing.

The train crew jumped in time to save themselves. But what a time they had trying to make the boss believe their story when they tried to explain the loss of their train! Finally, the boss fined them each a dollar and a quarter. Being as train men were kinda hard to get those days, he hated to fire them.

But poor Knute! It was easy enough for him to digest the freight cars, which were loaded with meat for the army posts. But when he finally digested the boilers, all that steam turned loose in his stomach gave him a bad stomach ache. At first, the steam had a pressure of one hundred and ninety pounds to the inch, just as it came from the boilers. But the indigestion gave him fever, and the fever made more steam, and so it went. Before long, he had three hundred pounds pressure and it was still a-going up. He felt pretty bad.

He had to have something done, but he couldn't go to the Indian medicine men. They were scared stiff at the sight of him. Then he thought of Paul Bunyan, the great inventor and logger. As far as anyone knows, Paul never found a problem he couldn't solve. So Knute tore out for Paul's camp.

Paul listened to the snake's story and let out a low whistle that blew in the windows of the Sunshine Café in Sabinal, Texas, which wasn't there yet.

This was the kind of a problem he liked. So he thought even faster than usual. Even so, he had chewed his nails till the scraps were piled round him nearly to his knees, and his hands were all tangled up in his whiskers, before he thought of anything. By that time Ole, the Big Swede, had gotten back from replacing the windows of the Sunshine Café. Paul right away put him to work taking a safety valve and whistle off an old donkey engine back of the blacksmith shop. Ole was as good a plumber as ever wore hair, so he had no trouble connecting these things up to Knute's neck.

Right away, the snake felt better. The valve was set to keep the pressure at one hundred and ten pounds. That was just enough to keep his stomach warm. And he was as tickled with the whistle as a kid with a new red wagon. He wanted to pay Paul for curing him, but Paul wouldn't hear of it. Said he was mighty obliged to Knute for bringing him such an interesting problem. Folks all over the country would be telling that story for years.

A few days later, Knute was back in camp with another little problem for Paul. He said that, what with his getting along in years, his circulation wasn't what it used to be. His tail being so far from the rest of him, he was having considerable trouble keeping it warm. That one was nothing at all for Ol' Paul. He just had Ole run a pipe line for the steam from the whistle right down Knute's back to his tail. Along the last mile or two, he fastened a lot of old steam radiators he'd picked up somewhere or other. And though that was the beginning of the coldest winter the oldest Indians could remember, Knute came through without a single chilblain.

And more than that, the heat attracted antelope, buffalo, and jack rabbits by the thousands, making his hunting a cinch.

Paul, Knute, and the Queen of Spain

Naturally, this was the beginning of a very fine friendship that lasted for many years. Knute got into the habit of dropping into camp every now and then with fresh meat for the men's Sunday dinner. So he was right popular with everyone, even the cooks, and that was something. For it's very, very seldom that anyone is popular with a camp cook.

A couple of years later, Ol' Paul was dickering with the Queen of Spain on a lumber deal. It seems there were about four states that she wanted to have logged off. The price she offered was about right, but the time limit on the job was so short that Johnnie Inkslinger, the bookkeeper, was worried. He advised Paul not to try it.

But Paul just grinned in his whiskers and reckoned that he'd try it. He said that if he needed more men there were plenty of good ones yet in Sweden. In the meantime, he just sat around whittling. Occasionally he went out to the blacksmith shop where Ole, the Big Swede, and a lot of helpers were working on something in the way of a secret contraption. And Johnnie was worrying himself sick.

A few days later, a timber cruiser came into camp with the news that Sowbelly Burke, Paul's old enemy, had heard of the deal, and had sent his straw boss, Mike Fink by name, to Sweden and hired all the Swedes there. Johnnie was about fit to be tied by this time, but Paul just sat and whittled.

Later the same day, one of Sowbelly's men came in with a message for Paul. It seems that Burke was ready to bet a dollar and a quarter that Paul couldn't finish on time.

Paul sent word back that he'd take the bet and raise a quarter. This puzzled Burke. Under the terms of the contract, Ol' Paul had to pay a whale of a penalty if he was late, and he had less than half enough men for a job that size.

By this time, the story had spread to every lumber camp and mill town in the country. Bets were being made everywhere on the outcome. Lots of folks thought that at last Sowbelly had gotten the best of Paul. But Paul's men stayed loyal, taking all bets. Even Hot Biscuit Slim bet a dime. But they were worried. They thought a lot of Paul.

However, a couple of weeks later, the straw bosses told the men at breakfast to pack their lunch buckets and get their axes. Work had finally started on the Queen's job.

When they came out of the mess hall, there was Knute waiting for them. But the way he was duded up was a caution. Right back of his shoulder blades were strapped two saw blades, each forty feet long. Down his back were the bunks and stakes off three trains of log cars. And there was also a donkey engine and a boom for loading logs from the ground.

Rope ladders hung down his sides, and the men climbed these to find places on his back. Ole was sitting by the whistle. When everyone was loaded, he blew the whistle twice and they tore out.

The two saw blades cut a swath through the timber like a mowing machine. Every little way, they dropped a crew to top and trim the fallen timber so it would be ready to load on the way back.

That way, timber was cut faster than it ever had been before. But after a few days, Knute began to limp from the wear and tear of hauling such heavy loads through rough country. So Ole shod him, nailing ninety-three thousand and fourteen pairs of sharp shoes on his belly scales. From then on, there was no trouble.

It was really a stirring sight to see ol' Knute come dusting into camp at night. As far back as you could see was bend after bend of him swinging round the curves of the tote road. And on his back were loads and loads of good saw logs, with the men riding on top waving their fur caps and hollering. The sparks from his shoes hitting the frozen ground made a solid line of fire the full length of him. The steam flying back from his nostrils almost hid Ole, who rode on Knute's head, holding a lantern and blowing the whistle every forty rods.

After they unloaded, it took nine hundred and forty-four men an hour and a quarter to rub him down and cool him out so he would not catch cold.

All winter, they worked like that. The job was finished with three days to spare, winning many bets for the men as well as bonuses all round. But Paul had to chase Sow-belly clear to the Gulf of Mexico to collect his. Even then, he only got about six bits. Burke had had to pay the Swedes all winter even though they didn't work, so he was broke.

The Queen of Spain wrote Paul a long letter afterwards, and we all figgered that she probably said some mighty nice things about him. But being as how the letter was written in Spanish, we never did find out. Nor did Paul. But the story of how Paul gave Sowbelly Burke his come-uppance was told for years in all the lumber camps in the country.

Dr. Dolittle and
the Pushmi-Pullyu

Hugh Lofting

Dr. John Dolittle lived in a little town called Puddleby-on-the-Marsh. He kept his house so full of pets that his patients stopped coming to him. So he became an animal doctor and learned to speak animal languages. Chee-Chee, his pet monkey, received word of a terrible sickness among the monkeys of Africa. So the good Doctor traveled to Africa and cured the monkeys.

John Dolittle told the monkeys that he must now go back to Puddleby.

They were very surprised at this; for they had thought that he was going to stay with them forever. And that night all the monkeys got together in the jungle to talk it over.

And the Chief Chimpanzee rose up and said,

"Why is it the good man is going away? Is he not happy here with us?"

But none of them could answer him.

Then the Grand Gorilla got up and said,

"I think we should all go to him and ask him to stay. Perhaps if we make him a new house and a bigger bed, and promise him plenty of monkey servants to work for him and to make life pleasant for him—perhaps then he will not wish to go."

Then Chee-Chee got up, and all the others whispered, "Sh! Look! Chee-Chee, the great Traveler, is about to speak!"

And Chee-Chee said to the other monkeys, "My friends, I am afraid it is useless to ask the Doctor to stay. He owes money in Puddleby; and he says he must go back and pay it."

And the monkeys asked him, "What is *money?*"

Then Chee-Chee told them that in the Land of the White Men you could get nothing without money; you could *do* nothing without money—that it was almost impossible to *live* without money.

And some of them asked, "But can you not even eat and drink without paying?"

But Chee-Chee shook his head. And then he told them that even he, when he was with the organ-grinder, had been made to ask the children for money.

And the Chief Chimpanzee turned to the Oldest Orang-outang and said, "Cousin, surely these Men be strange creatures! Who would wish to live in such a land? My gracious, how paltry!"

Then Chee-Chee said,

"When we were coming to you, we had no boat to cross the sea in and no money to buy food to eat on our journey. So a man lent us some biscuits; and we said we would pay him when we came back. And we borrowed a boat from a sailor; but it was broken on the rocks when we reached the shores of Africa. Now the Doctor says he must go back and get the sailor another boat—because the man was poor and his ship was all he had."

And the monkeys were all silent for a while, sitting quite still and thinking hard.

At last the Biggest Baboon got up and said, "I do not think we ought to let this good man leave our land till we have given him a fine present to take with him, so that he may know we are grateful for all that he has done for us."

And a little, tiny red monkey who was sitting up in a tree shouted down,

"I think that too!"

And then they all cried out, making a great noise, "Yes, yes. Let us give him the finest present a White Man ever had!"

Now they began to wonder and to ask one another what would be the best thing to give him. And one said, "Fifty bags of coconuts!" And another—"A hundred bunches of bananas! At least he shall not have to buy his fruit in the Land Where You Pay To Eat!"

But Chee-Chee told them that all these things would be too heavy to carry so far and would go bad before half was eaten.

"If you want to please him," he said, "give him an animal. You may be sure he will be kind to it. Give him some rare animal they have not got in the menageries."

And the monkeys asked him, "What are *menageries?*"

Then Chee-Chee explained to them that menageries were places in the Land of the White Men, where animals were put in cages for people to come and look at. And the monkeys were very shocked, and said to one another,

"These Men are like thoughtless young ones—stupid and easily amused. Sh! It is a prison he means."

So then they asked Chee-Chee what rare animal it could be that they should give the Doctor—one the White Men had not seen before. And the Major of the Marmosettes asked,

"Have they an iguana over there?"

But Chee-Chee said, "Yes, there is one in the London Zoo."

And another asked, "Have they an okapi?"

But Chee-Chee said, "Yes. In Belgium, where my organ-grinder took me five years ago, they had an okapi in a big city they call Antwerp."

And another asked, "Have they a pushmi-pullyu?"

Then Chee-Chee said, "No. No White Man has ever seen a pushmi-pullyu. Let us give him that."

A Strange Beast

Pushmi-pullyus are now extinct. That means there aren't any more. But long ago, when Doctor Dolittle was alive, there were some of them still left in the deepest jungles of Africa; and even then they were very, very scarce. They had no tail, but a head at each end, and sharp horns on each head. They were very shy and terribly hard to catch. The black men get most of their animals by sneaking up behind them while they are not looking. But you could not do this with the pushmi-pullyu—because, no matter which way you came towards him, he was always facing you. And besides, only one half of him slept at a time. The other head was always awake—and watching.

This was why they were never caught and never seen in Zoos. Though many of the greatest huntsmen and the cleverest menagerie-keepers spent years of their lives searching through the jungles in all weathers for pushmi-pullyus, not a single one had ever been caught. Even then, years ago, he was the only animal in the world that had two heads.

Well, the monkeys set out hunting for this animal through the forest. After they had gone a good many miles, one of them found peculiar footprints near the edge of a river; they knew that a pushmi-pullyu must be very near that spot.

Then they went along the bank of the river a little way and they saw a place where the grass was high and thick; and they guessed that he was in there.

So they all joined hands and made a great circle around the high grass. The pushmi-pullyu heard them coming; and he tried hard to break through the ring of monkeys. But he couldn't do it. When he saw that it was no use trying to escape, he sat down and waited to see what they wanted.

They asked him if he would go with Doctor Dolittle and be put on show in the Land of the White Men.

But he shook both his heads hard and said, "Certainly not!"

They explained to him that he would not be shut up in a menagerie but would just be looked at. They told him that the Doctor was a very kind man but hadn't any money; and people would pay to see a two-headed animal

and the Doctor would get rich and could pay for the boat
he had borrowed to come to Africa in.

But he answered, "No. You know how shy I am—I hate
being stared at." And he almost began to cry.

Then, for three days they tried to persuade him.

And at the end of the third day he said he would come
with them and see what kind of a man the Doctor was,
first.

So the monkeys traveled back with the pushmi-pullyu.
And when they came to where the Doctor's little house
of grass was, they knocked on the door.

The duck, who was packing the trunk, said, "Come in!"

And Chee-Chee very proudly took the animal inside and
showed him to the Doctor.

"What in the world is it?" asked John Dolittle, gazing at the strange creature.

"Lord save us!" cried the duck. "How does it make up its mind?"

"It doesn't look to me as though it had any," said Jip, the dog.

A New Pet for the Doctor

"This, Doctor," said Chee-Chee, "is the pushmi-pullyu —the rarest animal of the African jungles, the only two-headed beast in the world. Take him home with you and your fortune's made. People will pay any money to see him."

"But I don't want any money," said the Doctor.

"Yes, you do," said Dab-Dab, the duck. "Don't you remember how we had to pinch and scrape to pay the butcher's bill in Puddleby? And how are you going to get the sailor the new boat you spoke of—unless we have the money to buy it?"

"I was going to make him one," said the Doctor.

"Oh, do be sensible!" cried Dab-Dab. "Where would you get all the wood and the nails to make one with?—And besides, what are we going to live on? We shall be poorer than ever when we get back. Chee-Chee's perfectly right: take the funny-looking thing along, do!"

"Well, perhaps there is something in what you say," murmured the Doctor. "It certainly would make a nice new kind of pet. But does the er—what-do-you-call-it really want to go abroad?"

"Yes, I'll go," said the pushmi-pullyu, who saw at once, from the Doctor's face, that he was a man to be trusted. "You have been so kind to the animals here—and the monkeys tell me that I am the only one who will do. But you must promise me that if I do not like it in the Land of the White Men you will send me back."

"Why, certainly—of course, of course," said the Doctor. "Excuse me, surely you are related to the Deer Family, are you not?"

"Yes," said the pushmi-pullyu—"to the Abyssinian Gazelles and the Asiatic Chamois—on my mother's side. My father's great-grandfather was the last of the Unicorns."

"Most interesting!" murmured the Doctor; and he took a book out of the trunk which Dab-Dab was packing and began turning the pages. "Let us see if Buffon says anything—"

"I notice," said the duck, "that you only talk with one of your mouths. Can't the other head talk as well?"

"Oh, yes," said the pushmi-pullyu. "But I keep the other mouth for eating—mostly. In that way I can talk while I am eating without being rude. Our people have always been very polite."

When the packing was finished and everything was ready to start, the monkeys gave a grand party for the Doctor, and all the animals of the jungle came. And they had pineapples and mangoes and honey and all sorts of good things to eat and drink.

After they had all finished eating, the Doctor got up and said,

"My friends: I am not clever at speaking long words after dinner, like some men; and I have just eaten many fruits and much honey. But I wish to tell you that I am very sad at leaving your beautiful country. Because I have

things to do in the Land of the White Men, I must go.
After I have gone, remember never to let the flies settle on
your food before you eat it; and do not sleep on the ground
when the rains are coming. I—er—er—I hope you will all
live happily ever after."

When the Doctor stopped speaking and sat down, all
the monkeys clapped their hands a long time and said
to one another, "Let it be remembered always among our
people that he sat and ate with us, here, under the trees.
For surely he is the Greatest of Men!"

And the Grand Gorilla, who had the strength of seven
horses in his hairy arms, rolled a great rock up to the head
of the table and said,

"This stone for all time shall mark the spot."

And even to this day, in the heart of the jungle, that
stone still is there. And monkey-mothers, passing through
the forest with their families, still point down at it from the
branches and whisper to their children, "Sh! There it is—
look—where the Good White Man sat and ate food with us
in the Year of the Great Sickness!"

Then, when the party was over, the Doctor and his pets
started out to go back to the seashore. And all the monkeys
went with him as far as the edge of their country, carrying
his trunk and bags, to see him off.

THE END

PIANOS

About Elizabeth Eliza's Piano

Lucretia P. Hale

The Peterkins as a family were not noted for their brains. Indeed, if it hadn't been for the lady from Philadelphia, who was visiting in their town, the Peterkins would have had a hard time.

Elizabeth Eliza had a present of a piano. She was to take lessons from the postmaster's daughter.

They decided to have the piano set across the window in the parlor. The carters brought it in, and went away.

After they had gone, the family all came in to look at the piano. But they found the carters had placed it with its back turned towards the middle of the room, standing close against the window.

How could Elizabeth Eliza open it? How could she reach the keys to play upon it?

Solomon John proposed that they should open the window. Agamemnon could do this with his long arms. Then Elizabeth Eliza should go round upon the piazza, and open the piano. Then she could have her music-stool on the piazza, and play upon the piano there.

So they tried this. They all thought it was a very pretty sight to see Elizabeth Eliza playing on the piano, while she sat on the piazza, with the honeysuckle vines behind her.

It was very pleasant, too, moonlight evenings. Mr. Peterkin liked to take a doze on his sofa in the room. The rest of the family liked to sit on the piazza. So did Elizabeth Eliza, only she had to have her back to the moon.

All this did very well through the summer. But, when the fall came, Mr. Peterkin thought the air was too cold from the open window. The family did not want to sit out on the piazza.

Elizabeth Eliza practiced in the mornings with her cloak on. But she was obliged to give up her music in the evenings, the family shivered so.

One day, when she was talking with the lady from Philadelphia, she spoke of this trouble.

The lady from Philadelphia looked surprised. Then she said, "But why don't you turn the piano around?"

One of the little boys pertly said, "It is a square piano."

But Elizabeth Eliza went home directly, and, with the help of Agamemnon and Solomon John, turned the piano round.

"Why did we not think of that before?" said Mrs. Peterkin. "What shall we do when the lady from Philadelphia goes home again?"

Jimmy Takes Vanishing Lessons

Walter Brooks

The school bus picked up Jimmy Crandall every morning. Every afternoon it dropped him again. And so twice a day, on the bus, he passed the entrance to the mysterious road.

It wasn't much of a road any more. It was choked with weeds and blackberry bushes. The woods on both sides pressed in so closely that it was dark and gloomy, even on bright days. The bus driver once pointed it out.

"There's a haunted house about a quarter of a mile down that road." He paused. "But you ought to know about that, Jimmy. It was your grandfather's house."

Jimmy knew about it, and he knew that it now belonged to his Aunt Mary. But Jimmy's aunt would never talk to him about the house. She said the stories about it were silly nonsense and there were no such things as ghosts. If all the villagers weren't a lot of superstitious idiots, she would be able to rent the house. Then she would have enough money to buy Jimmy some decent clothes and take him to the movies.

Jimmy thought it was all very well to say that there were no such things as ghosts. But how about the people who had tried to live there? Aunt Mary had rented the house three times, but every family had moved out within a week. They said the things that went on there were just too queer.

Jimmy thought about the house a lot. If he could only prove that there wasn't a ghost . . . And one Saturday when his aunt was in the village, Jimmy took the key to the haunted house from its hook on the kitchen door, and started out.

It had seemed like a fine idea when he had first thought of it—to find out for himself. Even in the silence and damp gloom of the old road, it still seemed pretty good. Nothing to be scared of, he told himself. Ghosts aren't around in the daytime. But when he came out in the clearing and looked at those blank, dusty windows, he wasn't so sure.

"Oh, come on!" he told himself. And he squared his shoulders and waded through the long grass to the porch.

Then he stopped again. His feet did not seem to want

to go up the steps. But when at last they did, they marched right up and across the porch to the front door. Jimmy set his teeth hard and put the key in the keyhole. It turned with a squeak. He pushed the door open and went in.

He was in a long dark hall with closed doors on both sides. On the right, the stairs went up. He had left the door open behind him, and the light from it showed him that, except for the hatrack and table and chairs, the hall was empty. And then as he stood there, listening to the bumping of his heart, gradually the hall grew darker and darker —as if something huge had come up on the porch behind him. He swung round quickly, but there was nothing there.

He drew a deep breath. It must have been just a cloud passing across the sun. But then the door, all of itself, began to swing shut. And before he could stop it, it closed with a bang. And it was then that Jimmy saw the ghost.

It behaved just as you would expect a ghost to behave. A tall, dim, white figure, it came gliding slowly down the stairs towards him. Jimmy gave a yell, yanked the door open, and tore down the steps.

He didn't stop until he was well down the road. Then he had to get his breath. He sat down on a log. "Boy!" he said. "I've seen a ghost! Golly, was that awful!" Then, after a minute, he thought, "What was so awful about it? He was trying to scare me, like that smart aleck who was always jumping out from behind things. Pretty silly business for a grown-up ghost to be doing."

It always makes you mad when someone deliberately tries to scare you. And Jimmy began to get angry. And pretty soon he got up and started back. "I must get that key, anyway," he thought, for he had left it in the door.

This time he approached very quietly. He thought he'd just lock the door and go home. But as he tiptoed up the steps and reached out cautiously for the key, he heard a faint sound. He drew back and peeked around the side of the door.

The ghost was going back upstairs, but he wasn't gliding now. He was doing a sort of dance. Every other step he would bend double and shake with laughter. His thin cackle was the sound Jimmy had heard. Evidently he was enjoying the joke he had played.

A Timid Ghost

That made Jimmy madder than ever. He yelled "Boo!" at the top of his lungs. The ghost gave a thin shriek and leaped two feet in the air. Then he collapsed on the stairs.

As soon as Jimmy saw he could scare the ghost even worse than the ghost could scare him, he wasn't afraid any more. The ghost was hanging on to the banisters and panting. "Oh, my goodness!" he gasped. "Oh, my gracious! Boy, you can't do that to me!"

"I did it, didn't I?" said Jimmy. "Now we're even."

"Nothing of the kind," said the ghost crossly. "Ghosts are supposed to scare people. People aren't supposed to scare ghosts." He glided down and sat on the bottom step. "But look here, boy. This could be pretty serious for me if people got to know about it."

"You mean you don't want me to tell anybody about it?" Jimmy asked.

"Suppose we make a deal," the ghost said. "You keep still about this, and in return I'll—well, let's see. How would you like to know how to vanish?"

"Oh, that would be swell!" Jimmy exclaimed. "But—can you vanish?"

"Sure," said the ghost, and he did. All at once he just wasn't there. Jimmy was alone in the hall.

But the ghost's voice went right on. "It would be pretty handy, wouldn't it?" he said persuasively. "If your aunt called you to do something—well, she wouldn't be able to find you."

"I don't mind helping Aunt Mary," Jimmy said.

"H'm. High-minded, eh?" said the ghost. "Well, then—"

"I wish you'd please reappear," Jimmy interrupted. "It makes me feel funny to talk to somebody who isn't there."

"Sorry, I forgot," said the ghost. There he was again, sitting on the bottom step. Jimmy could see the step, dimly, right through him. "Good trick, eh? Well, maybe I could teach you to go through keyholes. Like this." He floated over to the door and went right through the keyhole, the way water goes down the drain. Then he came back the same way.

"That's useful, too," he said. "Getting into locked rooms and so on. You can go anywhere the wind can."

"No," said Jimmy. "There's only one thing you can do to get me to promise not to tell about scaring you. Go live somewhere else. There's Miller's, up the road. Nobody lives there any more."

"That old shack!" said the ghost, with a nasty laugh. "Doors and windows half off, roof leaky—no thanks! Peace and quiet, that's really what a ghost wants out of life."

"Well, I don't think it's very fair," Jimmy said, "for you to live in a house that doesn't belong to you and keep my aunt from renting it."

"Pooh!" said the ghost. "I'm not stopping her from renting it. I don't take up any room. It's not my fault if people get scared and leave."

"It certainly is!" Jimmy said angrily. "You don't play fair. I'm going to tell everybody how I scared you."

"Oh, you mustn't do that!" The ghost seemed quite disturbed and he vanished and reappeared rapidly several times. "If that got out, every ghost in the country would be in terrible trouble."

So they argued about it. The ghost said if Jimmy wanted money he could learn to vanish. Then he could join a circus and get a big salary. Jimmy said he didn't want to be in a circus. He wanted to go to college and learn to be a doctor. He was very firm. And the ghost began to cry. "But this is my *home,* boy," he said. "Thirty years I've lived here. Now you want to throw me out into the cold world! And for what? A little money! That's pretty heartless." And he sobbed, trying to make Jimmy feel cruel.

Jimmy didn't feel cruel at all. But he didn't really think it would do much good for him to tell anybody that he had scared the ghost. How could he prove it? So after a minute he said, "Well, all right. You teach me to vanish and I won't tell." They settled it that way.

Jimmy didn't say anything to his aunt. But every Saturday he went to the haunted house for his vanishing lesson. It is really quite easy when you know how. In a couple of weeks he could flicker. In six weeks the ghost gave him an examination and he got a B plus, which is very good for a human. So he thanked the ghost and shook hands with him and said, "Well, good-by now. You'll hear from me."

"What do you mean by that?" said the ghost suspiciously. But Jimmy just laughed and ran off home.

Jimmy Plans a Campaign

That night at supper, Jimmy's aunt said, "Well, what have you been doing today?"

"I've been learning to vanish."

His aunt smiled and said, "That must be fun."

"Honestly," said Jimmy. "The ghost up at grandfather's taught me."

"I don't think that's very funny," said his aunt. "And will you please not—why, where are you?" she demanded, for he had vanished.

"Here, Aunt Mary," he said as he reappeared.

"Merciful heavens!" she exclaimed. She rubbed her eyes hard. Then she looked at him again.

Well, it took a lot of explaining and he had to do it twice more before he could persuade her that he really could vanish. But at last she calmed down and they had a long talk. Jimmy kept his word and didn't tell her that he had scared the ghost, but he said he had a plan. At last she agreed to help him.

So, the next day, she went up to the old house and started to work. She opened the windows and swept and dusted and aired the bedding, and made as much noise as possible. This disturbed the ghost. Pretty soon he came floating into the room where she was sweeping. She was scared all right. She gave a yell and threw the broom at him. As the broom went right through him and he came nearer, waving his arms and groaning, she shrank back.

And Jimmy, who had been standing there invisible all the time, suddenly appeared and jumped at the ghost with a "Boo!" And the ghost fell over in a dead faint.

As soon as Jimmy's aunt saw that, she wasn't frightened any more. She found some smelling salts and held them under the ghost's nose, and when he came to she tried to help him into a chair. Of course, she couldn't help him much because her hands went right through him. But at last he sat up and said reproachfully to Jimmy, "You broke your word!"

"I promised not to tell about scaring you," said the boy.

"But I didn't promise that I wouldn't scare you again."

And his aunt said, "You really are a ghost, aren't you?
I thought you were just stories people made up. Well, excuse me, but I must get on with my work." And she began
sweeping harder than ever.

The ghost put his hands to his head. "All this noise,"
he said. "Couldn't you work more quietly, ma'am?"

"Whose house is this, anyway?" she demanded. "If you
don't like it, why don't you move out?"

The ghost sneezed violently several times. "Excuse me,"
he said. "You're raising so much dust. Where's that boy?"
he asked suddenly. For Jimmy had vanished again.

"I'm sure I don't know," she replied. "Probably getting
ready to scare you again."

"You ought to have better control of him," said the
ghost severely. "If he was my boy, I'd take a hairbrush
to him."

"You have my permission," she said. She reached right
through the ghost and pulled the chair cushion out from
under him and began banging the dust out of it. "What's
more," she went on, as he got up and glided wearily to
another chair, "Jimmy and I are going to sleep here nights
from now on. I don't think it would be very smart of you
to try any tricks."

"Ha, ha," said the ghost nastily. "He who laughs last—"

"Ha, ha, yourself," said Jimmy's voice from close behind
him. "And that's me laughing last."

The ghost muttered and vanished.

Jimmy's aunt put cotton in her ears and slept that night in the best bedroom with the light lit. The ghost screamed for a while down in the cellar. Nothing happened, so he came upstairs. He thought he would appear to her as two glaring, fiery eyes, which was one of his best tricks. But first he wanted to be sure where Jimmy was. He hunted all over the house, and though he was invisible himself, he got more and more nervous. He kept imagining that at any moment Jimmy might jump out at him. Finally, he got so jittery that he went back to the cellar and hid in the coal bin all night.

The following days were just as bad for the ghost. Several times he tried to scare Jimmy's aunt while she was working, but she didn't scare worth a cent. Twice, Jimmy managed to sneak up on him and appear suddenly with a loud yell, frightening him dreadfully. He was, I suppose, rather timid even for a ghost. He began to look quite worn out. He had several arguments with Jimmy's aunt, in which he wept and appealed to her sympathy. But she was firm. There was the abandoned Miller farm two miles up the road. Why didn't he move there?

When the house was all in apple-pie order, Jimmy's aunt went down to the village to see a Mr. and Mrs. Whistler, who were living at the hotel because they couldn't find a house to move into. She told them about the old house, but they said, "No thank you. We've heard about that house. It's haunted. I'll bet," they said, *"you* wouldn't dare spend a night there."

She told them that she had spent the last week there, but they evidently didn't believe her. So she said, "You know my nephew, Jimmy. He's twelve years old. I am so sure that the house is not haunted that I will let Jimmy stay there with you every night until you are sure everything is all right."

"Ha!" said Mr. Whistler. "The boy won't do it."

They sent for Jimmy. "Why, I've spent the last week there," he said. "Sure, I'd just as soon."

A Ghost Goes West

So the Whistlers moved in. Jimmy stayed there for a week, but he saw nothing of the ghost. And then one day one of the boys in his grade told him that somebody had seen a ghost up at the Miller farm. So Jimmy knew the ghost had taken his aunt's advice.

A day or two later, he walked up to the Miller farm. There was no front door and he walked right in. There was some groaning and thumping upstairs, and then after a minute the ghost came floating down.

"Oh, it's you!" he said. "Goodness sakes, boy, can't you leave me in peace?"

Jimmy said he'd just come up to see how the ghost was getting along.

"Getting along fine," said the ghost. "From my point of view, it's a very desirable property. Peaceful. Quiet. Nobody playing silly tricks."

"Well," said Jimmy, "I won't bother you if you don't bother the Whistlers. But if you come back there—"

"Don't worry," said the ghost.

So, with the rent money, Jimmy and his aunt had a much easier life. They went to the movies sometimes twice a week. Jimmy had all new clothes, and on Thanksgiving, for the first time in his life, Jimmy had a turkey.

Once a week, he would go up to the Miller farm to see the ghost. They got to be very good friends. The ghost even came down to the Thanksgiving dinner, though of course he couldn't eat much. He taught Jimmy several more tricks. The best one was how to glare with fiery eyes, which was useful later on when Jimmy became a doctor and had to look down people's throats to see if their tonsils ought to come out.

The ghost was really a pretty good fellow as ghosts go, and Jimmy's aunt got quite fond of him. When the real winter weather began, she even used to worry about him, because of course there was no heat in the Miller place. And when he accepted their invitation for Christmas dinner, she knitted him some red woolen slippers. He was so pleased that he broke down and cried. And that made Jimmy's aunt so happy, *she* broke down and cried.

Jimmy didn't cry, but he said, "Aunt Mary, don't you
think it would be nice if the ghost came down and lived
with us this winter?"

"I would feel very much better about him if he did,"
she said.

So he stayed with them that winter, and then he just
stayed on. It must have been a peaceful place, for the last
I heard he was still there.

Well-Loved Tales

In dreams, I sometimes make my way
To the Limpopo, green and gray;
Or aim the arrow, speed it well,
With great, heroic William Tell;
Drink in the tales told at the feast
Of Sinbad in the gorgeous East;
And look with hopeful eyes upon
Each duckling that may be a swan.

—*Dorothy Hall*

Master of All Masters

Joseph Jacobs

A girl once went to the fair to hire herself for a servant. At last, a funny-looking old gentleman engaged her, and took her home to his house. When she got there, he told her that he had something to teach her. In his house, he said, he had his own names for things.

He said to her, "What will you call me?"

"Master or mister, or whatever you please, sir," said she.

He said, "You must call me 'master of all masters.' And what would you call this?"—pointing to his bed.

"Bed or couch, or whatever you please, sir."

"No, that's my 'barnacle.' And what do you call these?" said he, pointing to his pantaloons.

"Breeches or trousers, or whatever you please, sir."

"You must call them 'squibs and crackers.' And what would you call her?"—pointing to the cat.

"Cat or kit, or whatever you please, sir."

"You must call her 'white-faced simminy.' And this now," showing the fire, "what would you call this?"

"Fire or flame, or whatever you please, sir."

"You must call it 'hot cockalorum,' and what this?" he went on, pointing to the water.

"Water or wet, or whatever you please, sir."

"No, 'pondalorum' is its name. And what do you call this?" asked he as he pointed to the house.

"House or cottage, or whatever you please, sir."

"You must call it 'high topper mountain.' "

That very night the servant woke her master up in a fright and said, "Master of all masters, get out of your barnacle and put on your squibs and crackers. For white-faced simminy has got a spark of hot cockalorum on its tail, and unless you get some pondalorum high topper mountain will be all on hot cockalorum." . . . That's all.

The Apple and the Arrow

Mary and Conrad Buff

William Tell, a legendary hero of Switzerland, stands for the heroic spirit of the Swiss people when they were trying to gain their independence from Austria. The best-known tale about the bowman, Tell, concerns his refusal to obey the hated ruler, Gessler. It happened on a day when Tell and his son were visiting the town of Altdorf, where Gessler dwelt.

Suddenly Walter saw his father and grandfather step from the inn. His father looked very angry. Even his grandfather did not smile as Walter ran up to him.

"Come at once, Son. Let us go," was all that his father commanded. "Quiet, and stay beside me."

"Yes," Walter answered, wondering. They passed through a narrow way between high houses, and soon the village square or market place opened before them. Walter saw the familiar fountain in the center of the square. To-day, two soldiers were beside it. One of them, an old fellow, was munching an apple. The other soldier was whittling on a stick with his dagger. They looked tired and bored.

Then Walter noticed a long pole set in the ground beside the fountain. He had never seen that before. On the top of the pole fluttered a velvet hat with a feather in it, such a hat as Walter had often seen well-born people wear. He wondered why no children were playing in the fountain. No dogs lay in the dirt. No women came with water jars to draw water and to gossip together.

Then a well-dressed villager passed by. Nodding to the soldiers, he doffed his cap and bent his knee to the hat on the pole. Walter felt his father's hand stiffen against his and heard him mutter, "Traitor!" Nevertheless, William Tell walked proudly on, looking neither to left nor to right. His great bow hung from one sturdy shoulder. Past the fountain he strode, Walter clinging to him—past the soldiers, past the pole with the hat on it.

Suddenly Walter heard the younger soldier shout, "Stop, you! Are you blind? See that hat on the pole, *you*. That's the hat of Austria, the ducal hat."

But father and son walked on. The soldier munching the apple grabbed his spear and ran toward the mountaineer, yelling, "You knave, you blockhead, *bow to that hat!* Or I'll run you through with this." And he lowered his great spear.

Only then did William Tell stop and eye the soldier fearlessly, as he shouted, "Hat, what hat? I see no hat. I have business with the tanner."

Tell's words made the soldiers very angry. One yelled, "Bend your knee to that hat, or we will crush your skull like a nutshell." The mountaineer took one more step forward without answering, but the shouting of the soldiers had brought many townsfolk into the square. His way was blocked by soldiers with spears and by shouting people.

Suddenly a guard blew on his bugle. Other soldiers streamed in from narrow streets. Walter and his father were surrounded by a mob of people.

"Now for the last time, bow before the ducal hat of Austria. Show you are a loyal subject of our governor, Gessler."

The name of Gessler seemed to make Tell even more rebellious. He laughed in defiance, as Walter clung to him and shrank back before the lowered spears of the soldiers. "Why should I bow before a silly hat? A hat is not a lord. A hat is a thing of rags and feathers. It is nothing to bow down before."

The mountaineer held his son's hand tightly and shouted these words so that all heard. The townsfolk milled around the soldiers in a crowd.

"Poor wretch, he'll get it now," said a villager.

"Take your hands from me," commanded Tell as a guard seized him. "I have done no wrong. Take your hands from me, I say. I will not bow before that hat. We've had enough of bowing and scraping in the land of Uri."

As they heard his scornful words, three angry soldiers grabbed the mountain man and pinned back his arms. "We dare you to insult the governor thus, you herder of goats!"

A bugle sounded again. The crowd scattered as mounted knights galloped into the market place. "Out of our way, you dumb brutes," they commanded. Walter, almost in tears now, glanced up at them. And then he saw Gessler— the governor, Gessler. It could be no one else. The knight wore fine clothing, and rode a beautiful and spirited horse. But Walter thought he looked evil.

"What goes on here?" demanded Gessler. The crowd was now deathly quiet. "Oh, so it is you, William Tell, the man of the mountains," jeered Gessler. "In trouble again, I see. For what do my men now hold you?"

The mountaineer did not reply. Then a soldier spoke. "He will not bow before the ducal hat, my lord."

"Oh, so he is too fine to bow before the hat of Albrecht of Austria, is he? Bow, I say, or we will run you through," warned Gessler.

Tell was silent. He did not move. He looked at Gessler and his eyes were like black coals, burning with hatred. Walter trembled. But he held himself proudly, like his father.

"So you have no tongue now. Speak, or you will be sorry."

Now the great bowman was really angry. He bellowed like a mad bull. The people could hear every word that he said.

"I will not bend my knee before a hat. I will bow only to those more truly noble than I. Men of gentle birth. Wise men. The man of God and the good Lord Himself. I will not bend my knee before a hat of rags and feathers. A hat is nothing to worship. A well-born man, a noble, is something else."

How angry Gessler became at these words! He knew that Tell was jeering at his common birth.

Trial by Arrow

"Oh, so you are too fine to bow!" snarled Gessler, white with fury. Then a sly look came into his face. He glanced sharply down at Walter, who was clinging to his father.

"Who is that cowardly brat that clings to you, Tell?" asked Gessler.

"My son, Walter. My elder son," replied Tell, looking at Walter and pressing his hand.

"I see you have your crossbow with you, Tell. I have heard it said you are a good bowman, the best in the canton of Uri. Is that true?"

"I know not if it is true," answered Tell, modestly. "There are many good bowmen in Uri. But some folk have said so."

A townsman shouted, "Tell is the best of us all."

"Let us see, then, how good a bowman you really are. Take that cowardly boy, men, and place him against yonder linden tree. Put an apple on his head. Tell, if you can shoot the apple from your son's head, you shall go free. But . . . if any harm comes to the boy or you miss the apple, you will *both* die."

A gasp of horror went through the crowd. Walter heard people cry, "The wretch . . . knave . . ." But Gessler only smiled an evil smile as he pointed to the linden tree.

At last Tell found his voice. "You cannot ask this of me, Governor," he pleaded. "This is an innocent lad, and my first-born. He has done no harm to anyone."

"But I thought you were such a great bowman, Tell," retorted the governor. "I see you are just a bag of wind with the face of a lion and the heart of a deer."

At these stinging words, Walter shouted in his high boyish voice, so that all heard—"Father, I am not afraid. I will stand at the linden tree and they need not bind me. I will stand as still as a rock. You will hit the apple, Father. I am not afraid."

"See the boy, Gessler, how he believes in his father!" shouted a woman. The soldiers seized Walter and bound him to the linden tree, while mothers clutched their children to them, as if to protect them from the evil governor.

As a guard placed a large apple upon Walter's head, the boy could see the townsfolk brandishing sticks and threatening the knights. A boy threw a stone and a horse reared.

Gessler commanded, "Quiet, you people of Altdorf. Quiet." Then, looking down at Tell, he said, "This is your chance to show how skilled you are with the bow."

The soldiers freed the mountaineer. He slipped his bow from his shoulder and raised it. He placed the arrow. Then, standing quietly, he looked at his son tied to the linden tree.

William Tell knelt on the ground. He raised his heavy crossbow to his shoulder and took careful aim. Not a sound was heard. Even the dogs stopped barking; the horses prancing. The mountaineer was about to press the trigger of his crossbow, when the sight of his slender son, standing so quietly at the linden tree, overcame him. He put down his bow and groaning aloud, he pleaded, "My lord, have pity. Spare my son. I cannot do this to an innocent, trusting child. I cannot. Have pity on us, my lord."

"Ho, ho, so it is 'my lord' at last, Tell. So you cannot. The strong mountain man cannot. He trembles like the leaves of that linden tree yonder. See how pale he is! What a rare sight! Tell is trembling like a frightened woman. Where is your boasted skill with the bow, Tell?"

As Walter heard these bitter words, he shouted above the noise, "Shoot, Father. God is watching over us."

Walter's voice seemed to bring back his father's courage. Tell took another arrow from his quiver and slipped it into his girdle. Then he quickly raised the heavy crossbow to his shoulder as muscles rippled on his brown arms. He sighted the apple on his son's head. He pulled back the drawstring. Many of the townsfolk were now on their knees praying. Gessler eyed every move that Tell made.

Then, with a grim smile and almost without warning, the great bowman quickly and surely squeezed the trigger of his bow. The arrow sped like a ray of light. Walter suddenly felt the apple on his head split, tremble, and fall to the ground. The nose of the arrow buried itself in the gnarled trunk of the old tree.

A great sigh of relief, like a sudden wind, passed over the heads of the people. Then all at once sounds of jubilation burst forth. "The mighty Tell! Tell, the hero!" the people shouted, surging toward the bowman as he stood there, his dark body glistening with sweat. The people tried to reach him to carry him on their shoulders, but soldiers barred their way.

When guards unbound Walter, he picked up the two halves of the apple and ran toward his father, crying, "See, Father, you cut the apple in two pieces!"

A soldier blew on a horn to quiet the crowd. In the silence, Walter heard Gessler shout, "You *are* a bowman, Tell, as men say. But what of that second arrow you thrust so quickly into your girdle?"

William Tell, feeling suddenly weak and tired, just looked at the governor. He said, "That is the custom of bowmen."

"Answer me, Tell. I want the truth. Why was the second arrow hidden in your girdle?"

William Tell was a simple, trustful man of the mountains. So he replied honestly, "Had I killed my son, Governor, this arrow would have found your heart."

The Elephant's Child

Rudyard Kipling

In the High and Far-Off Times the Elephant, O Best Beloved, had no trunk. He had only a blackish, bulgy nose, as big as a boot, that he could wriggle about from side to side; but he couldn't pick up things with it. But there was one Elephant—a new Elephant—an Elephant's Child— who was full of 'satiable curtiosity, and that means he asked ever so many questions. *And* he lived in Africa, and he filled all Africa with his 'satiable curtiosities.

He asked his tall aunt, the Ostrich, why her tail-feathers grew just so, and his tall aunt the Ostrich spanked him with her hard, hard claw. He asked his tall uncle, the Giraffe, what made his skin spotty, and his tall uncle, the Giraffe, spanked him with his hard, hard hoof. And still he was full of 'satiable curtiosity! He asked his broad aunt, the Hippopotamus, why her eyes were red and his broad aunt, the Hippopotamus, spanked him with her broad, broad hoof; and he asked his hairy uncle, the Baboon, why melons tasted just so, and his hairy uncle, the Baboon, spanked him with his hairy, hairy paw. And *still* he was full of 'satiable curtiosity! He asked questions about everything that he saw, or heard, or felt, or smelt, or touched, and all his uncles and his aunts spanked him. And still he was full of 'satiable curtiosity!

One fine morning in the middle of the Precession of the Equinoxes this 'satiable Elephant's Child asked a new fine question that he had never asked before. He asked, "What does the Crocodile have for dinner?" Then everybody said, "Hush!" in a loud and dretful tone, and they spanked him immediately and directly, without stopping, for a long time.

By and by, when that was finished, he came upon Kolokolo Bird sitting in the middle of a wait-a-bit thorn-bush, and he said, "My father has spanked me, and my mother has spanked me; all my aunts and uncles have spanked me for my 'satiable curtiosity; and *still* I want to know what the Crocodile has for dinner!"

Then Kolokolo Bird said, with a mournful cry, "Go to the banks of the great gray-green, greasy Limpopo River, all set about with fever-trees, and find out."

That very next morning, when there was nothing left of the Equinoxes, because the Precession had preceded according to precedent, this 'satiable Elephant's Child took a hundred pounds of bananas (the little short red kind), and a hundred pounds of sugar-cane (the long purple kind), and seventeen melons (the greeny-crackly kind), and said to all his dear families, "Good-bye. I am going to the great gray-green, greasy Limpopo River, all set about with fever-trees, to find out what the Crocodile has for dinner." And they all spanked him once more for luck, though he asked them most politely to stop.

Then he went away, a little warm, but not at all astonished, eating melons, and throwing the rind about, because he could not pick it up.

He went from Graham's Town to Kimberley, and from Kimberley to Khama's Country, and from Khama's Country he went east by north, eating melons all the time, till at last he came to the banks of the great gray-green, greasy Limpopo River, all set about with fever-trees, precisely as Kolokolo Bird had said.

Now you must know and understand, O Best Beloved, that till that very week, and day, and hour, and minute, this 'satiable Elephant's Child had never seen a Crocodile, and did not know what one was like. It was all his 'satiable curtiosity.

The first thing that he found was a Bi-Colored-Python-Rock-Snake curled round a rock.

" 'Scuse me," said the Elephant's Child most politely, "but have you seen such a thing as a Crocodile in these promiscuous parts?"

"*Have* I seen a Crocodile?" said the Bi-Colored-Python-Rock-Snake, in a voice of dretful scorn. "What will you ask me next?"

" 'Scuse me," said the Elephant's Child, "but could you kindly tell me what he has for dinner?"

Then the Bi-Colored-Python-Rock-Snake uncoiled himself very quickly from the rock, and spanked the Elephant's Child with his scalesome, flailsome tail.

"That is odd," said the Elephant's Child, "because my father and my mother, and my uncle and my aunt, not to mention my other aunt, the Hippopotamus, and my other uncle, the Baboon, have all spanked me for my 'satiable curtiosity—and I suppose this is the same thing."

So he said good-bye very politely to the Bi-Colored-Python-Rock-Snake, and helped to coil him up on the rock again, and went on, a little warm, but not at all astonished, eating melons, and throwing the rind about, because he could not pick it up, till he trod on what he thought was a log of wood at the very edge of the great gray-green, greasy Limpopo River, all set about with fever-trees.

Really the Crocodile

But it was really the Crocodile, O Best Beloved, and the Crocodile winked one eye—like this!

" 'Scuse me," said the Elephant's Child most politely, "but do you happen to have seen a Crocodile in these promiscuous parts?"

Then the Crocodile winked the other eye, and lifted half his tail out of the mud; and the Elephant's Child stepped back most politely, because he did not wish to be spanked again.

"Come hither, Little One," said the Crocodile. "Why do you ask such things?"

" 'Scuse me," said the Elephant's Child most politely, "but my father has spanked me, my mother has spanked me, not to mention my tall aunt, the Ostrich, and my tall uncle, the Giraffe, who can kick ever so hard, as well as my broad aunt, the Hippopotamus, and my hairy uncle, the Baboon, *and* including the Bi-Colored-Python-Rock-Snake, with the scalesome, flailsome tail, just up the bank, who spanks harder than any of them; and *so*, if it's quite all the same to you, I don't want to be spanked any more."

"Come hither, Little One," said the Crocodile, "for I am the Crocodile," and he wept crocodile-tears to show it was quite true.

Then the Elephant's Child grew all breathless, and panted, and kneeled down on the bank and said, "You are the very person I have been looking for all these long days. Will you please tell me what you have for dinner?"

"Come hither, Little One," said the Crocodile, "and I'll whisper."

Then the Elephant's Child put his head down close to the Crocodile's musky, tusky mouth, and the Crocodile caught him by his little nose, which up to that very week, day, hour, and minute, had been no bigger than a boot, though much more useful.

"I think," said the Crocodile—and he said it between his teeth, like this—"I think today I will begin with Elephant's Child!"

At this, O Best Beloved, the Elephant's Child was much annoyed, and he said, speaking through his nose, like this, "Led go! You are hurtig be!"

Then the Bi-Colored-Python-Rock-Snake scuffled down from the bank and said, "My young friend, if you do not now, immediately and instantly, pull as hard as ever you can, it is my opinion that your acquaintance in the large-pattern leather ulster" (and by this he meant the Crocodile) "will jerk you into yonder limpid stream before you can say Jack Robinson."

This is the way Bi-Colored-Python-Rock-Snakes always talk.

Then the Elephant's Child sat back on his little haunches, and pulled, and pulled, and pulled, and his nose began to stretch. And the Crocodile floundered into the water, making it all creamy with great sweeps of his tail, and *he* pulled, and pulled, and pulled.

And the Elephant's Child's nose kept on stretching; and the Elephant's Child spread all his little four legs and pulled, and pulled, and pulled, and his nose kept on stretching; and the Crocodile threshed his tail like an oar, and *he* pulled, and pulled, and pulled, and at each pull the Elephant's Child's nose grew longer and longer—and it hurt him hijjus!

Then the Elephant's Child felt his legs slipping, and he said through his nose, which was now nearly five feet long, "This is too butch for be!"

Then the Bi-Colored-Python-Rock-Snake came down from the bank, and knotted himself in a double-clove-hitch around the Elephant's Child's hind legs, and said, "Rash and inexperienced traveler, we will now seriously devote ourselves to a little high tension, because if we do not, it is my impression that yonder self-propelling man-of-war with the armor-plated upper deck" (and by this, O Best Beloved, he meant the Crocodile) "will permanently vitiate your future career."

This is the way all Bi-Colored-Python-Rock-Snakes always talk.

So he pulled, and the Elephant's Child pulled, and the Crocodile pulled; but the Elephant's Child and the Bi-

Colored-Python-Rock-Snake pulled hardest; and at last the Crocodile let go of the Elephant's Child's nose with a plop that you could hear all up and down the Limpopo.

Then the Elephant's Child sat down most hard and sudden; but first he was careful to say "Thank you" to the Bi-Colored-Python-Rock-Snake; and next he was kind to his poor pulled nose, and wrapped it all up in cool banana leaves, and hung it in the great gray-green, greasy Limpopo to cool.

"What are you doing that for?" said the Bi-Colored-Python-Rock-Snake.

" 'Scuse me," said the Elephant's Child, "but my nose is badly out of shape, and I am waiting for it to shrink."

"Then you will have to wait a long time," said the Bi-Colored-Python-Rock-Snake. "Some people do not know what is good for them."

How To Use a Trunk

The Elephant's Child sat there for three days waiting for his nose to shrink. But it never grew any shorter, and, besides, it made him squint. For, O Best Beloved, you will see and understand that the Crocodile had pulled it out into a really truly trunk, same as all Elephants have today.

At the end of the third day a fly came and stung him on the shoulder, and before he knew what he was doing he lifted up his trunk and hit that fly dead with the end of it.

" 'Vantage number one!" said the Bi-Colored-Python-Rock-Snake. "You couldn't have done that with a mere-smear nose. Try and eat a little now."

Before he thought what he was doing, the Elephant's Child put out his trunk and plucked a large bundle of grass, dusted it clean against his fore-legs, and stuffed it into his own mouth.

" 'Vantage number two!" said the Bi-Colored-Python-Rock-Snake. "You couldn't have done that with a mere-smear nose. Don't you think the sun is very hot here?"

"It is," said the Elephant's Child, and before he thought what he was doing he schlooped up a schloop of mud from the banks of the great gray-green, greasy Limpopo, and slapped it on his head, where it made a cool schloopy-sloshy mud-cap all trickly behind the ears.

" 'Vantage number three!" said the Bi-Colored-Python-Rock-Snake. "You couldn't have done that with a mere-smear nose. Now how do you feel about being spanked again?"

" 'Scuse me," said the Elephant's Child, "but I should not like it at all."

"How would you like to spank somebody?" said the Bi-Colored-Python-Rock-Snake.

"I should like it very much indeed," said the Elephant's Child.

"Well," said the Bi-Colored-Python-Rock-Snake, "you will find that new nose of yours very useful to spank people with."

"Thank you," said the Elephant's Child, "I'll remember that; and now I think I'll go home to all my dear families and try."

So the Elephant's Child went home across Africa frisking and whisking his trunk. When he wanted fruit to eat, he pulled fruit down from a tree, instead of waiting for it to fall as he used to do. When he wanted grass, he plucked grass up from the ground, instead of going down on his knees as he used to do. When the flies bit him, he broke off the branch of a tree and used it as a fly-whisk; and he made himself a new, cool, slushy-squashy mud-cap whenever the sun was hot. When he felt lonely walking through Africa, he sang to himself down his trunk, and the noise was louder than several brass bands. He went especially out of his way to find a broad Hippopotamus (she was no relation of his), and he spanked her very hard, to make sure that the Bi-Colored-Python-Rock-Snake had spoken the truth about his new trunk. The rest of the time he picked up the melon rinds that he had dropped on his way to the Limpopo—for he was a Tidy Pachyderm.

One dark evening he came back to all his dear families, and he coiled up his trunk and said, "How do you do?" They were very glad to see him, and immediately said, "Come here and be spanked for your 'satiable curtiosity."

"Pooh," said the Elephant's Child. "I don't think you peoples know anything about spanking; but *I* do, and I'll show you."

Then he uncurled his trunk and knocked two of his dear brothers head over heels.

"O Bananas!" said they. "Where did you learn that trick, and what have you done to your nose?"

"I got a new one from the Crocodile on the banks of the great gray-green, greasy Limpopo River," said the Elephant's Child. "I asked him what he had for dinner, and he gave me this to keep."

"It looks very ugly," said his hairy uncle, the Baboon.

"It does," said the Elephant's Child. "But it's very useful," and he picked up his hairy uncle, the Baboon, by one hairy leg, and hove him into a hornet's nest.

Then that bad Elephant's Child spanked all his dear families for a long time, till they were very warm and greatly astonished. He pulled out his tall Ostrich aunt's tail-feathers; and he caught his tall uncle, the Giraffe, by the hind-leg, and dragged him through a thorn-bush; and he shouted at his broad aunt, the Hippopotamus, and blew bubbles into her ear when she was sleeping in the water after meals; but he never let any one touch Kolokolo Bird.

At last, things grew so exciting that his dear families went off one by one in a hurry to the banks of the great gray-green, greasy Limpopo River, all set about with fever-trees, to borrow new noses from the Crocodile. When they came back nobody spanked anybody any more; and ever since that day, O Best Beloved, all the Elephants you will ever see, besides all those that you won't, have trunks precisely like the trunk of the 'satiable Elephant's Child.

The Second Voyage of Sinbad the Sailor

From *The Arabian Nights*

In the magnificent city of Bagdad, in the reign of the good Caliph Haroun-al-Raschid, there lived a merchant named Sinbad. He had sailed around the world, men said. He was enormously wealthy. Every day at his house a banquet was spread, with the finest and most tempting foods, and beautiful and agreeable music.

Now one day, a poor porter named Hinbad happened to be in that part of town where Sinbad had his home. Only wealthy people lived in that quarter, and Hinbad's errands seldom took him there. So when he saw the fine large mansion of Sinbad, and smelled the rich food and heard the music, he had to ask a servant at the gate whose house it was.

"Do you live in Bagdad and not know the house of Sinbad, the famous sailor?" asked the servant, amazed.

"Oh, Heaven!" exclaimed the porter. "Everyone has indeed heard of Sinbad. And why should it be that every day I must labor, and scarcely get bread for myself and my family, while Sinbad may spend vast riches and lead a life of pleasure?"

Picking up his load, Hinbad was about to go on. Just then a servant came out of the house and stopped him.

"My master, Sinbad, desires to speak with you," said the servant. And he led the poor porter through the courtyard into the dining hall. There sat a large company of people richly dressed, around a table loaded with good things. And at the head of the table was Sinbad himself, in a gorgeous turban, with many servants behind him.

Hinbad trembled with fear and embarrassment. But Sinbad called Hinbad to a seat at his own right hand. He himself served Hinbad with the best and most delicious food. And after the meal was over, Sinbad asked Hinbad his name and business.

"My lord, I am a poor porter. They call me Hinbad."

"And perhaps you would repeat for me the words you spoke in the street a while ago." For Sinbad had happened to overhear Hinbad complaining, through the window, and had sent the servant out to fetch him.

Hinbad was more embarrassed than ever. "My lord," he said, hanging his head, "my weariness made me say what I should not have said. I beg you to pardon me."

"I am not so unjust as to be angry with you," said Sinbad. "But I was just going to relate to this company the story of my second voyage. Stay and hear. Then you can judge for yourself whether my riches were acquired without labor, and whether I deserve the life of ease and pleasure which I now enjoy."

So saying, Sinbad settled himself more comfortably. All the company stopped talking and looked at him, waiting to hear the tale.

"After my first voyage, of which I told you yesterday," Sinbad began, "I planned to spend the rest of my days in Bagdad. But I soon grew weary of doing nothing. So I bought goods for a voyage, and gathered together a company of merchants upon whom I could depend.

"From island to island we sailed, trading with great

profit. One day we landed on an island fair to see, but apparently uninhabited by man or beast. We wandered about, each at his own pleasure, some here and some there. I ate my noon meal, and lay down in the shade to sleep. But when I awoke, alas, the ship was gone! I ran down to the shore. Her sail was just disappearing over the horizon.

"I was ready to die of grief. I tore my beard, threw dust upon my head, and lay down upon the ground in despair. Why had I not been content to stay at home, with the riches already acquired? Now it was too late.

"At length I felt calmer. Girding my robes about me, I climbed to the top of a tall tree to look about. Toward the sea, I could see nothing but sky and water. Looking over the land, however, I could see, far off, something white. Coming down from the tree and gathering up the scraps from my meal into a leather bag, I started off toward it.

"As I came up to the thing after a long while, I thought it was some sort of great white dome. I touched it. The walls were very smooth. I walked around it. But there was no door, no window, nor any other opening. Nor was there any way of climbing up the side.

"It was nearly sunset. All of a sudden the sky was darkened, as if by a thick black cloud. I looked up. There, flying toward me, was a bird of enormous size.

"Suddenly I remembered hearing sailors speak of a marvelous great bird called the roc. Immediately I saw that the white dome must be the creature's egg. I crept close to the egg. Soon one of the bird's legs, as big as the trunk of a tree, was beside me. I tied myself firmly to the leg with my unrolled turban, gave myself into the hands of Heaven, and went to sleep.

The Vale of the Serpents

"The next morning, before it was yet full day, the bird rose from the egg and flew away. She carried me so high I could not see the earth. Then she came down so rapidly that I lost my senses. Presently I found myself on the ground and hastily untied myself. The roc, having taken up an enormous serpent in her bill, flew away.

"I found myself within a fearful and gloomy valley. On all sides, the mountains rose up so high that their tops were in the clouds. Their sides were too steep to climb. There seemed to be no way to escape.

"As I walked about, I found that the floor of the valley

was paved with sharp jagged stones. Looking closer, I discovered that the stones were diamonds, larger and more beautiful than any I had ever seen. But I had no pleasure in walking among the diamonds, since the valley was likely to be my grave.

"Then I became aware that in the valley also were great numbers of enormous serpents, like the serpent the roc had carried away. Now that day had come, they had stolen away to their dens. The smallest of them could easily have swallowed an elephant.

"All that day I wandered sadly about. When night fell, I went into a cave and rolled a stone into the opening. I ate some of the scraps of food in my leather sack, and tried to sleep. But now the serpents had come from their dens. They hissed so fearfully that I could only lie there trembling. When day broke and I could at last come out of the cave, I was so weary that I lay down in the open and at once went to sleep.

"But suddenly I was awakened by a loud noise. Several large pieces of raw meat had been thrown from the cliffs above, and one had fallen very near me.

"I had heard stories before of this valley, and had always thought them to be idle tales. But now I remembered that to get the diamonds, merchants were said to throw down large pieces of meat, to which the diamonds would stick. Eagles living in the mountains would snatch the meat for their young ones. Then the merchants, who had climbed up to the nests, would drive away the eagles with shouts, and take the diamonds from the meat.

"Now I saw how I should be saved. I began to gather the largest diamonds I could find, and put them in the leather sack in which my food had been. Then, tying the sack and the largest piece of meat firmly to me by my girdle, I lay face down and waited.

"Almost at once, the eagles came. One of the strongest seized the piece of meat to which I was fastened, and carried me off to his nest on the top of the mountain. The merchants began shouting to frighten the eagles away, and one of the merchants soon came to the nest where I was.

"Seeing me, he was alarmed and angry. 'Why did you come here?' he asked. 'Was it to steal my goods?'

" 'You will not be angry with me when you have heard my story,' I replied calmly. 'I have here enough diamonds for both of us, more than all the other merchants together. They have only the diamonds that stuck to their meat. But I gathered these myself in the bottom of the valley.'

"The other merchants came up, then. They were surprised to see me, but even more surprised when I had told my story.

"At their camp, I opened the leather sack and showed them the diamonds I had brought. All the merchants said they had never seen such diamonds before—no, not in all their travels to foreign courts and places. I begged the merchant who had rescued me to take as many of the diamonds for his share as he pleased. However, he would take only one, and that the very smallest. 'This will be enough,' he said, 'to make my fortune for the rest of my days.'

"A day or two later, the merchants being satisfied with their luck, we left that place. We took ship at the first port we reached, and sailed away to the Isle of Roha, where the camphor trees grow. The tree is bored and the camphor juice is collected in a vessel. Then the tree withers and dies.

"On this island I exchanged some of my diamonds for goods to trade, and we went for a time from port to port. At length, enormously wealthy, I again reached Bagdad. Immediately, I gave large presents to the poor, and then lived honorably upon the riches I had acquired with so much risk. I think even you, friend Hinbad, will agree that I have done something to deserve the ease which I now enjoy."

So saying, Sinbad gave the poor porter a hundred pieces of gold. "Come tomorrow, friend Hinbad, and hear the tale of my third voyage," Sinbad invited him. And Hinbad left, scarcely able to believe in his good fortune, and that it was not all a dream.

The Ugly Duckling

Hans Christian Andersen

It was summer. The country was lovely. Golden wheat
and green oats ripened in the fields, and the rich green
meadows were dotted with haystacks. Beyond the fields
and meadows stretched wide woods, hiding deep lakes.

In the bright sunshine stood an old castle, surrounded
by a deep moat, and all overgrown with burdock. Down
at the moat, the thicket was just as wild as in the deepest
woods. And there a duck was sitting on her nest, hatching
her young. She was growing weary of it, because it took
so long.

But now, one after another, the eggs cracked open.
"Peep, peep," said the babies. "Quack, quack," said
Mother Duck. The babies all scrambled out from under
her, looking in wonder at the green world. Mother let
them have a good look, for she knew how good green is
for the eyes.

"How large the world is!" said her babies.

"So you think this is the whole world? Let me tell you, the world stretches far and wide," she said. "Why, it goes as far as the other side of the garden and over to the church-yard."

She got up and said, "I hope all the eggs are hatched. Oh, my, the largest egg is still there. I am sick and tired of it." But she sat down again.

"How are you coming along?" asked the old duck who stopped in to visit.

"The last egg is taking so long," said Mother Duck. "It just won't crack. But look at the others. They are the handsomest ducklings I've ever seen."

"I'm sure the egg that won't crack is a turkey egg," said the old duck. "I was fooled just the same way once. Did I have trouble with that brood! They are afraid of the water, you see. I scolded them and pecked them, but no, they wouldn't go into it. Now, let me look. Yes, that certainly *is* a turkey egg. Leave it alone and go teach the others to swim."

"Oh, I think I'll sit here just a little longer."

"Do as you please. I don't care," said the old duck, and she left.

And then the big egg cracked. "Peep, peep," it said, and out came the last child. It was big and ugly.

Mother Duck looked at it and said, "This really is awfully big for a duckling. Can it be a turkey chick? We'll soon find out. It shall go into the water even if I have to push it in myself!"

The next day was perfectly beautiful. Mother Duck came down to the water with all her family. She splashed in first. "Quack, quack," she commanded, and they all followed. They all swam admirably, even the ugly gray one.

"That surely is no turkey chick," said Mother. "Just look how prettily it uses its legs and how straight it holds itself. It *is* my very own child! Now come, children, and I'll show you the world and introduce you in the duck yard. Keep near me so that no one kicks you, and beware of the cat!"

So they came into the duck yard. There was a noise and a din going on, for two families were fighting over an eel's head. But the cat stole it and went off with it.

"That's how things go in the world," said Mother Duck. "Now pull yourselves together and curtsy nicely before that old duck there at the back. She is the most distinguished of us all, being of Spanish ancestry. That's why she is so fat. And if you look closely, you'll see she's wearing a red string around her leg. That's something very beautiful and the highest distinction a duck can get. It means that no one shall overlook her and that all animals, including men, shall know her. Come on, now. And don't turn your toes in! A well-educated duckling turns his toes out in walking, just as his father and mother do. Now, make a bow and say 'Quack.' "

And so they did. But the ducks of the yard looked them over, saying, "Goodness gracious! Do we have to have this brood here too? Look at that ugly one! No, no, we won't have that!" And one of them came right over and bit the ugly duckling's neck.

"Leave him alone," said Mother Duck. "He doesn't harm anybody, does he?"

"But he is so big and strange," said the duck who bit him. "So he must be cuffed about!"

"She really has nice children," said the old duck, "except that one. That one didn't turn out so well."

"He has been too long in the egg, that's why," said the mother. "He may not be handsome, but he's kindhearted. And he swims as well as the rest. And what's more, he's a drake. So his looks don't matter so much."

"Make yourselves at home, now," said the old duck. "And if you happen to find an eel's head, you may bring it to me."

They felt quite at home, except the ugly one who had been hatched last. He was bitten and teased by all the ducks and the hens in the yard.

Things went from bad to worse. Everybody chased the poor duckling wherever he went. Even his sisters and brothers treated him miserably. The ducks would bite him, the hens peck him, and the girl kick him when she came with their feed.

In the Marsh

The duckling couldn't bear it any longer, and ran away. As he flew over the fence, the little birds fluttered out of the bushes in fright.

"It's my ugliness that frightens them," the duckling thought. Closing his eyes, he kept running till he reached the great marsh where the wild ducks lived. There he rested for the night, tired and discouraged.

In the morning, when the wild ducks saw the newcomer, they asked, "What kind of bird are you? You certainly are ugly! But little do we care as long as you don't marry into our tribe."

Poor duckling! He didn't even dream of marriage. All he wanted was to be allowed to lie in the reeds and have a sip of marsh water now and then.

He had been there for a couple of days when two wild geese—or rather, ganders—came by.

"Listen, young fellow," they said, "you are so ugly it even makes us like you. Don't you want to come with us and be a rover?"

Just then, "Bang, bang!" rang out above their heads, and two shots brought down the two ganders. "Bang! Bang! Bang!" Flocks of wild geese flew up from the reeds. A great hunt was on. The bird dogs—the setters—splashed through the marsh, right through the mud and rushes.

The poor duckling trembled with fear. He twisted his head to hide it under his wing, but right at his side appeared a big setter with frightfully glaring eyes and sharp, bright teeth. He looked and sniffed, and "Splash, splash!"—off he went without harming the duckling.

"Thank heaven," sighed the duckling. "I'm so ugly that even the dogs won't bite me." And he lay quite still while the shots whizzed through the reeds.

It was late afternoon before all became quiet again. The poor duckling looked around cautiously and then hurried out of the marsh, across fields and meadows, as fast as his legs would carry him. Out in the open, the wind was very strong. He could hardly struggle along.

Before dusk, he reached a peasant's hut. It was so ramshackle it didn't know which way to fall—and that's why it still stood. The wind grew stronger and stronger. The duckling noticed that the door to the hut was hanging on only one hinge, leaving a crack, through which he quickly slipped into the room.

In the hut lived an old woman with a tomcat and a hen.

The tomcat, called "Sonny," could arch his back and purr —and even make his fur spark, though for that stunt you had to stroke his fur the wrong way. The hen had very short legs, so she was called "Chicky Shortleg." She was an excellent egg-layer, and the woman loved her as she would have loved a child.

The Cat and the Hen

In the morning, they all noticed the little stranger right away. The cat began to purr and the hen to cluck.

"Well, what do we have here?" said the old woman, looking at the duckling. But her eyesight was not good. She thought it was a fat duck who had got lost. "I call that good fortune," she said. "Now I can have duck eggs, too— if it doesn't turn out to be a drake. We'll have to try it."

The cat was master, and the hen mistress, in this house.

"Can you lay eggs?" the hen asked the duckling.

"No."

And the cat asked, "Can you arch your back and purr, and send sparks off your fur?"

"No."

Timidly the poor duckling sat down in a corner. He began to think of the fresh air and the sunshine outdoors, and such a longing came over him to be in the water that he could not help telling the hen about it.

"Are you crazy?" she said. "That's what comes of doing nothing. Lay eggs or purr, and then this whim of yours will quickly pass."

"But it's so wonderful to swim!" said the duckling. "So wonderful when you dive to the bottom and feel the water closing over your head!"

"What a pleasure *that* must be!" said the hen. "You must be completely out of your mind. Ask the cat, who is the wisest creature I know, whether he can swim or dive. Not to mention myself. Ask our mistress, the old woman. No one on earth is wiser than she. Do you believe she'd like to swim and let the water close over her head?"

"You don't understand," said the duckling.

"My, if we don't, who would?" said the hen. "You don't mean to say you are wiser than the cat and the old woman— not to mention myself? Stop boasting, youngster, and thank heaven you are here. And now see to it that you lay eggs. And learn to purr and make sparks."

"I think I'd prefer to go out into the world," said the duckling.

"All right, then—go!" said the hen.

And the duckling went. He swam and he dived marvelously. But no animal paid any attention to him because he was so ugly.

Autumn came, and the leaves in the woods turned yellow and brown. The dark clouds threatened hail and snow. On the fence sat the crow, cawing of cold. The poor duckling had a hard time of it.

One evening, as the sun was setting in splendor and glory, there came a flock of fine large birds out of the bushes. Such beautiful birds the duckling had never seen before.

They were swans, dazzling white, with long, graceful necks. They spread their wide, wide wings and flew off with a strange cry. They soared up so high that the duckling felt strangely moved.

He swam round and round in the water, craning his neck after them, himself uttering so strange and eerie a cry that it made him shiver with fright.

When he could no longer see the swans, he dived deep down to the bottom, and he was still all upset when he came up again. He loved these birds as he had never loved anything before. He did not envy them their beauty—how could he ever think of even wishing such beauty for himself? He, poor ugly creature, would have been happy had the ducks let him stay among them!

The winter was so cold, so bitter cold, that the duckling had to swim round and round to keep the water from freezing over. But night after night, the hole where he swam got smaller and smaller. The duckling couldn't let his legs rest for a moment, lest the water freeze entirely. But at last his strength failed him, and he lay quite still, frozen fast in the ice.

In the early hours of the morning, a peasant came by. Seeing what had happened, he went out, cracked the ice with his wooden shoe, lifted the duckling out, and carried him home to his wife. And they brought him back to life.

The children would have liked to play with him, but the duckling thought they wanted to harm him. Afraid, he flew away from them and right into the milk pail, spilling the milk all over the floor. The woman threw her hands up in despair. The duckling flew into the kneading trough—right into the butter—and then into the meal tub. He certainly looked awful now! The woman shrieked and chased him with the fire tongs. Laughing and screaming, the children ran into one another trying to catch him. By luck, he found the door open. He fluttered out and lay underneath the bushes in the fresh snow, almost unconscious.

It would be too distressing to tell of all the misery he had to suffer through that winter. He lay in the reeds of the marsh when the sun began to shine warm again. The larks sang a joyful greeting to the glorious spring.

All at once, the duckling lifted his wings. Their beat was much more powerful than ever before. They carried him aloft, and before he knew it he landed in a big garden. There the apple trees were in full bloom, and the sweet scent of lilacs filled the air. It was beautiful here—fresh and lovely along the winding channels of a little stream, overhung by clusters of blossoming lilac.

And then, out from the thicket right in front of him, appeared three lovely white swans. Their wing feathers rustled as they moved over the water. The duckling recognized these marvelous birds, and a strange sadness took hold of him.

"I shall fly over to these royal birds," he said to himself. "They will surely peck me to death for having dared to show myself before them in all my ugliness. But that won't matter. Better to end amongst them than to be nipped by the ducks, pecked by the hens, and kicked by the hen-yard girl."

And he flew over to them. The swans saw him coming and with rustling wings sailed toward him.

"Kill me!" said the poor duckling, and he bent his head down to the water to wait.

But what did he see in the clear mirror below? His own reflection! No longer did it show a dark, ugly, and unlovely bird. No, he himself was a swan!

The big swans pressed close to him, stroking him with their bills. Children came into the garden to throw the swans bread and seeds. And the smallest child cried, "Look, a new one is here!"

The others echoed, "Yes, yes, a new one has come!" They clapped their hands and danced merrily and ran to tell their father and mother, "The new one is the loveliest of all!" And the old swans bowed before him.

He felt bashful and happy, but not a bit haughty. With his feathers rustling and his graceful neck up high, he said from the bottom of his heart, "Of so much happiness I dared not even dream, when I was the ugly duckling!"

Other Lands and Other Faces

Other lands and other faces,
  Other names and ways,
Strange processions in strange places,
  Other nights and days . . .

Same imagining and dreaming—
  Courage, friends, and fame—
Hearts, no matter what the seeming,
  Everywhere the same.

—*Dorothy Hall*

The Shark

Armstrong Sperry

Mafatu was a boy of the South Seas. His mother had been drowned in a storm when he was a baby, and he was deathly afraid of the ocean. Cowards were not liked among Mafatu's people. All the boys made fun of him. Finally, in desperation, he sailed in a boat to a far, uninhabited island, to prove to himself his own courage. His only companion was his dog, Uri.

One morning, far down the beach, Mafatu came upon a sheltered cove. His heart gave a leap of joy; for there, white-gleaming in the sun, was all that remained of the skeleton of a whale. It might not have meant very much to you or to me. But to Mafatu it meant knives and fishhooks, bone for darts and spears, a shoulder blade for an ax. It was a real treasure. The boy leaped up and down in his excitement. "Uri!" he shouted. "We're rich! Come— help me drag these bones home!"

His hands seemed all thumbs in his eagerness. He tied as many bones as he could manage into two bundles. One bundle he shouldered himself. The other, Uri dragged behind him. And thus they returned to the camp, weary but filled with happiness. Even the dog seemed to have some understanding of what this discovery meant, or he was at least excited by his master's high spirits. He leaped about like a puppy, yapping until he was hoarse.

Now began the long task of grinding the knife and the ax. Hour after long hour, squatting before a slab of rock, Mafatu worked and worked, until his hands were raw and blistered and the sweat ran down into his eyes. The knife came first, since that was the most needful. Its blade was ten inches long, its handle a knob of bone. It was sharp enough to cut the fronds of coconut trees, to slice off the end of a green nut. *Ai*, but it was a wonderful knife! All Mafatu's skill went into it. It would be a fine weapon as well, the boy thought grimly, as he ground it down to a sharp point. Some sea robber had been breaking into his bamboo trap, and he was going to find out who the thief was! Was it that old hammerhead shark who was always swimming around, just as if he owned the lagoon?

Fishing with a line took too long when you were working against time. Mafatu could not afford to have his trap robbed. Twice it had been broken into, the bamboos crushed, and the fish inside it eaten. It was the work either of a shark or of an octopus. That was certain. No other fish was strong enough to snap the bamboo.

Mafatu's mouth was set in a grim line as he worked away on his knife. That old hammerhead—of course he *was* the thief! Mafatu had come to know him; for every day when the boy went out with his trap, that shark, larger than all the others, was circling around watchfully. The other sharks seemed to treat the hammerhead with great respect.

Hunger alone drove Mafatu out to the reef to set his trap. He knew that if he was to keep his strength to do all that lay ahead, he must have fish to add to the fruit he ate. But often, as he set his trap far out by the reef, the hammerhead would approach and roll over slightly in passing. The cold gleam of its eye filled Mafatu with fear and anger.

"Wait, you!" the boy threatened darkly, shaking his fist at the *ma'o* (shark). "Wait until I have my knife! You will not be so brave then, Ma'o. You will run away when you see it flash."

The Test of Courage

But the morning that the knife was finished, Mafatu did not feel so brave as he would have liked. He hoped he would never see the hammerhead again. Paddling out to the reef, he glanced down from time to time at the long-bladed knife where it hung about his neck by a cord. It wasn't, after all, such a dangerous weapon. It was only a knife made by a boy from a whale's rib.

Uri sat on the edge of the raft, sniffing at the wind. Mafatu always took his dog along, for Uri howled loudly if he were left behind. And Mafatu had come to depend on the companionship of the little yellow dog. The boy talked with the animal as if he were another person, consulting with him, playing when there was time for play. They were very close, these two.

This morning, as they approached the spot where the fish trap was, Mafatu saw the polished dorsal of the hated hammerhead circling slowly in the water. It was like a black triangle, making a little furrow in the water as it passed.

"*Aiá*, Ma'o!" the boy shouted roughly, trying to get up his courage. "I have my knife today, see! Coward who robs traps—catch your own fish!"

The hammerhead approached the raft without haste; it rolled over slightly, and its jaws seemed to curve in a grin. Uri ran to the edge of the raft, barking furiously. The hair on the dog's neck stood up stiffly. The shark, paying no attention, moved away. Then, with a whip of its powerful tail, it rushed at the bamboo fish trap and grabbed it in its jaws. Mafatu was struck dumb. The hammerhead shook the trap as a dog might shake a rat. The boy watched, fascinated, unable to make a move. He saw the muscles work in the fish's neck as the great tail beat the water to foam. The trap splintered into bits, while the fish within escaped, only to vanish into the shark's mouth. Mafatu was filled with helpless anger. The hours he had spent making that trap! But all he could do was shout threats at his enemy.

Uri was running from one side of the raft to the other, furious with excitement. A large wave sheeted across the reef. At that second, the dog's shift in weight tipped the raft dangerously. With a yelp, Uri slid off into the water. Mafatu sprang to catch him, but he was too late.

Instantly, the hammerhead whipped about. The wave pushed the raft away. Uri, swimming frantically, tried to regain it. There was desperation in the brown eyes so faithful and true. Mafatu leaned forward. His dog, his companion. . . . The hammerhead was moving in slowly. A mighty anger stormed through the boy. He gripped his knife. Then he was over the side in a clean-curving dive.

Mafatu came up under his enemy. The shark whirled

about. Its rough hide scraped the flesh from the boy's shoulder. In that instant, Mafatu stabbed. Deep, deep into the white belly. There was a terrific shock. Water lashed to foam. Gasping, the boy fought for life and air.

It seemed that he would never reach the surface. *Aué,* his lungs would burst! . . . At last his head broke water. Putting his face to the surface, he saw the great shark turn over, fathoms deep. Blood flowed from the wound in its belly. Instantly, gray shapes rushed in—other sharks, tearing the wounded hammerhead to pieces.

Uri—where was he? Mafatu saw his dog then. Uri was trying to pull himself up on the raft. Mafatu caught him by the neck and dragged him up to safety. Then he pulled his dog to him and hugged him close, talking to him foolishly. Uri yelped for joy and licked his master's cheek.

It wasn't until Mafatu reached shore that he realized what he had done. He had killed the *ma'o* with his own hand, with nothing but a bone knife. He could never have done it for himself. Fear would have robbed his arm of all strength. He had done it for Uri, his dog. And he felt suddenly humble, with gratitude.

At the Grandfather's House

Johanna Spyri

Heidi's parents had died when she was a baby, and her Aunt Dete had taken care of her. Now Dete wished to take a new job. So she brought Heidi to her grandfather's. The old man had lived by himself for many years high on one of the beautiful Swiss mountains, and was thought to be fierce and stern. The people in the village below were worried about how he would treat the little girl.

After Dete had gone, the grandfather sat down again on the bench. He smoked his pipe without saying a word, his eyes fixed on the ground. In the meantime, Heidi was busily looking about her. She saw the goats' shed near the hut and peeped into it. It was empty.

Continuing to explore, she came to the fir trees back of the hut. The wind was blowing hard. It roared through the branches, high up in the very tops. Heidi stood still and listened. When the sound died down a little, she went on around to the other side of the hut, coming back to her grandfather. She stood directly in front of him, put her hands behind her back, and gazed steadily at him. Her grandfather looked up.

"What do you want?" he asked.

"I want to see what you have inside the house," said Heidi.

"Come along, then!" And the grandfather got up and started to go in.

"Bring your bundle of clothes," he said, as he reached the door.

"I won't need them any more," replied Heidi.

The old man turned around and looked sharply at the child. Her black eyes sparkled as she waited to see what was inside the house.

"She's not stupid," he said, half to himself. Then he
asked aloud, "Why won't you need them any more?"

"Because I want to go like the goats, with their thin,
quick legs."

"So you shall. But bring the things anyhow," commanded the grandfather. "We can put them away in the
cupboard."

Heidi obeyed. The old man opened the door, and Heidi
followed him into a fairly large room. The room made up
the whole hut. It was furnished with a table and a chair,
and—in one corner—the grandfather's bed. In another
corner was the fireplace, where a large kettle hung. On the
other side of the room, in the wall, was a door. The grandfather opened the door, and there was the cupboard. His

clothes hung there. On one shelf were his shirts, stockings, and linen. On another shelf stood plates, cups, and glasses. On the highest shelf of all were a loaf of bread, smoked meat, and cheese. As soon as he opened the door, Heidi hurried in with her bundle and pushed it as far back as she could, so that it would be hard to find again.

Then, looking carefully around the room, she asked, "Where shall I sleep, Grandfather?"

"Wherever you like," was the answer.

The idea suited Heidi. She examined every corner of the room. Beside her grandfather's bed was a little ladder, leading up to the hayloft. Heidi climbed the ladder. The loft was full of fresh, fragrant hay. Through a round window, she could see far down into the valley below.

A Room With a View

"I'll sleep up here," Heidi called down. "It is beautiful! Just come and see how beautiful it is here, Grandfather."

"Oh, I know all about it," the grandfather's voice said from below.

"I'm going to make me a bed," called out the child again, trotting busily to and fro in the loft. "But you must come up and bring a sheet. The bed needs a sheet for me to sleep on."

"Well, well," said the grandfather, below. He went to the cupboard and rummaged about. Finally, he pulled out from under his shirts a coarse, heavy piece of cloth, which might do for a sheet. When he came up the ladder, he found that Heidi had indeed made a very neat little bed. It was turned so that she could look from it straight out through the round open window.

"That is very nicely made," said the grandfather. "Next comes the sheet—but wait a moment—". And he took up a big armful of hay and made the bed twice as thick, so that Heidi would not feel the hard floor through it. "There, now put the sheet on."

Heidi quickly took hold of the cloth, but she could not lift it because it was so heavy. However, this was all to the good, because the sharp ends of hay could not prick through its firm weave. So Heidi and the grandfather together spread the sheet over the hay, and Heidi tucked the ends under. It looked quite nice, and Heidi stood gazing at it thoughtfully.

"We have forgotten something, Grandfather," she said.

"And what is that?" he asked.

"The cover. When we go to bed, we creep in between the sheet and the cover."

"Is that so? But what if I haven't any cover?"

"Oh, that's all right," said Heidi, soothingly. "We can use more hay for a cover." She was about to run to the piled hay again, but her grandfather stopped her.

"Wait a minute," he said, and disappeared down the ladder to his own bed. When he came back, he laid a large, heavy linen sack on the floor.

"Isn't that better than hay?" he asked her. Heidi pulled

at the sack as hard as ever she could, trying to straighten it out. Her grandfather helped, and when it, too, was spread out on the bed, everything looked very neat and comfortable. Heidi regarded it admiringly. "That is a splendid cover," she said, "and the whole bed is beautiful! I wish it were night so that I could sleep in it!"

"I think we might have some lunch first," said the grandfather. "What do you say?"

Heidi had been so excited about the bed that she had forgotten everything else. But now that food was mentioned, she was suddenly very hungry. She had eaten nothing but a piece of bread and a cup of weak coffee early in the morning, and on top of that she had made a long journey. "Yes, I think so, too."

"Well, since we think the same thing, let us go down," said the old man. Following Heidi down the ladder, he went to the fireplace, pushed aside the large kettle, and pulled forward the little one that hung on the chain. He sat down on a three-legged wooden stool and built a fire. After a while, the kettle began to boil, and the old man toasted a large piece of cheese over the fire, at the end of a long iron fork. He turned the cheese this way and that, until it was golden yellow on all sides.

Heidi watched him. Suddenly an idea came to her. She jumped up and ran to the cupboard, and made several trips between it and the table. When the grandfather brought the toasted cheese, the table was already neatly laid with the round loaf of bread, two plates, and two knives. Heidi's bright eyes had seen everything in the cupboard. She knew what would be needed for the meal.

"That is right, to see for yourself what has to be done," said the grandfather. He laid the cheese on the bread and put the teapot on the table. "But there is still something else."

Heidi ran back to the cupboard. She spied a small bowl, and behind it, two glasses. She came back at once with the bowl and the glasses, and put them on the table also.

"Very good. But where are you going to sit?"

The grandfather himself was sitting in the only chair. Heidi flew like an arrow to the fireplace, carried back the little three-legged stool, and sat down on it.

"Well, you have a chair, sure enough. But it is rather a low one," the grandfather said.

He got up, filled the little bowl with milk, put it on his own chair, and pushed it up to the three-legged stool, so that Heidi had a table in front of her. He put a large slice of bread and a piece of the golden cheese on the chair and said, "Now eat!"

Sitting on the corner of the table, the grandfather began his own dinner. Heidi picked up the bowl of milk and drank and drank without stopping. Drawing a long breath, she finally set the bowl down.

"Do you like the milk?" her grandfather asked.

"I never tasted such good milk before," Heidi told him.

"Then you must have some more." The grandfather filled the bowl again and put it in front of the child. Contentedly, she began to eat her bread, spreading it with the toasted cheese, soft as butter. It tasted very good, with frequent drinks of milk.

When lunch was over, the grandfather went out to clean the goat-shed. Heidi watched while he swept it with a broom and laid down fresh straw for the animals to sleep on. Then he went into his little workshop. He found some round sticks, cut and shaped a board, bored some holes in it, and put the round sticks into them. Suddenly it was a stool like the fireplace one, only higher. Heidi was speechless with amazement.

"Do you know what this is, Heidi?" asked the grandfather.

"It is a stool for me. I know, because it is so high. You made it so quickly!" said the child. She was still deeply astonished.

"She understands what she sees. Her eyes are in the right place," the grandfather said to himself. He went around the hut, driving a nail here and there, and mending wherever it was needed. Heidi followed him step by step, and watched every move.

The Goats

Evening was coming on. The sound was getting deeper in the old fir trees, for a strong wind had come up and was blowing through their thick tops. To Heidi, the sound was so beautiful that she skipped and jumped in delight, under the trees. The grandfather stood in the doorway, watching the child.

Suddenly, there came a shrill whistle. Down from the mountain above, the goats came leaping, with Peter in the midst of them. With a shout of joy, Heidi rushed in among them.

At the hut, two pretty, slender goats—one white, the other brown—left the others and went over to the grandfather. They licked his hands, in which he had brought some salt to welcome them, as he did every evening. Peter went on with his flock. Heidi gently petted first one goat and then the other. She was wild with delight.

"Are they ours, Grandfather? Are they both ours? Will they sleep in the shed? Will they stay with us for always?" asked Heidi.

When the goats had finished their salt, the old man said, "Go and bring out your little bowl and the bread."

Heidi obeyed and came back at once. Milking one of the goats, the grandfather filled the bowl and cut off a piece of bread. "Now eat your supper and go on up to bed!" he said. "Your Aunt Dete left another bundle for you. Your nightgown and other night things are in it. You will find it in the cupboard. I must take care of the goats now, so sleep well!"

"Good-night, Grandfather! Good-night—oh, what are their names, Grandfather? What are they called?" cried the child, running after the old man and the goats as they went into the shed.

"The white one is called Little Swan. The brown one is Little Bear," answered the grandfather.

"Good-night, Little Swan! Good-night, Little Bear!" Heidi sang after them. Sitting down on the bench, she ate the bread and drank the milk. But the wind was so strong that it almost blew her off the seat. So she hurried to finish; then went in and climbed the ladder to her bed. At once she fell asleep, and slept as soundly and as well as if she had been in the bed of some royal princess.

An Iceland Christmas

Steingrimur Arason

Nonni lived on a little Iceland farm with his father,
Erik, and his mother, Helga. To these people, the festival
of Christmas, coming in the cold winter gloom, was one
of the most beautiful times of the year.

When Christmas was still a whole month away, everyone
began talking about it. Old Gudda, one of the house
servants, was suddenly the most important person in the
household. She was the only one who could remember
what *Jól* (Yule) had been like in the old days.

All day long, her half-querulous voice could be heard
in the kitchen. "Not that way. It was not like that we did
it when I was young." Once, when Nonni was slow in
moving to do some errand, she said, "Gryla will surely put
you in her bag and carry you away."

Of course, Nonni had long since stopped being frightened by such tales, but he liked to think about them. No

one believed any longer in Gryla's thirteen sons, the Christmas goblins who appeared, one at a time, the thirteen days before *Jól* and left, one at a time, the thirteen days afterward. But it was fun to pretend the wicked lads were about. And it was convenient to blame spilled milk or other accidents on them. They were very big and ugly, and their feet were round like pancakes. Gudda always made sure the Christmas goodies were put out of their way.

Helga laughed at this part of Christmas, but she admitted it was fun. Long ago, she said, the Vikings had sailed to Ireland. Many of the Irish had joined them on their return voyages to Iceland. Irish ideas about Christmas had become mixed up with the Norse customs. This accounted for the fairy lore, which used to be so important a part of the Christmas season. It was dying out now. But Gudda wanted *Jól* to be just as she had known it when she was young; so, to please her, the people at Fairdale kept up the old customs.

At Christmas time, in contrast with the usual plainness of winter meals, there was always all the food one could want. Even the animals were given double feedings on Christmas Eve. The kitchen was filled all day long with the smell of baking. Even Nonni had a hand in it. Covered from chin to toe in one of Helga's aprons, he spent one afternoon making the *laufabraud*. Everyone, including Erik, worked in the kitchen making his own pile of these little flour cakes, each as big around as a plate.

There was so much laughter and loud talk that Skuggi, the dog, became too excited. He had to be put outside, with flour on the end of his nose. Behind him, he left a perfect pawmark in the center of one of the beautiful cakes of Sigga, the maid! She was about to toss it into the scrap pail. But a chorus of protest came from all sides.

"No, no, Sigga! That's a lovely one."

"That is Skuggi's *laufabraud*. It has a better design than any of ours."

"We will give it to him on Christmas Eve."

Sigga laughed, then, and gave it to Helga, who fried it with the others in sizzling sheep's fat. It was put away with the rest, to be brought out on Christmas Eve, along with the platters of smoked rib meat, fat sausages, and smoked leg of lamb.

The days that followed were busy, happy ones. Nonni helped Sigga and his mother give the house a brisk cleaning. He helped in the making of the candles. He went

with Erik up into the hills to get ground pine to trim the
badstofa (sleeping-living room). He spent some time with
Glaesir each day, in the stable, combing and brushing the
pony's white coat.

At last, it was the day before Christmas. No one but
Gudda had discovered any traces of the visits of the Christmas goblins, but she declared it was plain as day they were
around. Two cakes had disappeared from the storeroom.
Sigga looked meaningly at Thor, and he grinned a little
slyly. One of Gudda's stockings had disappeared, and it
was found mysteriously on the floor of the stable. Nonni
spoke to Skuggi about this. But the dog looked at the limp
stocking so innocently that nothing could be proved.

As Christmas Eve approached, Gudda began to look a
little anxious. "Are you going to invite the fairies this
year, Helga Magnusdoter?"

Helga, who liked to tease the old woman herself, but
allowed no one else to, answered with an uninterested
air. "Oh, I don't believe that will be necessary, Gudda.
There haven't been any fairies around for a long time."

Nonni felt disappointed for a moment. Then he caught
the smile in his mother's eyes and decided she meant to
do it, after all.

But Gudda was instantly indignant. "No fairies! And
it was only a week ago that they helped me churn the
butter, when you couldn't make it come!"

Helga couldn't help smiling. "The fairies, Gudda? It

was because I had sprained my wrist that I couldn't churn the butter. But we shall see. If there is time after the candles are put around, I might manage to invite the fairies."

Gudda's face took on a look of righteousness. "When I was young, we attended to the important matters first."

Inviting the Fairies

Gudda had her way, as she always did. When dusk was just settling over the farmhouse and the day was beginning to be "holy," Helga set lighted candles in every room, in every window, on tables and shelves, and even in the long turf-lined hallway. Then she walked sunwise around the house, chanting the old rhyme which she had known since her childhood:

> Come, those who want to come;
> Stay, those who want to stay;
> Go, those who want to go,
> Without harm to me or mine.

Nonni loved this. Ever since he was small, it had made him feel safe and happy.

By six o'clock, the outside work was finished. The entire
household was crowded into the *badstofa*. Helga opened
a large bundle and gave out the new garments, one to each
person, for everyone must wear something new at *Jól*. The
men received knitted socks, and the women new shawls—
all except Gudda, who was given a pair of woolen stockings to replace those she believed stolen by the goblins.
For Nonni, there was a beautiful new sweater with red
embroidery across the shoulders.

Erik brought out the Bible, and read the Christmas story
aloud, while everyone kept very still, watching the flower-
like candle flames. When the story was ended, everyone
joined in a song. The candle flames stirred and danced
with their singing. Then there was handshaking all
around, and everyone wished everyone a *"Gledileg Jól"*
(joyful Christmas). The plates, heaped high with good
things to eat, were brought in. Skuggi received his very
own *laufabraud*, which he gulped down without even
taking the time to admire his beautiful pawmark.

When Nonni awoke the next morning, he lay staring out of the little window in his parents' room and saw stars all over a dark blue sky. Through and over it all, trembled the northern lights.

"Just as I wanted it," he thought happily. He left his warm bed and dressed quickly.

"Nonni, do you think you can feed the cows?" Helga said. She and Sigga were making up the beds. "It is eight o'clock now. If we all work hard, we can get through our work in an hour, have breakfast, and go to church."

"I'll be ready," Nonni promised. He hurried through the pitch-dark passageway to the stable. The cows began to low at his approach.

"Be quiet. You will get your breakfast in a minute. You had extra food last night. You are not so hungry."

The women had finished breakfast and were combing out their long hair. While he ate his own breakfast, Nonni watched them braiding it into fancy coils. Then he dressed in his best clothes and was ready.

When they left the house, there was a rim of dawn above the eastern mountains. The ice on the lowlands shone dark as a mirror. The mountains were white with snow.

"Let me fetch Glaesir, Father," Nonni begged.

"Yes, but be careful when you mount him."

Erik was helping Snorri carry out several large trunks. They were to be lashed on the sledge to serve as seats.

Nonni came back rather suddenly on Glaesir, who was eager for a run. When Erik put on the harness, he laid back his ears and showed plainly that he was not going to like this. Erik backed him skillfully into place between the shafts. When the pony was firmly harnessed, he seemed to decide in favor of it, after all. He stood quietly and held his head high. It was an honor, of course, to be selected from among all those other ponies for this important task.

Helga came out with an armful of eider-down quilts. The trunks were spread with woolly sheepskins. Then everyone was seated, wrapped snugly in eider down. Erik looked at Nonni with a smile and motioned him into the driver's seat, himself taking the seat behind. Nonni grew red with pleasure. Without a word, but very proudly, he lifted the reins. At that moment Skuggi, a delighted grin all over his face, came rushing around the corner of the house and leaped into the sledge.

Everyone laughed, and Erik called to the foreman, "Shut him in the house till we are out of sight. I don't like to have dogs around the churchyard."

Skuggi was dragged out, looking very disappointed. Nonni was sorry for him; but not even Skuggi's bad luck could spoil his pleasure in this trip. He was to drive Glaesir for the first time! The pony stamped and threw his head sideways. He wanted to be off. Erik nodded, and the sledge shot forward. The snow flew up in a stinging spray on either side. Behind him, Nonni could hear the women laugh and squeal as they shielded their faces.

"It is a good custom," Erik said, "to go slowly at the start of a journey."

Nonni pulled at the reins, and Glaesir slowed a little—lifting his feet high, one at a time. Each shoe rang sharply as he set it down, and the mountains echoed the sound. Erik had put sharp points at the heel of each shoe, and an edge in front, so Glaesir would not slip on the icy road.

The Runaway

They had not gone half the distance to church when a queer sound behind them made Glaesir lay back his ears. Before anyone could say a word or look around, the pony was flying over the ice. The ground slid away so quickly under the sledge that it made Nonni breathless and dizzy. He hung onto the reins and tried not to look down. Behind him, he could hear his father trying to scramble to his aid.

But the sledge was swaying and tilting dangerously, while Glaesir flew like a bird. No one made a sound. They were too frightened to cry out. Glaesir ran as though he were alone, as though the sledge whizzing along behind him had no weight at all.

Nonni felt the reins slipping from his hold, and he saw how dangerous this would be. The sledge would turn over. They would be dragged along on the sharp ice and snow.

It seemed to Nonni that he sat there a long time hanging on to the reins that pulled, nevertheless, away from him. He could not understand why his father was so slow. They would all be killed and it would be his—Nonni's—fault for being such a poor driver that he could not even hang on to the reins. With a little moan, he managed to thrust his arm through the sliding loop and was instantly jerked from his seat.

"Steady, steady, boy. Easy now . . . slow, slow."

Erik's arm was around Nonni, holding him tight, and Erik's big hands caught the reins in front of Nonni's. Nonni sank back gratefully, feeling that he would never want to drive again. He was weak with relief. Erik's hands, pulling the reins with a steady pressure, told the pony he was not alone. He ran with more smoothness now. The sledge stopped tilting and settled down on its runners. Behind him, Nonni heard his mother draw in her breath. Still no words were spoken.

As Nonni felt the strength return to his arms and legs,

he dared not look around. He had been so sure that he could bring them all proudly into the churchyard. Now he had failed and had risked all their lives. His father would never let him drive Glaesir again. He was so ashamed that his cheeks burned.

"Is Nonni all right?" his mother called anxiously.

"He's fine," Erik answered. Glaesir was trotting calmly now. "He used his head and hung on to the reins when another would have lost them. I hate to think what might have happened if he hadn't."

Nonni heard these words and felt better. He was glad he had done that much, anyway.

"I never was so frightened in all my life," Sigga said. "Nonni, you were brave to hold on like that. I would have fainted dead away."

Nonni still could not trust himself to answer. His arms ached. He was shivering from the strain.

Erik smiled at him. "After this, son, the homeward trip will seem tame. Think you'll be interested enough to try it?"

Nonni struggled with his answer. He had had enough of driving Glaesir, but he was surprised and delighted to find his father was still willing to trust him.

"I guess so," he answered shakily.

"I wonder what could have frightened him so?" Helga said. They had almost forgotten that strange sound behind them. Now they turned to look. Away in the distance, but gaining on them like a little whirlwind, was Skuggi! It was the sound of his claws on the icy road, and his panting breath, that had frightened the pony.

"He's all tired out, but look at him come. I'd make him run all the way home, too," Snorri said. "It would teach him a lesson, maybe."

"And have him frighten the pony again?" Helga asked in horror. "Not if I have to hold the big creature on my lap all the way."

Nonni, watching Skuggi running so hard to catch up with them, would have liked to stop and take him in the sledge. But the church was in sight and he knew the others would not sympathize. No, poor Skuggi would have to go all the way to the churchyard on his own four legs.

As soon as the sledge stopped, Nonni jumped down and gathered the tired dog up in his arms. Skuggi was panting hard. He tried to twist about and lick Nonni's chin, but everyone said, "Bad dog!" Nonni lifted him into the sledge and put him down on a warm sheepskin. He lay there breathing hard in great gasps, but his eyes shone with the pride of achievement.

Glaesir was unharnessed, and Nonni led the pony over to a shed where he would be protected from the cold wind. He gave him some hay and fed him a huge herring he had brought as a special treat.

"Going home, I will drive you again," he told him, "and there had better be no more nonsense. I will drive you so well you will know there is nothing to fear."

The church bells were ringing now. People were arriving from all directions. Nonni went back to his family, and the little group entered the church together. Inside, nearly every seat was taken. Hundreds of candles held their steady flames. As the group found places, the deep organ tones filled the room and everyone burst forth singing.

Jiya Makes a Choice

Pearl S. Buck

A big tidal wave from the ocean has taken the lives of Jiya's family. Now Jiya, a Japanese boy, is living with his friend Kino and Kino's family, who have a farm high up on the mountain.

While Kino and his father were talking, the dusk had deepened. Now, coming up the mountainside, they saw a flickering light. This light was steadily climbing the pathway toward their house.

"I wonder who comes!" Kino exclaimed.

"A visitor," his father replied. "But who can it be?"

In a few minutes, they saw the visitor was Old Gentleman, coming from the castle. His manservant carried the lantern, but Old Gentleman walked behind him very sturdily, with the help of a long staff. They heard Old Gentleman's voice in the dusk.

"Is this the house of Uchiyama the farmer?" Old Gentleman asked.

"It is," his servant replied. "And the farmer sits there at his door with his son."

At this, Kino's father stood up, and Kino stood up too.

"Please, Honored Sir," Kino's father said, "what can I do for you?"

Old Gentleman came forward. "Do you have a lad here by the name of Jiya?"

"He lies sleeping inside my house," Kino's father said.

"I wish to see him," Old Gentleman said. Anyone could see that this old gentleman was one who expected to be obeyed. But Kino's father only smiled.

"Sir, the lad is asleep and I cannot wake him. He suffered the loss of his whole family when the big wave came. Now sleep heals him."

"I will not wake him," Old Gentleman said. "I only want to see him."

So Kino's father led Old Gentleman tiptoe into the room where Jiya slept. Kino went too. The servant held the light, shaded by his hand so it would not fall on Jiya's closed eyes.

Old Gentleman looked down on the sleeping boy. Jiya was very beautiful, even though so pale and weary. He was tall for his age and his body was strong, and his face showed intelligence as well as beauty.

Old Gentleman gazed at him and then motioned to the servant to lead him away. They went again to the dooryard and there Old Gentleman turned to Kino's father.

"It is my habit when the big wave comes to care for those who are orphaned. Three times the wave has come.

Three times I have searched out the orphans and the widows and I have fed them and sheltered them. But I have heard of this boy Jiya and I wish to do more for him. If he is as good as he is handsome, I will make him my own son."

"But Jiya is ours!" Kino cried.

"Hush," his father cried. "We are only poor people. If Old Gentleman wants Jiya, we cannot say we will not give him up."

"Exactly," Old Gentleman said. "I will educate him and give him fine clothes and send him to a good school. He may become a great man and an honor to our whole province and even to the nation."

"But if he lives in the castle we can't play together any more," Kino said.

"We must think of Jiya's good," Kino's father said. Then he turned to Old Gentleman. "Sir, it is very kind of you to propose this for Jiya. I had planned to take him for my own son, now that he has lost his birth parents. But I am only a poor farmer. I cannot pretend that my house is as good as yours, or that I can afford to send Jiya to a fine school. Tomorrow when he wakes, I will tell him of your kind offer. He will decide."

"Very well," Old Gentleman said. "But let him come and tell me himself, so that I will know how he feels."

"Certainly," Kino's father replied proudly. "Jiya will speak for himself."

How unhappy Kino was to think that Jiya might leave this house and go and live in the castle! "If Jiya goes away, I shan't have a brother," he told his father.

"You must not be so selfish, Kino," his father replied.
"You must allow Jiya to make his own choice. I forbid you
to speak to Jiya of this matter. When he wakes, I shall
speak to him myself."

When his father was so stern, Kino did not dare to dis-
obey, and so he went sadly to bed. He thought, when he
drew his quilt over him, that he would not sleep all night.
But being young and tired, he slept almost at once.

Day of Decision

Yet, as soon as Kino woke in the morning, he remembered Jiya and the choice he had to make. He got up and
washed and dressed and folded his quilt and put it into
the closet where it stayed during the day. His father was
already out in the field, and there Kino went and found
him. It was a beautiful, mild morning. A soft mist covered
the ocean so that no water could be seen.

"Is Jiya awake yet?" Kino asked his father, when they
had exchanged morning greetings.

"No, but he will wake soon, I think," his father replied.
He was weeding the cabbage bed carefully. Kino knelt
down to help him.

"Must you tell him about Old Gentleman today?" Kino
pleaded.

"I must tell him as soon as he wakes," his father replied.
"It would not be fair to let Jiya grow used to thinking of
this as his home. He must make the choice today, before
he has time to put down his new roots."

"May I be there when you talk with him?" Kino asked next.

"No, my son," his father replied. "I shall talk to him alone and tell him all the benefits that a rich man like Old Gentleman can give him and how little we who are poor can give him."

Kino could not keep from wanting to cry. He thought his father was very hard. "But Jiya will certainly want to go away!" he sobbed.

"Then he must go," his father said.

They went into the house to have breakfast, but Kino could scarcely eat. After breakfast, he went back to the field. His father stayed in the house, and they could hear Jiya getting up.

For a long time, Kino stayed in the field working alone. The warm tears dropped from his eyes upon the earth. When the sun was nearing its height, he heard his father's voice. He got up at once and walked along the path between the terraces until he reached the doorway. There his father stood with Jiya. Jiya's face was still pale and his eyes were red.

The father turned to Kino. "I have told Jiya that he must not decide until he has seen the inside of the castle. I want him to see all that Old Gentleman can give him for a home. Jiya, you know how our house is—these four rooms and the kitchen, this little farm, upon which we have to work so hard for our food. We have only what our hands can earn for us."

Kino's father held out his two hard, work-worn hands. Then he went on, "Kino, you are to go with Jiya. When you see the castle, you must persuade him to stay there, for his own sake."

Kino felt the task laid upon him was very hard. But he only said, "I will go and wash myself, Father, and put on my good clothes."

"No," his father said. "Go as you are—you are a farmer's son."

So the two boys went down the mountainside. Avoiding

the empty beach, they climbed to the castle. The gate was open and the garden was most beautiful. A gardener was sweeping the green moss.

When he saw them he came over to them. "What do you want?" he asked.

"My father sent us to see the honored Old Gentleman," Kino faltered.

"Are you the Uchiyama boy?" the gardener asked.

"Yes," Kino replied, "and this is Jiya, whom Old Gentleman wants to come and live here."

"Follow me, if you please," the gardener said. He bowed to Jiya and his voice was polite.

The two boys followed him along a wide, pebbled path. Over their heads, the ancient pines leaned their crooked branches. In the distance beyond the forest, the sun poured down upon a flower garden and a pool with a waterfall.

"How beautiful it is!" Kino whispered sadly.

Jiya did not answer. He walked along, his head held high. When they reached the house, they took off their shoes and followed the gardener through a great door. Inside this, the gardener paused. A manservant came forward and asked what they wanted. The gardener whispered and the manservant nodded. "Follow me," he said to the boys.

In the Castle

So they followed him through wide passageways. The walls were of fine polished wood, unpainted, but smooth and silvery. Under their feet, fine-woven, padded mats were softer than the moss beneath the trees. On both sides of this passageway, panels slid back to show beautiful rooms. In each room were a vase of flowers, an exquisite scroll, a few pieces of dark polished furniture. Neither Jiya nor Kino had ever seen such a house. Kino was speechless. How could he hope now that Jiya would not want to stay in the castle?

Then, far in the distance, they saw Old Gentleman sitting beside a small table. The table was set in front of the open sliding panels that looked into the garden. Old Gentleman was writing. He held a brush upright in his right hand and he was carefully painting letters on a scroll, his silver-rimmed spectacles sliding down on his nose.

When the two boys came near, he looked up and took off his spectacles and laid down his brush. "Would you like to know what I have been writing?" he asked.

Neither Kino nor Jiya could answer. The great house, the silence, the beauty—all of this fell into place as the background for Old Gentleman himself. He was tall and thin, and his hair and beard were white. His face and hands were beautiful. The bones were delicate and the skin was smooth and brown. He looked as proud as a king, but his dark eyes were wise as an old scholar's eyes are wise.

"It is not my own poem," he said. "It is the saying of a man of India. But I like it so much that I have painted it on this scroll to hang where I can see it every day." He took up the scroll and read these words:

> *The Children of God are very dear,*
> > *but very queer—*
> *Very nice, but very narrow.*

He looked at the boys. "What do you think of it?" he said.

They looked at one another. "We do not understand it, sir," Jiya said at last. Since he was a little older than Kino, he felt he should speak.

Old Gentleman shook his head and laughed softly. "Ah, we are all the children of God," he said. Then he put on his spectacles and looked hard at Jiya. "Well?" he said. "Will you be my son?"

Jiya turned very red. He had not expected to have the question put to him so suddenly and so directly.

Old Gentleman saw he found it hard to speak. "Say yes or no," he told Jiya. "Those are not hard words to say."

"I will say—no!" Jiya said. Then he felt this was harsh. "I thank you but I have a home—on the farm," he added.

Ah, how Kino felt when he heard these words! He forgot entirely about the big wave and all the sorrow it had brought. For a moment, he was filled with pure joy. Then he remembered the small farmhouse, the four little rooms and the old kitchen.

"Jiya," he said solemnly, "remember how poor we are."

Old Gentleman was smiling a half-sad little smile. "They are certainly very poor," he said to Jiya. "And here, you know, you would have everything. You can even invite this farm boy to come and play sometimes, if you like. And I am quite willing for you to give the family some money. It would be suitable, as my son, for you to help the poor."

"Where are the others who were saved from the big wave?" Jiya asked suddenly.

"Some wanted to go away, and the ones who wanted to stay are out in the back yard with my servants," Old Gentleman replied.

"Why do you not invite them to come into this big house and be your sons and daughters?" Jiya asked.

"Because I don't want them for my sons and daughters," Old Gentleman replied rather crossly. "You are a bright, handsome boy, and they told me you were the best boy in the village."

Jiya looked about him. Then he shook his head again. "I am no better than the others," he said. "My father was a fisherman."

Old Gentleman took up his spectacles and his brush again. "Very well," he said. "I will do without a son."

The manservant motioned to them and they followed. Soon they were out in the garden again.

"How foolish you are!" the manservant said to Jiya.

"Our Old Gentleman is very kind indeed. You would have everything here."

"Not everything," Jiya replied.

They went out of the gate and across the hillside again, back to the farmhouse. Setsu, Kino's little sister, was outside. She came running to meet them, the sleeves of her bright kimono flying behind her and her feet clattering in wooden sandals.

"Jiya has come back home!" she cried. "Jiya—Jiya—"

And Jiya, seeing her happy little face, opened his arms and gave her a great hug. For the first time, he felt comfort creep into his sad heart, and this comfort came from Setsu, who was like life itself.

Go West, Young Man

There was a wise fellow
   Who said, "It is best
For ambitious young folks
   To go West, West, West."

Out where the plains
   And the coyotes are,
The eye of a man
   Can see far, far, far.

Out where the mountains
   Stand bare of a tree,
The soul of a man
   Can feel free, free, free.

—*Dorothy Hall*

Riding the Pony Express

Marion Garthwaite

Sally Mason was baking cinnamon rolls. Her brother,
Randy, would enjoy something warm and good when he
rode in, late in the afternoon, to change horses. It would
be his last lap before he turned the mail over to the next
Pony Express rider at Placerville.

Randy would stop only long enough to fling the saddle
and its heavy pouches of mail from the tired horse to a
fresh one, before he would hit leather and be off again.
Mrs. Mason always had a cup of hot coffee for him, with
cake or rolls to be taken along. But Sally's mother was
away with a sick neighbor. Twelve-year-old Sally was trying to take her place.

Sally pulled the pan of cinnamon rolls out of the oven
just as a shadow appeared in the doorway. It was the
Indian squaw, Old Suzy, as broad as she was high. She
was carrying a basket.

"Oh, Suzy!" cried Sally, "you're going for thimble-berries! There's time enough. I'll get a pail and go with you."

Sally put two of the hot rolls in the Indian woman's basket. Old Suzy's face crinkled up until her beady black eyes disappeared. Her face was burned almost black by years of mountain sun, and so wrinkled that it was hard to see the blue tattoo marks on her chin.

Old Suzy and Sally climbed the hill behind the stable. The wind was blowing in strong gusts. Sally was panting, but Old Suzy climbed steadily upward, the full skirt of her dirty, torn Mother Hubbard caught up over her arm. They stopped at a high meadow.

Suzy's basket was nearly full, and Sally's pail half full, when Old Suzy straightened her back and pointed.

"Rain come," she said, and started down the mountain.

Sally followed. Old Suzy turned off below the meadow. In a clearing by the stream, there was a tumble-down log cabin. As they reached it, the big drops of rain began to splash down on the shaky roof. In a few seconds the downpour was deafening, and Old Suzy shut the sagging door against it. It was dark in the cabin with only the light coming through the cracks between the logs.

Old Suzy stood by the door looking through one of these chinks. Suddenly she caught Sally's arm and half pulled, half pushed her down into a corner, dragging an old packing box and a broken chair in front of them.

"Black Jack come," grunted Old Suzy. "Him bad."

Sally heard voices, and two men stumbled into the dark cabin.

"Lucky you knew this was here!" said the smaller of the two men.

"Pays to know good hideouts in these parts," answered the man, whom Sally knew as Black Jack, a reckless gambler.

The two men stood in the doorway.

"This is as good a place as any to talk," said Black Jack. "Randy Mason comes through here around four. I've heard he's carrying a lot of money this trip. I plan to stop him at the Arch Rock."

"But Jack," said the other man, "that's U. S. mail."

"It's the money I'm after," said Black Jack. "If he hands that over, he can have the mail. If he doesn't . . ." Black Jack shrugged.

Sally stirred. Suzy's hard fingers pressed tight into her knee.

"I don't like it." The smaller man spat out into the rain.

"It's easy money," said Black Jack. "There's just one chance. That's why you're in on this. Randy may take the cutoff back of his place. 'Specially since this rain came. He might figger the ford's high. If he does, he'll come out just below the Gap. You wait there. Shoot him as he comes onto the trail. Or—if you're chicken—stick him up and hold him till I get there. I may have trouble getting through the ford myself. If you let him get by, I'll cut out your gizzard."

"It's risky," whined the other man.

"So's pannin' gold. So's everything. Come on, the rain's lettin' up. You can cache your share here till the hullabaloo blows over."

After the two men had gone, Old Suzy held Sally back for several minutes. Then she let her go. Sally plunged down the mountain, forgetting her pail of berries. She built up the fire with trembling hands. She put on the coffee and slid the pan of rolls into the warm oven. It seemed no time at all before she heard the wild coyote yell Randy always gave as he came down the trail.

Sally met him at the corral. While he pulled his saddle and blanket from the heaving back of the foam-flecked pony and tossed it onto his fresh horse, Sally poured out her story. Randy gulped down the hot coffee and stuffed the rolls into a leather pouch slung over his deerskin shirt.

"Good kid!" he said, with a grin. "I'll take the cutoff. I meant to, anyway, after this storm. Besides, I'd rather face the other man on the upper trail than Black Jack at the Arch Rock. Black Jack is too good a shot. Now listen, Sally."

Sally put out a protesting hand, but he shook her off. "Listen carefully," he said. "The Express money is sewn into the saddle lining. The pouches that usually carry the mail are stuffed with old letters. The regular mail is rolled in my saddle blanket. I'll throw him the pouches and I may get through."

"And Find Out Why"

Randy handed Sally the empty mug. "You can see the Gap from here, Sal. Usually I make it in twenty minutes.

The mud will slow me down. Give me thirty minutes.
Saddle your horse as soon as I leave. Come out here where
you can see clearly. I'll wave my hat. If you don't see me
ride through that Gap in thirty minutes, you're to take
the cutoff and find out why."

With one motion he turned his horse, was in the saddle,
and was gone down the trail in a spatter of mud.

"So long," he yelled, waving to her as his pony plunged
into the trees.

Sally saddled her horse. She changed her cotton print
dress for a pair of Randy's doeskin trousers and a leather
shirt. She tucked her curls into one of Randy's hats. She
had kept careful track of the time. When there was just
five minutes to go, she walked the horse out to the gate,
where she had a clear view of the Gap. In her hand was
her father's little minute glass. She watched the Gap, keeping half an eye on the sifting sand. Five times she turned

the little glass. Then she jumped on her horse and started up the cutoff trail.

She found Randy on the main trail below the Gap. The short man she had seen at the cabin lay face down in a puddle of mud. Randy's horse was dead. Randy lay on the ground beside his horse, frantically trying to get the saddle blanket untied. He had fastened a leather thong about his leg above where the leather pants were soaked with blood. As Sally rode onto the trail, he whirled away from the horse and snatched his gun from the ground beside him.

"Oh, Sal!" he cried in relief. "You're in time. Get this blanket off and onto your horse. Never mind anything else. We can't get the saddle off. The horse is lying on it. Ride for all you're worth into Placerville. Turn the mail over to Rogers at the station."

"You're hurt!" said Sally. "I can't leave you here in this mud."

"You're to do as I say," Randy ordered. "Change this blanket over. Get going."

A figure glided out of the woods. Sally thought it was Black Jack and her heart jumped.

"Old Suzy!" cried Randy.

"How did you know where to come?" asked Sally.

"Suzy hear." The Indian woman stooped and lifted Randy like a sack of meal across her shoulder. She carried him into the woods. When she came back, she had Randy's gun belt strapped about her broad waist. She stripped the saddle off Sally's horse. Then she heaved the dead horse off the stirrup and tugged until she had freed Randy's saddle. She and Sally put the saddle on Sally's horse. They tied the blanket securely behind. Sally worked frantically. She expected Black Jack to come down the trail any moment.

"Black Jack come by and by," said Old Suzy.

"What's keeping him?" asked Sally.

Old Suzy shrugged. "Horse gone," she said. "He tie horse by tree. He go sit Arch Rock. Suzy chew reins off. Give him horse big slap." Her eyes were lost in a mass of crinkles.

Sally swung herself into the saddle. "Good Old Suzy!" she said.

Suzy grunted. Sally dug her heels in her horse's sides and started up the steep grade to the Gap.

Two hours later, she galloped into the mining town of Placerville and up to the Pony Express station.

"Thought you'd never git here," shouted the waiting rider, much annoyed. "Yer an hour late." And then, "I'll be hornswoggled! 'Tain't Mason. It's a gal. Who be ye?"

"I'm Sally, Randy's sister," said Sally, sliding out of the saddle. "It was a holdup. Randy's hurt and can't ride. The money's sewn inside the saddle, and the mail is in the blanket." Her knees were trembling. She could hardly stand.

With a practiced hand, the rider slid the saddle onto his fresh horse.

"You gotta place to stay?" he asked. "This town's plenty rough for a gal."

"I'll stay with the Gearys. They're kind of cousins."

He fastened the blanket behind his saddle, leapt upon the horse, and whirled away in a clatter of hoofs.

He waved. "Ye done all right fer a gal!" he shouted back to her. "Ridin' fer the Pony Express."

The Shindig

Shannon Garst

*Twelve-year-old Bob was spending the summer on his
Uncle John's Wyoming cattle ranch. Bob had never been
on a ranch before, and he had a lot to learn.*

One Saturday morning, Bob noticed that the Circle K
cowboys plunged into their work with unusual energy.
That night there was to be a big "shindig" at the neighboring Flying V Ranch. During breakfast, the men could
talk of nothing else. They gulped down hot cakes, bacon
and eggs, and scalding coffee, eager to get at their day's
work and finish it in plenty of time to slick up for the
occasion.

"What is a shindig?" Bob asked.

"You don't know what a shindig is?" Crowbait asked in amazement. And all the men looked shocked at such ignorance.

"I never heard of such a thing," Bob confessed.

Finally Montana took pity on him. "A shindig is—well, it's just a shindig," he said lamely. "A big hoedown. A get-together. Everyone comes from miles around. Some fellows bring their fiddles. Happy, here, will take his guitar. They play music for the square dances. The ladies and gals bring sandwiches and cakes and pies. And everyone has a high old time."

"It sounds like fun!" Bob turned to his uncle. "May I go to the shindig, Uncle John?" he asked eagerly.

John Benton pursed his lips and studied the matter for a long moment. Bob held his breath.

"He can go in the pickup truck with me," Happy offered. "I'll keep my eye on him."

"We-ll," the words came out slowly. "I believe he can go. I don't see how any harm can come to him."

"Oh, thanks!" Bob exclaimed.

Supper was a hurried affair that night, with much talk and banter about the shindig. Bob never had seen the men spend so much time cleaning themselves up. They polished their boots, doused oil on their hair, and put on their brightest silk shirts and neckerchiefs.

Most of the men rode horseback to the Flying V, but Happy drove the pickup because he was to take some of the food. Bob saw him wrap his guitar case tenderly in a blanket before he carefully stowed it away in the car.

"Aren't you going?" Bob asked his uncle.

"No," Mr. Benton said. "Someone has to stay at the ranch, and the job suits me very well. Have a good time, Bob. When you get tired, go out and sleep in the pickup. The boys always stay until morning."

Cookie rode with Bob and Happy. As they spun along, he and Happy told Bob that the Flying V was a dude ranch that made a business of entertaining city people who wanted a taste of ranch life without any of the hardships. Bob noticed a touch of scorn in their tone as they spoke of the Flying V hands as "dude wranglers."

When they got to the big barn where the dance was being held, the place was a gay sight. Electrically-wired lanterns hung from the rafters, and bales of hay had been placed along the walls for seats. Bob was amused to see that the dude wranglers were dressed much like the cowboys he had seen in the movies. They wore bright-colored, braid-trimmed silk shirts, brighter neckerchiefs, and tight-fitting trousers trimmed with braid. Their hats were extra wide, with fancy bands. Some of them wore chaps decorated with large silver conchas. Most of the dudes were also fixed up in fancy Western clothes.

"Howdy, stranger!" A voice beside him made Bob start. He turned to look into the most thoroughly freckled face he had ever seen, on a boy about his own age.

"Oh, howdy!" Bob returned, smiling.

"I'm Jerry Bates. I live on the ranch just north of your

uncle's," the freckled boy said with a friendly grin. "I hear you're spending the summer on the Circle K. Why don't you ride over sometime?"

Bob felt his face turn red. He didn't want to admit that he wasn't allowed to ride outside the ranch.

"Oh, I don't know my way around very well yet," he finally found words. "Why don't you ride over to the Circle K?"

"I might do that," Jerry answered.

Swing Your Partner!

The two boys stood watching the square dancers. Bob had never seen dancing like this before. The cowboys entered into the spirit of the thing with enthusiasm and considerable hilarity. The "caller" stood on a chair and bellowed directions:

> Rope your cow and brand your calf,
> Swing your honey a loop and a half.
> Come on now with the old mess wagon,
> Hind wheel's broke and the axle's draggin'.
> Swing, swing! Everybody swing!

The cowboys stamped and whooped to liven things up. Bob noticed that Shorty was the liveliest and noisiest of them all.

"He's really having a good time," Jerry observed.

Bob watched Montana, whirling around gracefully in the complicated figures of the square dances. It seemed only natural to him that the foreman should excel at everything he did. And he noticed that, although most of the musicians smiled and stamped their feet as they played, Happy strummed his guitar with as much dead seriousness as he did everything else.

As the two boys wandered around the great barn, Bob was surprised to see in one corner a dozen or more babies and small children, fast asleep on hard benches.

"I don't see how they do it," he said—"sleep with all this music and whooping and laughing going on!"

"I don't either," Jerry laughed, "but I used to do it myself. My folks began to drag me to these shindigs when I was only knee high to a grasshopper. So I practically grew up sleeping in places like this."

Bob stared down at the small children lying there.

"Ever hear how some cowpokes switched babies at one of these dances?" Jerry asked.

"No. Tell me about it."

"It really happened not very far from here," Jerry said. "My father read me the story out of a book called *The Virginian.* They had all the babies asleep in one of the bedrooms, and these fellows went in and changed the babies around. There was quite a mix-up when their mamas went to get them."

Bob laughed.

Jerry looked thoughtful for a moment. Then he whispered, "I have an idea. A humdinger!" He seized Bob's arm. "Come along with me."

Bob followed him outside. Near the barn there was a long rail to which the cowboys' horses were tied.

"We'll switch the ponies," whispered Jerry. "It's so dark out here the fellows can't see their animals. Each cowboy will just come to where he tied his pony and climb on without thinking. They dance till nearly daylight and by then the men are so dead tired they generally go to sleep while they're riding. They depend on their ponies to take them home."

Bob put his hand over his mouth to keep back a shout of mirth. "Most of the cowboys will wake up on some other ranch—not their own," he whispered.

"Yeh," Jerry chuckled. "Each pony will go to his home ranch. There'll be an awful mix-up of cowboys in the morning."

"This is a better joke than mixing up the babies," Bob said, in deep admiration over Jerry's genius. "This really should be in a book, too."

A Joke—and the Morning After

Bob settled himself cozily between Happy and Cookie as the shindig broke up in that dark hour just before dawn. Everyone was groggy with weariness and yawning widely as good nights were said.

Bob chuckled as he thought of the mixed-up horses.

"What's funny, partner?" Cookie asked.

"Oh, I just happened to think of something," Bob answered briefly.

Happy started to sing. Bob promptly went to sleep, to be awakened by Cookie's booming voice, "Here we are back on the home range. Wake up, Bob, and let's go!"

As Bob climbed stiffly from the pickup, Happy said mournfully, "There won't be time for any snoozing at all. When we have one of these all-night shindigs, we might as well count it a night's sleep lost and let it go at that."

"Then why don't people go home earlier?" Bob asked a trifle crossly. "Why do they stay all night?"

"Oh, we cowmen don't have many social events," Happy yawned. "So when we do, we have to make the most of it." He looked toward the eastern sky which the dawn was beginning to tinge with pink. "Just in time to get in the hosses," he added in gloomy tones.

"And Bob and I are just in time to get breakfast," said Cookie, as spryly as if he had had a full night's sleep. "Shake a leg there, partner, and get the wood and water in and set the places at the table."

Bob's feet dragged as he did his chores, though the smell of cooking bacon and coffee revived him a bit. He heard some of the men coming in, shouting at one another across the barnyard as cheerfully as though they were not tired at all.

As Bob slid sleepily into his place at the table, he suddenly remembered something. He looked about quickly. Then he gasped. He had taken pains to see that Crowbait's horse was changed, but there sat Crowbait, eating as though nothing unpleasant had ever happened to him. It was Montana who was missing! No one had seen him since the party.

"It's possible he might have got his hoss mixed up," Crowbait remarked, and Bob thought he felt a glance in his direction. "I noticed my pony was tied in a different place. Might be, the animals got tired of standing in the same spot and moved about just for fun. I was smart enough to notice. Probably a dumb guy like Montana wouldn't."

Almost as Crowbait spoke, Montana dragged himself into the room. He smiled rather sheepishly, but he looked half-dead with weariness.

A mighty guffaw of laughter greeted him.

Suddenly Bob didn't think the trick was clever at all. If it had been Crowbait who had made the useless ride to some far-away ranch, he wouldn't have minded. But not for anything would he have pulled a trick like this on his friend Montana.

"It's a wise man that knows his own hoss. Especially after a dance." Crowbait laughed in the disagreeable manner he had. "Me, I had sense enough to notice whether I was mounted on my own animal."

Montana grinned wearily. "I reckon I deserve your kidding," he said. "Any cowpoke that don't recognize his own hoss, even in the dark and when he's half asleep, deserves a lot of kidding. But I never thought anyone would pull a skunky trick like that."

He looked straight at Crowbait, and his eyes were like cold steel.

"Don't look at me," Crowbait shrugged. "Why don't you ask Bob if he knows anything about it?"

All eyes turned on Bob.

"You—of all people?" Montana cried.

Bob wished the floor would swallow him.

Montana said nothing more. He sat down and piled hot cakes on his plate. Everyone else went on eating.

When the men went outside, Bob tagged along after Montana. The cowboy paid no attention. Finally Bob plucked him by the sleeve.

"Sa-ay," he blurted, "I'm sure sorry about what I did last night. Changing horses, I mean—"

"Whose idea was it?" Montana asked sharply.

"It was Jerry's really," Bob admitted. "But I thought it was awfully good. That is, at first I did. But I didn't mean to play such a trick on *you*."

"O.K.," Montana said, and the old familiar grin came back to his face. "I've pulled too many tricks on other fellows to hold any grudge when I'm the victim. I reckon I can take a joke as well as play one."

Something welled up in Bob's heart that made it actually hurt. Gee, but Montana was a swell guy!

Texas Trains and Trails

Whenever I ride on the Texas plains
I never hear the couplings cluck,
I never hear the trains
Go chuck-a-luck, chuck-a-luck, chuck-a-luck,
I never hear the engine snort and snuffle,
I never see the smoke plume, I never watch the rails,
But I see the moving dust where the beef herds shuffle,
And I think I am a cowboy,
A rope and tie 'em cowboy,
Punching Texas longhorns
On the Texas trails.
And the engine goes *Whoop!*
Whoopee, whoopala!
And the cars go *Ki-yi,*
Ki-yi, ki-yi, coma-la ki-yi,
    Whoopala,
Ki-yi!
    Whoop!

No, I never hear the bell, nor the brakeman call
When I ride on the Texas trains;
But I hear the steers bellow and the yearlings bawl,
And the lone wolf howl on the wire grass plains.
And I never play I'm fireman, or anything like that,
For I'm playing I'm a cowboy,
A bronco-bustin' cowboy,
Riding Texas longhorns
In a ten-gallon hat.
And the trains go *Youpi-ya*,
Get a-long, dogies,
Get a-long, get a-long
Youpi-yi, youpi-ya,
Youpi-youpi-youpi-ya
Get a-long, get a-long,
Youpi-ya,
     Yo-o-u-u-p!

—*Mary Austin*

The Blizzard

Laura Ingalls Wilder

Seventy years ago, as now, winter on the Great Plains of the West could be cruelly long and cold. Ma, Pa, and the girls had moved from their Dakota homestead into the little prairie town near by, after an old Indian had warned them it was going to be a bad winter. Now, in October, Laura and Carrie were going to the town school.

Laura and Carrie were enjoying school so much that they were sorry when Saturday and Sunday interrupted it. They looked forward to Monday. But when Monday came, Laura was cross because her red flannel underwear was so hot and scratchy.

It made her back itch, and her neck, and her wrists, and where it was folded around her ankles, under her stockings and shoe-tops, that red flannel almost drove her crazy. At noon, she begged Ma to let her change to cooler underthings. "It's too hot for my red flannels, Ma!" she protested.

"I know the weather's turned warm," Ma answered gently. "But this is the time of year to wear flannels. You would catch cold if you took them off."

Laura went crossly back to school and sat squirming because she must not scratch. She held the flat geography open before her, but she wasn't studying. She was trying to bear the itching flannels. The sunshine from the western windows had never crawled so slowly.

Suddenly there was no sunshine. It went out, as if someone had blown out the sun like a lamp. The outdoors was gray, the windowpanes were gray, and at the same moment a wind crashed against the schoolhouse, rattling windows and doors and shaking the walls.

Miss Garland, the teacher, started up from her chair. One of the little Beardsley girls screamed. Carrie turned white.

Laura thought, "It happened this way on Plum Creek, the Christmas when Pa was lost." Her whole heart hoped and prayed that Pa was safe at home now.

Teacher and all the others were staring at the windows, where nothing but grayness could be seen. They all looked frightened. Then Miss Garland said, "It is only a storm, children. Go on with your lessons."

All the heads bent over the books as Teacher had told them to do. But Laura was trying to think how to get home. The schoolhouse was a long way from Main Street, and there was nothing to guide them.

All the others had come from the East that summer.

They had never seen a prairie blizzard. But Laura and Carrie knew what it was. Carrie's head was bowed limply above her book, and the back of it, with the white parting between the braids of fine, soft hair, looked small and helpless and frightened.

There was only a little fuel at the schoolhouse. The school board was buying coal, but only one load had been delivered. Laura thought they might outlive the storm in the schoolhouse, but they could not do it without burning all the desks.

Without lifting her head, Laura looked up at Teacher. Miss Garland was thinking and biting her lip. She could not decide to dismiss school because of a storm, but this storm frightened her.

"I ought to tell her what to do," Laura thought. But

she could not think what to do. It was not safe to leave the schoolhouse and it was not safe to stay there. Even the twelve desks might not last long enough to keep them warm until the blizzard ended. She thought of her wraps and Carrie's, in the entry. Whatever happened, she must somehow keep Carrie warm. Already the cold was coming in.

There was a loud thumping in the entry. Every pupil started and looked at the door.

It opened and a man stumbled in. He was bundled in overcoat, cap, and muffler, all solid white with snow driven into the woolen cloth. They could not see who he was until he pulled down the stiffened muffler.

"I came out to get you," he told Teacher. He was Mr. Foster, who had come in from his claim to stay in town for the winter at Sherwood's, across the street from Teacher's house.

Miss Garland thanked him. She rapped her ruler on the desk and said, "Attention! School is dismissed. You may bring your wraps from the entry and put them on by the stove."

Laura said to Carrie, "You stay here. I'll bring your wraps."

The entry was freezing cold. Snow was blowing in between the rough boards of the walls. Laura was chilled before she could snatch her coat and hood from their nail. She found Carrie's and carried the armful into the school-house.

Crowded around the stove, they all put on their wraps and fastened them. Cap Garland, Teacher's brother, did not smile. His blue eyes narrowed and his mouth set straight while Mr. Foster talked.

Laura wrapped the muffler snugly over Carrie's white face and took firm hold of her mittened hand. She told Carrie, "Don't worry. We'll be all right."

"Now, just follow me," said Mr. Foster, taking Teacher's arm. "And keep close together."

He opened the door and led the way with Miss Garland. Mary Power and Minnie each took one of the little Beardsley girls. Ben and Arthur followed them closely with the Wilmarth boys. Then Laura went out with Carrie into the blinding snow. Cap Garland shut the door behind them.

They could hardly walk in the beating, whirling wind. The schoolhouse had disappeared. Nothing could be seen but swirling whiteness and now and then a glimpse of each other, disappearing like shadows.

Laura felt that she was smothering. The icy particles of snow whirled scratching into her eyes and smothered her breathing. Her skirts whipped around her, now wrapped so tightly that she could not step, then whirled and lifted to her knees. She held tightly to Carrie. Carrie, struggling and staggering, was pulled away by the wind and then flung back against her.

"We can't go on this way," Laura thought. But they had to.

Lost in the Storm

She was alone in the whirling winds and snow except for Carrie's hand that she must never let go. The others must be somewhere ahead. She must keep up with them or she and Carrie would be lost. If they were lost on the prairie they would freeze to death.

But perhaps they were all lost. Main Street was only two blocks long. If they were going only a little way to north or south, they would miss the block of stores. Beyond was empty prairie for miles. Laura thought they must have gone far enough to reach Main Street, but she could see nothing.

The storm thinned a little. She saw shadowy figures ahead. They were darker gray in the whirling gray-whiteness. She went on as fast as she could, with Carrie, until she touched Miss Garland's coat.

They had all stopped. Huddled in their wraps, they

stood like bundles close together in the swirling mist. Teacher and Mr. Foster were trying to talk, but no one could hear what they said. Then Laura began to know how cold she was.

Her mittened hand was so numb that it hardly felt Carrie's hand. She was shaking all over and deep inside her there was a shaking that she could not stop. Only in her very middle there was a solid knot that ached, and her shaking pulled this knot tighter so that the ache grew worse.

She was frightened about Carrie. The cold hurt too much, Carrie could not stand it. Carrie was so little and thin, she had always been delicate, she could not stand such cold. They must reach shelter soon.

Mr. Foster and Teacher were moving again, going a little to the left. All the others hurried to follow them. Laura took hold of Carrie with her other hand. It had been in her coat pocket and was not quite so numb. Suddenly she saw a shadow go by them. She knew it was Cap Garland.

He was not following the others to the left. With hands in his pockets and head bent, he went trudging straight ahead into the storm. A fury of winds thickened the air with snow and he vanished.

Laura did not dare follow him. She must take care of Carrie, and Teacher had told them to follow her. She was sure that Cap was going toward Main Street. But perhaps she was mistaken.

She kept tight hold of Carrie and hurried to follow Mr. Foster and Teacher as fast as she could. Her chest sobbed for air and her eyes strained open in the icy snow-particles that hurt them like sand. Carrie struggled bravely, stumbling and flopping, doing her best to stay on her feet and keep going.

Laura felt that they were going in the wrong direction. She did not know why she felt so. No one could see anything. There was nothing to go by—no sun, no sky, no direction in the winds blowing fiercely from all directions. There was nothing but the dizzy whirling and the cold.

Then, out of the whiteness, something hit her. The hard blow crashed against her shoulder and all through her. She rocked on her feet and stumbled against something

solid. It was high, it was hard, it was the corner of two
walls. Her hands felt it, her eyes saw it. She had walked
against some building. With all her might she yelled,
"Here! Come here! Here's a house!"

Main Street at Last

At first no one heard her. She pulled the icy stiff muffler
from her mouth and screamed into the blinding storm.
At last she saw a shadow in it, two tall shadows thinner
than the shadowy wall she clung to—Mr. Foster and
Teacher. Then other shadows pressed close around her.
They were all there—Mary Power and Minnie, each with
a little Beardsley girl, and Arthur Johnson and Ben
Woodworth and the small Wilmarth boys. Only Cap
Garland was missing.

They followed along the side of that building till they came to the front of it. It was Mead's Hotel, at the very north end of Main Street. Beyond it was nothing but the railroad track covered with snow, the lonely depot and the wide, open prairie. If Laura had been only a few steps nearer the others, they would all have been lost on the endless prairie north of town.

For a moment, they stood by the hotel's lamplit windows. Warmth and rest were inside. But the blizzard was growing worse and they must all reach home.

Main Street would guide all of them except Ben Woodworth. No other buildings stood between the hotel and the depot where he lived. So Ben went into the hotel to stay till the blizzard was over. He could afford to do that because his father had a regular job.

Minnie and Arthur Johnson, taking the little Wilmarth boys, had only to cross Main Street to Wilmarth's grocery store. Their home was beside it. The others went down Main Street, keeping close to the buildings. They passed Royal Wilder's feed store, and then they passed Barker's grocery. The Beardsley Hotel was next and there the little Beardsley girls went in.

The journey was almost ended. They passed Couse's Hardware store and they crossed Second Street. Mary Power had only to pass the drugstore now. Her father's tailor shop stood next to it.

Laura and Carrie and Teacher and Mr. Foster had to cross Main Street now. It was a wide street. But if they missed Pa's house, the haystacks and the stable were still between them and the open prairie.

They did not miss the house. One of its lighted windows made a glow that Mr. Foster saw before he ran into it. He went on around the house corner with Teacher to go by the clothesline, the haystacks, and the stable to the Garland house.

Laura and Carrie were safe at their own front door. Laura's hands fumbled at the doorknob, too stiff to turn it. Pa opened the door and helped them in. He was wearing an overcoat and cap and muffler. He had set down a lighted lantern and dropped a coil of rope. "I was just starting out after you," he said.

Laura felt Ma's hands breaking away the icy muffler, and she said, "Is Carrie all right?"

"Yes, Carrie's all right," said Pa.

Ma took off Laura's hood and unbuttoned her coat and helped her pull out of its sleeves. Laura could hardly move, but she stooped and with her fingers dug out the caked snow that the wind had driven in between her woolen stockings and the tops of her shoes. Then she staggered toward the stove and sat stiffly down.

She felt numb and stupid. She rubbed her eyes and saw a pink smear on her hand. Her eyelids were bleeding where the snow had scratched them. The sides of the coal heater glowed red-hot and she could feel the heat on her skin, but she was cold inside. The heat from the fire couldn't reach that cold.

Pa sat close to the stove holding Carrie on his knee. He had taken off her shoes and held her wrapped in a shawl. The shawl shivered with Carrie's shivering. "I can't get warm, Pa," she said.

"You girls are chilled through. I'll have you a hot drink in a minute," said Ma, hurrying into the kitchen. She brought them each a steaming cup of ginger tea.

It was wonderful to be there, safe at home, sheltered from the winds and the cold. Laura thought that this must be a little bit like heaven.

"I'm glad you didn't have to come for us, Pa," Laura said drowsily. "I was hoping you were safe."

"So was I," Carrie told Pa, snuggling against him. "I

remembered that Christmas, on Plum Creek, when you didn't get home.''

"I did, too," Pa said grimly. "When Cap Garland came into Fuller's and said you were all heading out to the open prairie, you can bet I made tracks for a rope and lantern. We'd have had a posse out looking for you, though we'd have been hunting for a needle in a haystack.''

"Best forget about it," said Ma. "And now, Laura and Carrie, you're going to bed and get some rest. A good long sleep is what you need.''

Whitey and Jinglebob

Glen Rounds

At the time I speak of, Whitey was ten years old, or thereabouts. He had him a hand-me-down Stetson with a rattlesnake-skin hatband onto it, and a pair of Uncle Torwal's fancy stitched Fort Worth boots.

Jinglebob was about the same size and probably the same age. He got his name from the second-hand Stetson he wore. The brim of it had been tromped on by a horse at some time, so it sort of hung down on one side, the way a jinglebobbed calf's ear does. His father was a freighter. He had left the boy with Torwal and Whitey one trip, and Jinglebob'd just sort of stayed.

Torwal was an old-time cattle man, with legs that were bowed, a drooping red moustache, and a stiff arm from getting an Injun arrow in the early days.

These three lived by themselves, doing their own cooking, dish washing, and the like. They ran the ranch with the help of a sooner dog, name of Confusion.

This particular day, Torwal had gone to Lone Tree to get the mail and some other odds and ends. Whitey and Jinglebob were down in the corral practicing up on their rodeo stuff. You see, they were no great shakes for size, but none the less they figured they were top hands, almost. And it's a well-known fact that if you want to be a top hand in any business, you have to practice.

So, when Torwal came back that afternoon, he saw a considerable cloud of dust raising up over the corral where he was keeping a bunch of long yearlings and two-year-olds, fattening them up for shipping. As he rode closer, he could hear the excitement. He tied his horse and climbed up on the fence to watch.

Jinglebob had just roped a big yearling and got him snubbed up to the snubbing post in the middle of the corral. He held him there while Whitey put a rope around the critter and climbed onto his back. Jinglebob turned his rope loose, and the calf started an imitation of a Brahma bull at the rodeo. Whitey rode about three jumps and then was thrown. After he'd dusted himself off a little, he roped another calf and Jinglebob tried to ride it.

Both boys were plastered with sweat and dirt. The calves likewise. Some were standing around with the tips of their tongues showing and foam on their chops.

"We're practicing to be top hands," Whitey told Uncle Torwal.

"Yessir!" said Jinglebob. "We're practicing on roping and bareback riding today."

"Fat stock like that gets hot mighty easy," Torwal said, as they walked over to the windmill to get a drink.

"Yessir, it does for a fact," Whitey admitted.

"We'd sort of noticed that," said Jinglebob. "But if we are to be top hands, we have to keep in practice."

Uncle Torwal agreed that it was necessary for a top hand to keep in practice. But it occurred to him that such excitement wasn't exactly the best thing in the world for fattening calves.

Whitey and Jinglebob agreed that there was much in what he said. But how in the world were they to practice their riding, they wanted to know.

Uncle Torwal thought that over a while. Then he said, "It's too late to do anything about it today. But tomorrow, we'll build a contraption like one I saw down on the Reservation one time."

"I just don't see how we can learn to ride on a contraption," Whitey said. Jinglebob agreed with him.

"It'll give you a right brisk bit of practice, and not sweat the fat off the beef," Torwal assured him. From then on, he would tell no more about it.

They talked about the contraption while they peeled potatoes and sliced bacon for supper. Torwal listened to them as he mixed the biscuits, but wouldn't say anything. Even after they'd gone to bed, Whitey and Jinglebob talked of what kind of contraption Uncle Torwal could be thinking of. But they could make nothing of it. So they finally took their Stetsons off and went to sleep.

The next morning, as soon as they'd had breakfast and cleaned up the kitchen, Torwal took them out behind the blacksmith shop. He started the boys digging four deep post holes, set in a square some ten feet across, while he fastened four rings onto the ends of an old oil drum with strap iron and rivets. They finished the holes about the time he was done with the drum.

Then, from the pole pile, Torwal picked out four long, stout ash poles. He helped the boys set these up in the post holes and tamp them solid, after he'd fastened a good length of rope to the top of each. When that was done, he fastened the ropes to the rings in the drum, so it hung on its side some four feet off the ground. After he'd taken an old saddle and strapped it on the drum, he stepped back and looked the thing over.

"There's your contraption," he said, looking right pleased with himself. Whitey and Jinglebob looked at the contraption and then at each other.

After a while, Whitey spoke up. "It looks like a kids' play-toy to me," he said, looking right unhappy.

"Yessir! That's just the way it looks to me," Jinglebob said. "It'd be fine for kids to play with. But I don't see what we can do with it."

"Mebbe you won't feel so disappointed about it when you've given it a whirl," said Torwal. "Supposing you try it out first, Jinglebob."

Jinglebob wasn't at all enthusiastic. But he didn't want to hurt Uncle Torwal's feelings after he'd gone to so much trouble building the thing. So he said it was all right with him. He and Whitey both figured Uncle Torwal must be slipping. As a general thing, he understood how they felt about having to fool with kid stuff.

They hated to think how cowboys roundabout would laugh if the word got around they played with such a sissy contraption! But for now, there was nothing they could do but make the best of it. So Jinglebob climbed into the saddle. He sat there looking sheepish while Uncle Torwal took up the stirrups to fit him.

"All set?" Torwal asked after a bit.

"Yessir, I reckon so," Jinglebob said, without much enthusiasm.

"Well, hang onto your hat!" And Torwal and Whitey started shoving the limber poles one way and another.

The Lone Tree Killer

That was when Jinglebob got the surprise of his life. With the drum swung from the tops of those limber poles whipping in all directions, it proved to be anything but a solid proposition. In less than no time at all, Jinglebob sailed off and rolled head over heels.

He was somewhat surprised. So was Whitey, for that matter. They looked at one another. They looked at the contraption. Uncle Torwal just looked pleased with himself. "Still think it's a kids' play-toy?" he asked after a while.

"No, sir! That thing bucks worse than Black Diamond at Cheyenne! But of course I wasn't expecting anything so brisk. If I could try it again, I don't reckon I'd have any trouble staying with it."

But the second try was no better than the first. Then Whitey tried it and was piled. After that, they talked Torwal into trying it, and were mighty pleased when he was thrown almost as quick as they had been. They all took turns from then on. With practice, they found that they could make the contraption do just about anything an outlaw horse could do, and a few that would be right difficult for the best horse that ever wore hair.

While they were still experimenting with the contraption, Smoky Tom Nelson rode up with one of his cowboys to see Torwal about something or other. They were right pleased to see Torwal playing with a kids' contraption, they said, with wide grins.

After some talk back and forth, Torwal invited them to try a ride themselves, provided it was all right with Whitey and Jinglebob.

"Yessir! We'd be right pleased to have you try out our

play-toy!'' they both said, grinning happily at the idea.

"You try it first, Texas,'' Smoky said to the cowboy with him.

This cowboy was from Texas, where they go in more for fancy trimmings than is usual in Lone Tree County. Even for a Texas man, he was a sight for sore eyes. His saddle was crusted almost solid, wherever he wasn't sitting on it, with silver conchas and doo-dads of all kinds. He had little looking glasses set into the corners of his saddle skirts, in addition to the silver. His stirrups were covered with long *tapaderos* that near touched the ground. His Stetson was so tall and so wide in the brim, and had so many silver conchas on it, that Whitey and Jinglebob figured he must need both hands to take it off. Altogether, he was so loaded down that it seemed a wonder his horse wasn't sway-backed.

"I'm a man that will ride anything that has four legs and hair on the outside,'' the Texas man said. "When I set onto an outlaw's back, it's as if I'd suddenly growed there. Many a killer hoss has taken one look at me walking up to him and reformed on the spot, being from then on a perfect mount fer ladies, children, and *dee*-crepit Injuns. I've rode hosses that couldn't be rode, setting straight up, scratching them fore and aft according to Association rules, meanwhile reading the latest copy of *Grit*. But that's no hoss. It's nothing but a kids' contraption.''

"Of course, if you're not feeling good...'' Torwal began.

"I'm in fine fettle," the Texas man said. "Never felt better! Bright-eyed and bushy-tailed, that's me. But I still say that's a complete waste of time for a man of my talents!"

Whitey and Jinglebob were bug-eyed with excitement. They figured that if anybody could ride the contraption, it was the Texas man. A fellow that looked as grand and talked as fancy as that must be about the best in the country.

But the long and short of it was that after Torwal and Smoky talked the Texas man into trying just one ride, he did no better than anyone else. The first time the contraption flung him, he allowed it was an accident. He hadn't expected it to be so brisk, he said.

"Just what I said," Jinglebob whispered to Whitey.

But the second try was no better. The third was as bad. After that, he picked himself up and limped over to the contraption and looked it over close, while nobody said a word.

"Where in the name of all-get-out did you get this infernal machine? What do you use it for?"

"In this country we build such things for the children to learn to ride on," Torwal told him. "To sort of start them on something easy until they can handle a real horse."

The Texas man brushed dust off himself, then spoke up again. "Up to now I've rode everything that come down the pike," he said. "I've rode 'em saddled and I've rode 'em slick. I've rode big hosses down to nubbins and little hosses down to nuthin! And then I get flang by a kids' contraption! All I can say is, yuh should name it the Lone Tree Killer and enter it in the contest at Cheyenne this fall."

And from then on, the Lone Tree Killer's reputation spread. Any Sunday afternoon, you could find half the cowboys in Lone Tree County gathered around and waiting their turn to get thrown by it. Whitey and Jinglebob had to wait their turn at it like everyone else. They no longer felt it was a kids' contraption. And they had plenty of company when they practiced to be top hands.

Whistling Down the Street

If I've a tune to whistle
When hurrying down the street,
A rhythm to keep time to
With running, jigging feet—

I'll not be sad or lonely,
While there's a gay refrain
For whistling in the sunshine,
Singing in the rain.

—*Dorothy Hall*

Pure Foolishness

There was an old man who said, "How
Shall I flee from that horrible cow?
   I will sit on this stile
   And continue to smile,
Which may soften the heart of that cow."
              —*Edward Lear*

There was an old man on the Border
Who lived in the utmost disorder;
   He danced with the cat,
   And made tea in his hat,
Which vexed all the folks on the Border.
              —*Edward Lear*

There once was a man of Calcutta
Who spoke with a terrible stutter.
   At breakfast he said,
  "Give me b-b-b-bread,
And b-b-b-b-b-b-butter."
             —*Unknown*

There was a young lady of Niger
Who smiled as she rode on a tiger;
   They returned from the ride
   With the lady inside
And the smile on the face of the tiger.
            —*Cosmo Monkhouse*

The Puzzled Centipede

A centipede was happy quite,
Until a frog in fun
Said, "Pray, which leg comes after which?"
This raised her mind to such a pitch
She lay distracted in the ditch
Considering how to run.

—*Unknown*

The Lion

The Lion is a kingly beast.
He likes a Hindu for a feast.
And if no Hindu he can get,
The lion-family is upset.

He cuffs his wife and bites her ears
Till she is nearly moved to tears.
Then some explorer finds the den
And all is family peace again.

—*Vachel Lindsay*

The Melancholy Pig

There was a Pig, that sat alone,
  Beside a ruined Pump.
By night and day he made his moan:
It would have stirred a heart of stone
To see him wring his hoofs and groan,
  Because he could not jump.

—*Lewis Carroll*

The Pirate Don Durk of Dowdee

Ho, for the Pirate Don Durk of Dowdee!
He was as wicked as wicked could be,
But oh, he was perfectly gorgeous to see!
    The Pirate Don Durk of Dowdee.

His conscience, of course, was as black as a bat,
But he had a floppety plume on his hat
And when he went walking it jiggled—like that!
    The plume of the Pirate Dowdee.

His coat it was crimson and cut with a slash,
And often as ever he twirled his mustache
Deep down in the ocean the mermaids went splash,
    Because of Don Durk of Dowdee.

Moreover, Dowdee had a purple tattoo,
And stuck in his belt where he buckled it through
Were a dagger, a dirk and a squizzamaroo,
    For fierce was the Pirate Dowdee.

Oh, he had a cutlass that swung at his thigh
And he had a parrot called Pepperkin Pye,
And a zigzaggy scar at the end of his eye
   Had Pirate Don Durk of Dowdee.

He kept in a cavern, this buccaneer bold,
A curious chest that was covered with mould,
And all of his pockets were jingly with gold!
   Oh jing! went the gold of Dowdee.

His conscience, of course, it was crook'd like a
     squash,
But both of his boots made a slickery slosh,
And he went through the world with a wonderful
     swash,
   Did Pirate Don Durk of Dowdee.

It's true he was wicked as wicked could be,
His sins they outnumbered a hundred and three,
But oh, he was perfectly gorgeous to see,
   The Pirate Don Durk of Dowdee.
              —*Mildred Plew Meigs*

Water Noises

When I am playing by myself,
And all the boys are lost around,
Then I can hear the water go;
It makes a little talking sound.

Along the rocks below the tree,
I see it ripple up and wink;
And I can hear it saying on,
And do you think? And do you think?

A bug shoots by that snaps and ticks,
And a bird flies up beside the tree
To go into the sky to sing,
I hear it say, *Killdee, killdee!*

Or else a yellow cow comes down
To splash a while and have a drink.
But when she goes I still can hear
The water say, *And do you think?*

—*Elizabeth Madox Roberts*

Dust of Snow

The way a crow
Shook down on me
The dust of snow
From a hemlock tree

Has given my heart
A change of mood
And saved some part
Of a day I rued.
—*Robert Frost*

Song for a Little House

I'm glad our house is a little house,
Not too tall nor too wide;
I'm glad the hovering butterflies
Feel free to come inside.

Our little house is a friendly house,
It is not shy or vain;
It gossips with the talking trees,
And makes friends with the rain.

And quick leaves cast a shimmer of green
Against the whited walls,
And in the phlox, the courteous bees
Are paying duty calls.
—*Christopher Morley*

The Horseshoe

Wonder where this horseshoe went.
Up and down, up and down,
Up and past the monument,
Maybe into town.

Wait a minute. "Horseshoe,
How far have you been?"
Says it's been to Salem
And halfway to Lynn.

Wonder who was in the team.
Wonder what they saw.
Wonder if they passed a bridge—
Bridge with a draw.

Says it went from one bridge
Straight upon another.
Says it took a little girl
Driving with her mother.
                    —Edna St. Vincent Millay

Lonesome Train

The train that wails across the hills
Gathers in its cry
All the lonesomeness of dark,
The bigness of the sky.
Something deep inside me thrills
To hear a train go by.
                    —Dorothy Hall

Silver Ships

There are trails that a lad may follow
  When the years of his boyhood slip,
But I shall soar like a swallow
  On the wings of a silver ship,

Guiding my bird of metal,
  One with her throbbing frame,
Floating down like a petal,
  Roaring up like a flame;

Winding the wind that scatters
  Smoke from the chimney's lip,
Tearing the clouds to tatters
  With the wings of my silver ship;

Grazing the broad blue sky light
  Up where the falcons fare,
Riding the realms of twilight,
  Brushed by a comet's hair;

Snug in my coat of leather,
  Watching the skyline swing,
Shedding the world like a feather
  From the tip of a tilted wing.

There are trails that a lad may travel
  When the years of his boyhood wane,
But I'll let a rainbow ravel
  Through the wings of my silver plane.
                —*Mildred Plew Meigs*

Old Quin Queeribus

Old Quin Queeribus—
    He loved his garden so,
He wouldn't have a rake around,
    A shovel or a hoe.

For each potato's eyes he bought
    Fine spectacles of gold,
And mufflers for the corn, to keep
    Its ears from getting cold.

On every head of lettuce green—
    What do you think of that?—
And every head of cabbage, too,
    He tied a garden hat.

Old Quin Queeribus—
    He loved his garden so,
He couldn't eat his growing things,
    He only let them grow!

                —*Nancy Byrd Turner*

Tillie

Old Tillie Turveycombe
Sat to sew,
Just where a patch of fern did grow;
There, as she yawned,
And yawn wide did she,
Floated some seed
Down her gull-e-t;
And look you once,
And look you twice,
Poor old Tillie
Was gone in a trice.
But oh, when the wind
Do a-moaning come,
'Tis poor old Tillie
Sick for home;
And oh, when a voice
In the mist do sigh,
Old Tillie Turveycombe's
Floating by.

—*Walter de la Mare*

Autumn

The morns are meeker than they were,
The nuts are getting brown,
The berry's cheek is plumper,
The rose is out of town.

The maple wears a gayer scarf,
The field a scarlet gown.
Lest I should be old-fashioned,
I'll put a trinket on.

—*Emily Dickinson*

Snow

Oh the falling Snow!
Oh the falling Snow!
Where does it all come from?
Whither does it go?
Never never laughing,
Never never weeping,
Falling in its Sleep,
Forever ever sleeping—
From what Sleep of Heaven
Does it flow, and go
Into what Sleep of Earth,
The falling, falling Snow?

—*Eleanor Farjeon*

Stopping by Woods on a Snowy Evening

Whose woods these are I think I know.
His house is in the village though;
He will not see me stopping here
To watch his woods fill up with snow.

My little horse must think it queer
To stop without a farmhouse near
Between the woods and frozen lake
The darkest evening of the year.

He gives his harness bells a shake
To ask if there is some mistake.
The only other sound's the sweep
Of easy wind and downy flake.

The woods are lovely, dark and deep.
But I have promises to keep,
And miles to go before I sleep,
And miles to go before I sleep.

—Robert Frost

Ducks' Ditty

All along the backwater,
Through the rushes tall,
Ducks are a-dabbling,
Up tails all!

Ducks' tails, drakes' tails,
Yellow feet a-quiver,
Yellow bills all out of sight
Busy in the river!

Slushy green undergrowth
Where the roach swim—
Here we keep our larder
Cool and full and dim.

Everyone for what he likes!
We like to be
Heads down, tails up,
Dabbling free!

High in the blue above
Swifts whirl and call—
We are down a-dabbling
Up tails all!

—*Kenneth Grahame*

Swift Things Are Beautiful

Swift things are beautiful:
Swallows and deer,
And lightning that falls
Bright-veined and clear,
Rivers and meteors,
Wind in the wheat,
The strong-withered horse,
The runner's sure feet.
—Elizabeth Coatsworth

Dogs and Weather

I'd like a different dog
For every kind of weather—
A narrow greyhound for a fog,
A wolfhound strange and white
With a tail like a silver feather
To run with in the night,
When snow is still and winter stars are bright.

In the fall I'd like to see
In answer to my whistle,
A golden spaniel look at me.
But best of all for rain
A terrier, hairy as a thistle,
To trot with fine disdain
Beside me down the soaked, sweet-smelling lane.

—Winifred Welles

April Rain

It isn't raining rain for me,
It's raining daffodils;
In every dimpled drop I see
Wild flowers on the hills.

The clouds of gray engulf the day
And overwhelm the town;
It is not raining rain to me,
It's raining roses down.

It is not raining rain to me
But fields of clover bloom,
Where any buccaneering bee
Can find a bed and room.

A health unto the happy,
A fig for him who frets!
It is not raining rain to me,
It's raining violets.

—*Robert Loveman*

The Day Before April

The day before April
   Alone, alone,
I walked in the woods
   And sat on a stone.
I sat on a broad stone
   And sang to the birds.
The tune was God's making
   But I made the words.
        —Mary Carolyn Davies

Comparison

Apple blossoms look like snow,
They're different, though.
Snow falls softly, but it brings
Noisy things:
Sleighs and bells, forts and fights,
Cozy nights.
But apple blossoms when they go,
White and slow,
Quiet all the orchard space,
Till the place
Hushed with falling sweetness seems
Filled with dreams.
        —John Farrar

The Mist and All

I like the fall,
The mist and all.
I like the night owl's
Lonely call—
And wailing sound
Of wind around.

I like the gray
November day,
And bare, dead boughs
That coldly sway
Against my pane.
I like the rain.

I like to sit
And laugh at it—
And tend
My cozy fire a bit.
I like the fall—
The mist and all—
　　　—Dixie Willson

November Night

Listen . . .
With faint dry sound,
Like steps of passing ghosts,
The leaves, frost-crisp'd,
　　break from the trees
And fall.
　　　—Adelaide Crapsey

 "November Night" from VERSE by Adelaide Crapsey, Copyright 1915 by Algernon S. Crapsey, 1934 by Adelaide T. Crapsey; reprinted by permission of Alfred A. Knopf, Inc.

The Cat and the Broom

The broom looks tattered and tired today,
    The raggedest stick of a broom;
It couldn't reach up for a cobweb grey
    Or sweep out the smallest room.

And Trusty Tompkins, our little black cat,
    With fur like the finest silk,
Is curled up tight in a ball on the mat
    Too sleepy to drink his milk.

But the bad old broom looks rakish and sly,
    As if it had been on a spree;
And Puss from a narrow satin eye
    Looks wickedly out at me.

Ho, ho! I know what the rascal pair
    In the midnight hours were at;
It wasn't mousing or sweeping the stair
    That made them look like that.

I know by the old broom's battered plight
    And Tompkins' look of sin
They were both of them out with a witch last night,
    And they've only just got in.

—A. A. Kenny

The Raggle, Taggle Gypsies

There were three gypsies a-come to my door,
    And downstairs ran this lady, O.
One sang high and another sang low,
    And the other sang "Bonnie, Bonnie Biskay, O."

Then she pulled off her silken gown,
    And put on hose of leather, O.
With the ragged, ragged rags about her door
    She's off with the Raggle, Taggle Gypsies, O.

'Twas late last night when my lord came home,
    Inquiring for his lady, O.
The servants said on every hand,
    "She's gone with the Raggle, Taggle Gypsies, O."

"Oh, saddle for me my milk-white steed,
    Oh, saddle for me my pony, O.
That I may ride and seek my bride
    Who's gone with the Raggle, Taggle Gypsies, O."

Oh, he rode high and he rode low,
   He rode through woods and copses, O.
Until he came to an open field,
   And there he espied his lady, O.

"What makes you leave your house and lands?
   What makes you leave your money, O?
What makes you leave your new-wedded lord
   To go with the Raggle, Taggle Gypsies, O?"

"What care I for my house and lands?
   What care I for my money, O,
What care I for my new-wedded lord?
   I'm off with the Raggle, Taggle Gypsies, O."

"Last night you slept on a goose-feather bed,
   With the sheet turned down so bravely, O.
Tonight you will sleep in the cold, open field,
   Along with the Raggle, Taggle Gypsies, O."

"What care I for your goose-feather bed;
   With the sheet turned down so bravely, O?
For tonight I shall sleep in a cold, open field,
   Along with the Raggle, Taggle Gypsies, O."

              —*Old Folk Song*

The Cowboy's Life

The bawl of a steer,
To a cowboy's ear,
   Is music of sweetest strain;
And the yelping notes
Of the gay coyotes
   To him are a glad refrain.

For a kingly crown
In the noisy town
   His saddle he wouldn't change;
No life so free
As the life we see
   Way out on the Yaso range.

The rapid beat
Of his broncho's feet
   On the sod as he speeds along,
Keeps living time
To the ringing rhyme
   Of his rollicking cowboy song.

The winds may howl
And the thunder growl
   Or the breezes may safely moan;—
A cowboy's life
Is a royal life,
   His saddle his kingly throne.

           —*James Barton Adams*

Whoopee Ti Yi Yo

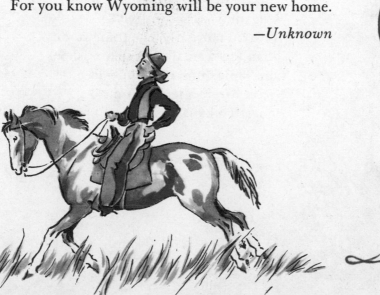

As I was a-walking one morning for pleasure,
I spied a cowpuncher all riding alone;
His hat was throwed back
   and his spurs was a-jinglin'
As he approached me a-singin' this song:

Whoopee ti yi yo, git along, little dogies;
It's your misfortune and none of my own.
Whoopee ti yi yo, git along, little dogies,
For you know Wyoming will be your new home.

Early in spring we round up the dogies,
Mark and brand and bob off their tails;
Round up our horses, load up the chuck wagon,
Then throw the dogies upon the old trail.

It's whooping and yelling
   and driving the dogies;
Oh, how I wish you would go on!
It's whooping and punching
   and go on, little dogies,
For you know Wyoming will be your new home.

—*Unknown*

Faith, I Wish
I Were a Leprechaun

Faith, I wish I were a leprechaun
Beneath a hawthorn tree,
A-cobblin' of wee, magic boots,
A-eatin' luscious, lovely fruits;
Oh, fiddle-dum, oh, fiddle-dee,
I wish I were a leprechaun
Beneath a hawthorn tree!

Faith, I wish I were a leprechaun
Beneath a hawthorn tree,
A-throwin' snuff into the eyes
Of young and old and dull and wise;
Oh, fiddle-dum, oh, fiddle-dee,
I wish I were a leprechaun
Beneath a hawthorn tree!

Faith, I wish I were a leprechaun
Beneath a hawthorn tree,
With no more irksome thing to do
Than sew a small, bewitchin' shoe;
Oh, fiddle-dum, oh, fiddle-dee,
I wish I were a leprechaun
Beneath a hawthorn tree!

—*Margaret Ritter*

Real People

These boys and girls
    were just as real as you—
Like you, they used to dream
    and eat and play;
Were mostly good,
    but full of mischief too—
Perhaps you'll grow up
    in a book some day!

—Dorothy Hall

Dick Whittington and His Cat

A Story of Old England

More than 500 years ago, there really was a Dick Whittington, who really did become Lord Mayor of London. Young people have always liked to believe that Dick's cat was real, too.

Once upon a time in England lived a boy called Dick Whittington. His father and mother died when he was young. All he had to eat and to wear was what the other poor folk in the village could spare him. And that was not very much.

One day, Dick watched a wagon drive down the village street. The eight horses all had bells on their heads. "That fine wagon must be going to London!" thought Dick. "Oh, if I could only go there, too!" Like all the country folk of his day, the poor boy was sure that London was a wonderful place, where the streets were paved with gold.

The wagoner was walking beside his horses, his whip in his hand. "Please, sir," said Dick timidly, "may I go with you to London town?" And when the kind wagoner learned that Dick had no parents to care, he was willing.

At last they got to London. Dick was in such a hurry to

see the gold-paved streets that off he ran without even saying goodbye. He ran and he ran and he ran. But alas! the streets were just as muddy and dirty as in his own village at home.

Poor Dick nearly starved in London. There was no work to be had. At last, when he had not eaten for three days, he lay down on a doorstep, weak and ill. Here he was spied by the cook, an ugly, bad-tempered old woman.

"For shame, you lazy beggar!" she scolded. "Be off or I'll give you a bath of hot dishwater!" Just then, the owner of the house himself appeared. He was Mr. Fitzwarren, a rich merchant.

At the sight of the ragged boy lying on his doorstep, Mr. Fitzwarren shook his head. Poor children were expected to work almost from the time they could toddle. Still, the merchant spoke kindly. "Why are you not at work, my boy?"

"Because I can get no work," Dick answered faintly. "And I am ready to die of hunger."

Mr. Fitzwarren had Dick brought in and fed and given an attic to sleep in. He was to clean the pans and run errands for the cook.

Dick would have been content if it hadn't been for the cook's bad temper. She worked him from dawn to dark, and often beat him. Besides, the merchant's house was old and overrun with mice. In his attic at night, Dick could hardly sleep for the scuffling and the squeaking. Finally, he decided to buy a cat.

With the only penny he had in the world, Dick went out into the streets. There he saw a little girl with a fine large cat in her arms.

"Little girl, will you sell me your cat for a penny?"

"Yes, I will," said the little girl. "And she is a good mouser, too."

So Dick took Mrs. Puss to his attic. From that day on, there was peace and quiet with the mice.

Some time later, Mr. Fitzwarren had a ship ready to set sail to foreign ports. And, as was his custom, he called all his servants together. Each one brought some money, or goods to send out for trade.

Only Dick did not appear. Miss Alice, Mr. Fitzwarren's daughter, guessed what the trouble was. She sent for the boy, saying, "Father, I will lay down some money for Dick, out of my own purse."

"No, daughter, that you may not do. The rule is, you know, that each must send something of his own."

Then Dick spoke up. "All I have in the world is a cat, which I bought for a penny from a little girl."

"Fetch your cat, then, my lad, and let her go."

So Dick fetched Mrs. Puss and gave her to the captain, while the others grinned. But Miss Alice saw that Dick hated to part with his cat. Secretly, she gave him some money to buy another.

After that, Miss Alice did many kind little things for Dick. It made the old cook so cross and jealous that she treated Dick worse than ever. At last, he thought he could not stand it any longer. So early one morning, the poor boy tied his few ragged clothes up into a bundle and crept softly out of the house.

He trudged as far as Halloway. There he sat down on a stone—to this day called Whittington's stone. As he sat there, the bells of Bow Church began to ring. And plain as plain, they said to Dick:

> Turn again, Whittington,
> Thrice Lord Mayor of London.

"Lord Mayor of London!" said Dick to himself. "To be Lord Mayor of London, and ride in a fine coach! Why, what is the cuffing and scolding of a poor old woman, if I am to be Lord Mayor of London at last?"

So, taking up his bundle, Dick returned. He was lucky enough to get into the house and start his work before the old cook came downstairs.

A Cat That Looked at a King

In the meantime, Mr. Fitzwarren's ship, the *Unicorn*, was driven by storms to the Barbary Coast of Africa, where English ships seldom came. The people there were Moors. They came down to the ship in throngs, to stare at the English sailors.

The captain sent samples of his cargo to the Moorish king, and in return was invited to visit the king and queen at the palace. There, he was received most politely, and food was brought. But hardly were the dishes on the table when a whole army of rats and mice rushed in, and made short work of the meal.

The captain was astonished. "Is this not—er, well, unpleasant—to His Majesty?" he asked cautiously.

"Oh, yes," the servants said. "The king would give half his treasure to be rid of these terrible pests."

Then the captain remembered Whittington's cat. "Your Majesty," he said, "on board my ship is a marvelous creature. It could soon deliver you from these rats."

The king jumped up and cracked his heels together for joy. "Bring the creature at once," he ordered. "If it can do what you say, I will load your ship with gold and jewels."

So the captain went off to the ship while the cooks prepared another meal. He got back with Mrs. Puss just as the rats and mice rushed out for the second time.

Mrs. Puss did not need to be told what to do. Jumping out of the captain's arms, she pounced right and left on her enemies. In a few minutes, those that were not dead had run squeaking to their holes. The king and queen were speechless with delight.

"Here, pussy, pussy!" the captain called. Mrs. Puss came up and rubbed around his feet, and the captain, taking her up, presented her to the queen.

At first, the queen was a little afraid. But when the captain stroked the cat and said, "Pussy, pussy," the queen also put out her hand and said, "Putty, putty!" And Mrs. Puss jumped into the queen's lap, purring, and settled down for a nap.

When the king learned that Mrs. Puss's kittens would keep not only his palace but the whole country free from rats, he bought the ship's cargo at a handsome price. But he gave ten times as much for Mrs. Puss as for all the rest.

One morning, Mr. Fitzwarren had gone early to his counting-house. He had had no word of the *Unicorn,* and was beginning to feel uneasy. Just then there was a knock at the door. "Who knocks?" he called.

"Your captain," came the answer. "I bring good news of the *Unicorn* and all her cargo."

When Mr. Fitzwarren heard the whole wonderful story, he could only exclaim over and over again. At last, he sent for all the household.

Again, Dick would have excused himself. But Mr. Fitz-warren insisted, and even had Dick sit down in a chair. At first, the poor boy thought everybody was making fun of him.

"Indeed, Mr. Whittington, we are not making fun of you," Mr. Fitzwarren said. "The captain has sold your cat to the King of Barbary for more than my whole for-tune." And he had the captain and his men open the treasure, to show Dick it was really true.

Dick wanted to share his riches with Mr. Fitzwarren and Miss Alice. But they would not accept any. He had to content himself with giving presents to the captain and the crew, and even to the old cook.

Then Dick had to send for a tailor, and dress like a gentleman. And when his face was washed and he was dressed in fine clothes, Miss Alice's liking for Dick turned into love. So they were married, and the Lord Mayor of London himself came to their wedding.

Dick was Sheriff of London and three times Lord Mayor, as the Bow Bells had foretold. He was also made a knight by the king. And for many years, the stone figure of Sir Richard Whittington, with his cat in his arms, could be seen over the doorway to one of the public buildings put up while he was Mayor.

Andy Stands Guard

Stanley Young

When Andrew Jackson was twelve years old, the American Revolution was coming in earnest to the Carolina frontier. Andy's father was dead, and his brother Hugh was fighting with the American army. No news of Hugh had come for a long time. So Andy's mother set out to look for him, with Andy's Uncle Crawford. Andy was left with his aunt, to guard the house.

Aunt Crawford and Andy watched them wind their way down the rough corduroy road. Then they turned to go into the house.

"Your mother's a brave woman," Aunt Crawford said, wiping her eyes on her apron.

Andy nodded. Secretly, he didn't see why his mother had to go looking for Hugh. Hugh was a soldier, a man now. He could look out for himself.

"Come now," Aunt Crawford said. "We've the dishes to do."

A frown broke over Andy's face. "Uncle said I was to guard the house."

"You can guard from the kitchen," Aunt Crawford said, smiling.

Andy took up his gun and reluctantly followed her. He dried the dishes faithfully, but down to the last pewter cup his eyes and mind were out of the window. He had set his gun up in one of the cabin rifle holes, ready for action. Every cabin, as well as every blockhouse, had these square openings about every five feet around the entire building. Andy kept darting from one hole to the other as if he expected a raid any minute. His jumping made his aunt nervous.

"You'll have me jumping next," she said. "Go on outside."

Andy grabbed up his rifle and tore for the door. There was a tall pine just outside. With his gun fastened to his belt with leather thongs, Andy shinnied up the pine, hugging the tree with his knees until his hands caught the first branch. He pulled himself up and climbed to the highest branch. Shading his eyes, he looked out over the landscape. Far below was Twelve Mile Creek, filled with logs pushing their slow way down the valley to the Catawba. Up the valley, right, he could see the smoke curling from Long Potter's house.

Andy looked away to the left. As far as he could see, the landscape lay peaceful in the gray morning light. But when he looked nearer he saw something that almost made him fall out of the tree. Not a hundred yards away, in the edge of the forest, he saw a man dodging from right to left and back again. The man was evidently pursuing something but Andy could not see what it was. The man wore buckskins like everyone else. But his face, at this distance, could not be recognized.

Behind the man, only a few steps now, Andy could see the copper-brown, half-naked figure of an Indian brave. The Indian was following the settler, step by step, and gaining on him. Andy saw the Indian raise his tomahawk high above his head. Almost instinctively, almost before he had time to be afraid, Andy pulled his rifle tight to his shoulder and fired.

The woods rang with the sound. Andy looked and saw that the Indian had disappeared and the white man was turning his head from side to side in surprise trying to locate the direction of the shot. Andy slid to the ground. He stopped long enough to ram fresh shot and powder into his gun. Then he hurried toward the spot where he had seen the Indian. Aunt Crawford came out of the house and called to him, but he ran on.

The Schoolmaster

It took Andy no more than a minute to reach the spot.
When he saw the white man's long black hair and his
hawkish nose he recognized him at once. Old Horn-Rim,
the schoolmaster. Andy ran up to him, shouting.

"Why, Master Jackson!" the schoolmaster exclaimed.
"Did you fire that shot just now?"

"I did, sir," Andy said.

"Well now, that's a pity. I was pursuing one of the
various diurnal lepidopterous insects that so abound in
this region—"

"And an Indian was after you," Andy said shortly. "I
shot at him from that tree. He was about to tomahawk
you."

The schoolmaster's eyes widened. Andy left him and
ran over to the tree close by where he saw the bark scarred.
His shot had hit the tree behind which the Indian had
hidden.

"Here," Andy said. "Here are his footprints, right enough."

"Well," the schoolmaster said. "Well, I thought the Indians were peaceable around here."

"There's a war on," Andy said. "The Redcoats get them stirred up."

There was a pause. The schoolmaster smiled down at the excited boy.

"Andy, I suppose if there's one person around here whose life you shouldn't be too particular about, it's the schoolmaster's."

Andy looked embarrassed, not knowing what to say. Old Horn-Rim was all right but he wasn't very exciting, as a rule.

"What did you say you were chasing?" Andy asked, anxious to change the subject. His eyes peered into the shadows of the forest.

"A butterfly," the schoolmaster said. "A very rare one." Wasn't that like Old Horn-Rim, Andy thought? Out chasing butterflies when there was a war going on! But the schoolmaster's next words changed Andy's opinion of him.

"Tomorrow I'm going East to fight. Colonel Davie is an old friend of mine," the schoolmaster said. "And the colonies need every last man of us," he added.

As if he had read Andy's thoughts, the schoolmaster took the rifle and tested it in his hands.

"Loaded?" he asked.

Andy nodded. The schoolmaster raised the gun to his shoulder.

"See that bare limb over there? That dead one on the poplar?" he asked.

Andy nodded again. Surely the schoolmaster wasn't going to try to hit that! It was too far.

When the schoolmaster fired Andy saw the branch on the poplar fall to the ground. He was speechless. The schoolmaster handed the gun back to Andy.

"Let's walk over to your house," he said. "I want to tell your aunt that her brave nephew saved my life."

Andy walked along with him in silence, thinking. Old Horn-Rim, what a shot! Never again would he judge anyone by his outward appearance. And never again would he make fun of the schoolmaster, or hide hoptoads in the three-legged desk. Andy decided that perhaps his mother was right in wanting him to be a schoolmaster. Or maybe he would be a lawyer, as Old Horn-Rim had so often suggested.

"If you'd been where I was you'd have hit that Indian, certain," Andy said.

"I wouldn't have tried to hit him. I'd have frightened him away, as you did, Andy," the schoolmaster replied.

Andy looked puzzled.

"The Indian is fighting for his land the same way we're fighting the British. No wonder they hate us, lad," the schoolmaster went on. "All the decent settlers—your father, your uncle, and most of them around here—bought their lands from the Indians. A lot of others just grabbed theirs, at the point of a rifle."

As the schoolmaster talked on, Andy forgot to be sorry over missing the Indian. He was glad now that he had only hit the tree. Maybe the Indians were like white men, some of them all right and some not.

"You'll probably have to fight Indians the rest of your life, if you choose to live in the wilderness," the schoolmaster said. "They're savages, there's no doubt of it. But don't just use them for rifle practice."

Aunt Crawford was halfway to the forest when Andy and the schoolmaster came out. Her eyes were questioning and fearful well before she spoke.

Andy told her, simply, what had happened and the schoolmaster offered to stay at the cabin until Mr. Crawford came home.

Andy protested against this. He assured his aunt that one man around the place was quite enough.

The schoolmaster smiled. "The Scotch-Irish are a stubborn lot," he said. "The salt of the earth, though. How do I know? I'm one myself."

And then shaking Andy's hand and thanking him again, elaborately and at length in three-syllable words, he started down the path toward Twelve Mile Creek. Andy looked after him and saw with amazement that the schoolmaster had begun to dodge back and forth, on and off the path, just as he had been doing when the Indian was after him.

"All that for a diurnal lepidopterous insect," Andy said.

Aunt Crawford stared at him with her eyes popping.

"What! Were you swearing, Andrew?" she asked severely.

"No'm," he said. "I was merely discussin' butterflies."

Aunt Crawford shrugged her shoulders and decided that the Indian affair had momentarily robbed her nephew of his wits. She turned and went into the house. Andy, his eyes on the forest, stood in silent watch by the door wondering what he would do if a Redcoat suddenly appeared over the hill.

Peregrine White and Virginia Dare

Virginia Dare was the first baby of English parentage to be born in this country—in 1587, in the "lost" colony of Roanoke, Virginia. Peregrine White was the first child born in the Pilgrim colony in Massachusetts in 1620.

Peregrine White
And Virginia Dare
Were the first real Americans
Anywhere.

Others might find it
Strange to come
Over the ocean
To make a home,

England and memory
Left behind—
But Virginia and Peregrine
Didn't mind.

One of them born
On Roanoke
And the other cradled
In Pilgrim oak.

Rogues might bicker
And good men pray.
Did they pay attention?
No, not they.

Men might grumble
And women weep
But Virginia and Peregrine
Went to sleep.

They had their dinner
And napped and then
When they woke up
It was dinner again.

They didn't worry,
They didn't wish,
They didn't farm
And they didn't fish.

There was lots of work
But they didn't do it.
They were pioneers
But they never knew it.

Wolves in the forest
And Indian drums!
Virginia and Peregrine
Sucked their thumbs.

They were only babies.
They didn't care.
Peregrine White
And Virginia Dare.

> —*Rosemary and Stephen Vincent Benét*

The Boy Who Loved Tools

Carolyn Sherwin Bailey

Perhaps your lucky family possesses a table, chair, or chest of drawers made by the famous Duncan Phyfe. This Scotch boy came to our country about a hundred and seventy years ago, when he was just a lad in his teens.

There was very little furniture in the turf cottage in Loch Fannich, Scotland, where the Phyfe family lived. The boy Duncan opened his eyes in a wooden cradle. His first steps took him from an old carved chest to a stool, and from there to a rough wood table. The Phyfes had little else except the straw beds. But when Duncan grew to be a boy, he found all the world of moor and hill waiting to be explored.

Gabel Phyfe, the father of Duncan, was a Scottish herdsman. Soon the boy was given a flock to care for. Following the sheep and lambs about their rocky pastures, he grew to know well the wind-swept trees, the waving grasses, the fields of purple heather and bluebells.

Coming down the hill pasture one night, gathering together the sheep with the help of his dog, Duncan started home through the sunset. There was no need of haste. The cottage with its candlelight and tomorrow's sheepherding would be no different from all his past. But before he had fastened the gate of the sheepfold, the boy knew that something had happened. The shrill sound of bagpipes came from the bench outside the cottage. There, a visiting soldier sat in kilts and tartan. Duncan's mother was busy packing the carved chest with the family's clothing. His father was counting the coins in his money bag. The younger children met Duncan with shining eyes.

"Father has sold the flock," they told him. "This soldier has told us of a new town in America—Albany, on the great Hudson River—where there are other Scottish people. We are leaving Scotland to find our fortunes in the new land."

In the next few months, there were unexpected hardships. There was the long trip by wagon, with their goods, to the seaport. The long voyage in a small sailing ship to New York took nearly all of Gabel Phyfe's money. The trip was stormy and hard to bear. Little Eliza Phyfe died at sea. When they reached the new land and started on a second journey by wagon trail and boat up the Hudson to Albany, the Phyfe family wondered if they had not been following a rainbow.

But they found the Albany of the year 1784 a busy town of little brick-and-stone houses. There was plenty of work for men and boys who knew how to use their hands.

One of the leading trades of Albany was the building of carts and wagons. Farm crops, flour, furs, clothing, and bricks had to be taken up and down the river, along the trails or by boat. The dock at Albany was crowded with carts. Roads going west were being rutted by great lumbering Conestoga wagons, big enough to hold a whole family and their goods. It seemed best to bind out Duncan Phyfe to a wagoner in Albany. From this man, he could learn about the different kinds of wood, and how to shape an axle and fit together the spokes of a wheel. It might lead to a knowledge of joinery (fine carpentry)—a good trade, one of the best. Duncan went to work almost as soon as the Phyfes reached Albany.

Duncan's father soon died, and the rest of the family scattered. There was need for him to learn a trade. Soon

Duncan was helping to make coaches. In these, the rich folk of Albany would ride down to New York for the gay parties that followed the election of George Washington as our first President. The trade of coach-making in our growing country was an art. The Scotch became leaders in it. Coach doors and windows were decorated with carving. And the boy found that the shapes he had known as a shepherd lad—wild flowers, leaves, the stars at night, and the moving branches of trees—were coming to life in wood under his skilled fingers and his carving tools.

At last, Duncan finished his apprenticeship. His brother John was driving one of the new horse-drawn omnibuses that carried people about in New York. Then, as now, this city lying on the great harbor drew young people to it. Duncan Phyfe packed his dearest possession, his tool-chest, and set out to walk to New York. When he could get a little repairing or furniture-making along the shores of the Hudson, he was able to earn his board and lodging. Sometimes he slept in the meadows or woods along the way.

New York was a town of craftsmen. Our country was still new. There was an ever-growing need for carriages, furniture, casks, cloth, bricks, boards—all the necessities of living and going about. John Jacob Astor, the fur prince of New York, had started big business and was now very wealthy. Shipbuilding and trade with the Indies were making New York very prosperous.

Broad Street, near the water, was the street of the joiners. Here, great planks of rare woods were brought from the ships, or from the forest lands of the North and the Jersey shore.

Within the shops, the pieces of furniture were shaped at the bench, on the lathe, and in the hands of the craftsmen—beautiful chests of drawers, Windsor chairs, four-poster beds, desks, tables, chests, sofas. American homes were being furnished almost as beautifully as those which the colonists had left in England and France.

We hear of Duncan Phyfe first in his own little joiner's

shop at 2 Broad Street. He worked modestly and by hand. He never put his name in the newspapers as the other furniture-makers of Broad Street did. Nor did Duncan Phyfe carve his name on the pieces, in the manner of the times. Designed and built by himself, strong enough to last hundreds of years, fair enough to find a place in a museum of art today, Duncan Phyfe's furniture was something to be proud of. But still he worked alone in his small shop and wore the old beaver hat he had brought from Albany, not troubling to make a show like his neighboring craftsmen.

Fame and Fortune

One day, a fine coach drove down Broad Street. It stopped near Duncan's shop. In flowered bonnet and silk cloak, out stepped the newly married daughter of the rich Mr. Astor, the fur merchant. Her name was Mrs. Langdon, and she was a great beauty. She was looking for furniture for her new house. She stopped at the door of Number 2, glancing in curiously at the man working there. Perhaps he was stretching damask over a sofa with claw legs and tiny curled rosettes at the back like the curved horns of one of his Scottish rams. Perhaps he was putting the last brass leaf against the front of a dark, polished highboy. Perhaps he was fitting together the parts of a long banquet table. The stories do not tell just what it was in Duncan Phyfe's shop that attracted the beautiful and rich Mrs. Langdon. But with a rustle of silk, and a cry of delight, she was across his threshold.

"I must have this . . . I want that . . . Could you make the furniture for my whole house?"

Duncan Phyfe was dazed, dumb. All he had been trying to do was to make strong, useful, beautiful furniture. Here he was, famous at the turn of a coach's wheels and the opened purse of a lovely lady.

It amused the daughter of Mr. Astor to take her friends to see the tiny shop of this dour Scotch craftsman. Sometimes he forgot to take off his old beaver hat when they rushed in upon him. And he would never be hurried in his work. It became the fashion to have as much of Duncan Phyfe's furniture in one's house as possible.

At last, he had to take in some apprentices and build a new shop. Then he built himself a house and a warehouse. All of these buildings were as plain and beautiful as his handcraft. They stood side by side on old Partition Street in New York. After Robert Fulton took his steamboat up the Hudson River, Partition Street was renamed Fulton Street. If you should go to New York today, remember that the great Hudson Terminal stands where Duncan Phyfe's Partition Street shop, warehouse, and home once stood.

Success had come to the Scotch shepherd boy. He always made his own drawings and plans, but soon he was sending his brother Lochlin to England for fine brass. He hired a large number of joiners, carvers, and polishers. The clipper ships brought him the finest of Santo Domingo and

Cuban mahogany for his lumber yard. In far-away tropic ports, the term "Phyfe logs" became known. Mr. Phyfe would pay one thousand dollars for one log if sound and well-grained. Soon, his craft made him an unusually rich man for those days.

But the very few records of Duncan Phyfe which we have show him as always busy, modest, and retiring. Designing and finishing his handsome, delicately carved pieces was his great reward. Until he was an old man, he could be seen daily talking with his apprentices or bent over his own bench carving a rosette or shaping a bit of brass.

After a while, the sign above the shop read, "Duncan Phyfe & Son." If a grown person wanted to see the great Duncan himself, he had a hard time. But children knew the way to his garden. In a little shop at one end of the garden, a small, plump old Scotch gentleman could be found at his bench, busily making sewing-tables for little girls, boxes to hold ribbons and beads, cradles and chests of drawers for dolls. Mr. Phyfe had about half a million dollars in the bank. But what he still valued most was his tool-chest and the feeling of a bit of wood in his fingers.

The President's Whiskers

Hertha Pauli

This story is a true one. Back in 1860, when Abraham Lincoln was running for President, a little girl named Grace Bedell wrote him a letter. In the letter, she said she thought he'd look a lot better with whiskers. Lincoln answered her letter, but Grace couldn't tell whether he planned to grow the whiskers.

Then Lincoln was elected. Grace was going to have a chance to see him!

The unforgettable date was February 16, 1861. On February 16, a special train would stop a few miles from Westfield—the train that was carrying Mr. Lincoln to the White House.

Grace hardly slept the night before. It was pitch dark when she wriggled into the sky-blue percale with the polkadots—her Sunday dress. She held the oil lamp up to the small mirror. Did she look like a real lady? No, the bonnet was missing. It had velvet ribbons and two pink flowers on top. In a moment, a perfect little lady smiled out of the mirror, and the flowers nodded approval.

The lady was satisfied. She put the lamp back on the table and leaned on the window sill, waiting impatiently for dawn to break.

Other windows began to light up in the village. Grace heard voices in the house, and the clatter of pots and pans. She got her warm cape and took a last look out of the window. A few high clouds were sailing slowly southward. It would be a beautiful day.

Downstairs, Mother was feeding the baby. Grace danced through the room. "Mother, does my skirt hang right?"

"Stand still a moment. Now turn, slowly. Yes, it's straight all around."

Grace's face fell suddenly. "There'll be so many people he won't even see me," she pouted.

"You're lucky to see him, dear," Mother said.

It was not yet sunup when the Bedells set out in the spring wagon. The older boys had gone ahead, but the rest of them sat under the tasseled top: Father holding the reins, Mother, Grace, Sam, even Kitty. The baby came along, too, asleep in Mother's arms, because Father insisted. "When she grows up," he said, "she'll want to tell she saw him, and she may not get another chance."

Grace could not sit still. "Look—" she pointed, jumping up and down triumphantly—"there are the Rices, but Bricktop is going to school today—"

If Grace was not quiet, Father said over his shoulder, *she* would be going to school today.

"Will you hold the baby awhile, dear?" Mother asked. Grace held the baby. She held it so quietly it did not even wake up.

Horses and vehicles crowded Main and North Portage streets. For days, Westfield had been in a dither; today it would be deserted. Shops were shut. On the post office door hung a big sign: "Closed for Business on February 16."

"Heavens, look at that crowd," said Mother. "Do drive carefully, Father."

The horse-and-buggy parade moved out of the village and westward. Harnesses glistened in the rising sun. Now and then, a farmer's wagon fell in from a side road, or a couple of men on horseback. There were more people on the road than for the fair.

They entered North East, crossing the tracks in the

center of the village. Another turn, and there was the depot, decked in red-white-and-blue bunting, with "Hail to the Chief" spelled out in big letters on a streamer across the tracks.

Mr. Bedell tied the horses to the hitchrail and put blankets on them so they would not freeze. The family headed for the depot, only to find a line of soldiers around it and no one permitted to pass except people with ribbons in their buttonholes. The Bedells had to stand in the crowd. Mother said they were lucky the ground was frozen or their dresses would be ruined.

Then—"They're coming!" Grace screamed.

Wagons came clattering up the road. Men jumped off and lined up as for a drill on the green. The fifes and drums played. There were the three older Bedell boys, and in front of them, barking commands just as if he were in the classroom, was Mr. Wedge! Grace felt actually proud of the assistant principal. Then came the carriages, led by Mr. Rice's. Mr. Rice drove his chestnuts himself, with a tall, gleaming stovepipe hat of black silk on his head. All the carriages were full of silk hats and beribboned button-holes. Father explained that these marks distinguished the reception committee for Mr. Lincoln.

The crowd was still growing. People kept pushing in front until Grace hardly saw the depot any more. Even the flag on the roof disappeared from time to time behind the feathered hat of a large lady.

Baby Sue started to cry, and Mother went back to the wagon with her and Kitty and Sam. Only Father stayed with Grace. They were far back in the crowd now.

"Will he come now?" she asked.

Mr. Bedell drew out his watch. "If the paper had the schedule right, the train is due in an hour."

It was the longest hour in Grace's life.

A gull shrieked. Or—? There was a sudden hush. The shriek came again. It was no gull. It was a steam whistle.

"Here she comes!" And everybody started pushing and craning necks. Grace held onto Father's hand. And yet she was swept forward and sideways and back. People began to yell, to cheer. Grace saw small clouds of black smoke rise into the blue sky, closer and closer. She stretched as high on her toes as she could and saw the top of a huge black funnel pass slowly behind many heads, hissing and puffing smoke, and then the flat roof of a car, and another, and a third with the Stars and Stripes fluttering over the rear platform.

The hat in front shifted a little. Grace had a glimpse of the platform. The noise was deafening.

When a Dream Comes True

One of the stovepipe hats had risen above the rest. A very tall, very black hat, quietly sticking out of a lot of fidgety black hats—this was all Grace could see, until the lady in front got so excited that her feathered headgear slipped to one side. Then she saw more. The calm hat was not half so shiny as the restless ones. It looked dusty and a bit wrinkled, pushed back on a head of black hair. Cries of "Speech! Speech!" rose. All around, there suddenly was dead silence.

"Ladies and gentlemen," someone said, "I have no speech to make and no time to speak in."

You could have heard a pin drop. And yet, the easy drawl rang as familiar as folks talking at any street corner. You almost thought you had heard the voice before.

"I appear before you that I may see you," it said, "and that you may see me."

Grace felt ice-cold. It was he. His voice. He was up there on the platform. She stretched so that it hurt, but all she saw was the wrinkled stovepipe hat.

"And I'm willing to admit that, so far as the ladies are concerned, I have the best of the bargain."

Some ladies tittered.

"Though I wish it to be understood that I don't make the same acknowledgment concerning the men."

Laughter rippled, swelled, burst through the crowd. Grace laughed and clapped her hands. In back of her, an old farmer slapped his thighs and cackled, "That's telling 'em, Abe." In front of her, the lady with the slipping feathers shrieked, "Hooray for President Lincoln!"

Father caught Grace up and set her on his shoulder.

Nothing but Old Glory on the roof of the car remained above the gaunt, shadowy face in the distance, and Grace thought, "My stars, I see them—the whiskers—"

He was speaking again. "I have but one question, standing here beneath the flag of our country: Will you stand by me as I stand by the flag?"

Why was the crowd so still? For an instant, Grace could see the whole figure, immensely tall, in deep black from his boots to the hat that made him look endless.

Someone shouted: "We sure will, Abe!"

The crowd took it up. Hands and hats and women's handkerchiefs rose into the air amid thundering echoes: "Yes—yes—we sure will, Abe!"

Slowly the shouting died. "I don't care for them great orators," Grace heard the farmer behind her. "I want to hear jist a plain, common feller like the rest of us, that I kin foller an' know where he's driving. Abe Lincoln fills the bill."

Grace felt herself sliding down. She was on the ground, hemmed in like a fish in a barrel. Surely it was all over, and the silent crowd was waiting only for the train to start.

Once more, she heard the voice that made you feel you had heard it all your life. "I have a little correspondent in this place," he said.

How simple it sounded! But Grace knew it could not be. She was dreaming again, as a moment back, when she thought she had seen the whiskers.

"This little lady," the voice went on, "saw from the first what great improvement might be made in my appearance—"

It was a lovely dream. You had to keep your eyes shut tight; if you looked, it would be time to get up and go to school.

"—and if she is present, I would like to speak to her."

Grace opened her eyes wide. She was not in bed. She was in a crowd at the North East depot, unable to move, to see, to make a sound.

"Tell us the name," people shouted. "The name!"

And Mr. Lincoln replied distinctly: "Her name is Grace Bedell."

It was Father who took her hand and led her forward.

She went without knowing how, without noticing that a path was opened for them. There were steps ahead, and Father gave her a boost up to the platform in sight of a thousand people, up to a pair of big, black-booted feet. Somewhere above, she heard a slow chuckle.

"She wrote me that she thought I'd look better if I wore whiskers—"

He stooped. Grace felt strong hands under her arms. Suddenly, as if she had no weight at all, she was raised high in the air, kissed on both cheeks, and gently set down again. And her cheeks burned not only from bliss but from a scratching. Up there, sprouting darkly all around the rugged face and covering cheeks and jaw, so that only the upper lip remained free, were the whiskers.

"You see, I let them grow for you, Grace," said Mr. Lincoln.

Grace's eyes traveled up along the black overcoat, all the way up to the whiskers and the wrinkled black hat. She could do nothing but look at the tall, gaunt, plain, familiar great man. She would have liked to stand and look forever and ever.

He took her hand. She heard him say that he hoped to see his little friend again some time; she understood that this moment had to end. He helped her down the steps and she went obediently, like a good girl, back to her proud father.

Grace's brothers, too, were suddenly there, and Mother, and Mr. Wedge, and the sour-faced Mr. Rice, and the postmaster, and Kitty, and a lot of yelling strangers. Grace saw them and did not see them. She heard cheers, yells, a shrill whistle, a rumbling and puffing and screeching. But her mind heard only three words, repeated over and over: "My little friend—my little friend . . ."

Abraham Lincoln

Remember he was poor and country-bred;
   His face was lined; he walked with awkward gait.
Smart people laughed at him sometimes and said,
   "How can so very plain a man be great?"

Remember he was humble, used to toil.
   Strong arms he had to build a shack, a fence,
Long legs to tramp the woods, to plow the soil,
   A head chuck full of backwoods common sense.

Remember all he ever had he earned.
   He walked in time through stately White House doors;
But all he knew of men and life he learned
   In little backwoods cabins, country stores.

Remember that his eyes could light with fun;
   That wisdom, courage, set his name apart;
But when the rest is duly said and done,
   Remember that men loved him for his heart.

                —*Mildred Plew Meigs*

Just Around
the Corner

Just around the corner
   And down Adventure Lane
Adventures are a-popping
   Like mushrooms after rain.

A sudden blackbird whistles,
   The day turns soft and fair—
And boys and girls come running
   To find adventures there.

—*Dorothy Hall*

Citronella Weather

Mildred Lawrence

"Hush, Malinda!" said Mother. "Daddy's writing an editorial."

Malinda hushed. When Daddy was writing an editorial, he absolutely, positively, must not be disturbed. But she did wish, when everybody else in the Rebel family had their name on the masthead of the *Argus,* that she could have hers there, too.

"Randolph Rebel, Editor and Publisher," it began. (That, of course, was Daddy.)

"Mrs. Randolph Rebel, Society Editor." (And that, of course, was Mother.)

"Junius Rebel, Advertising Manager." (Junius, Malinda's oldest brother, wrote things that said, "On Sale! This Week Only! Boots and Galoshes!")

"Jeremy Rebel, Custodian." (Jeremy, Malinda's second oldest brother, swept out the office and helped run the press when Big Eph didn't get there.)

"David Rebel, Circulation Manager." (David, Malinda's third-oldest brother, delivered all the papers every week.)

Only Malinda wasn't anybody at all. It made her feel very lonesome, like the orphan children that Mother sent the barrel of old clothes to every year.

"Please, please Daddy," begged Malinda, "can't I do something, too?"

"You're not old enough, Baby," said Daddy vaguely. But Malinda kept practicing writing news items and taking them out into the back room where Mr. Wooliver was setting type. Malinda liked talking to Mr. Wooliver. He was never too busy to pay attention. Besides, by sniffing around where Mr. Wooliver was, she could tell what the weather was that day.

If it was cold, Mr. Wooliver had a roll of cotton soaked in camphor behind each ear—"to ward off colds," he said. If it was warm, the cotton was soaked in citronella to keep the mosquitoes away.

"I never catch colds and I never get mosquito bites," said Mr. Wooliver, wiping enough ink off his hands so that he could pick up Malinda's news items.

" 'Annabelle Douglas's cat, Mee-Yow, has six baby kittens,' " he read. " 'One of them has six toes on its front feet.' Well, now, that's very good, young miss. Going to be a writer like your daddy, I see."

And so Malinda ran happily back to her favorite bench in the park and wrote down some more news.

"Clarinda Smith and Robby Holcomb found a hornets' nest down by the river last week," she wrote. "The hornets were not glad to see them. They got stung eight times."

She nibbled her pencil and looked down at the river far below. Nearly everybody in Riverdale lived down on the river bank. But the stores, and the churches, and the city hall, and the library were all at the top of the hill, a long climb even for Malinda.

"Lucius Wixby fell into the river Tuesday," wrote Malinda, "and spoiled his new suit that his mother bought at the bargain sale last week."

She ran back to the *Argus* to see if just this once Daddy would print some of her news items. But she had forgotten that this was the day when the rest of the family were going to the Press Club meeting at Highlands, across the river and sixty miles away. Malinda was to stay home with Great-aunt Essie.

Daddy rattled out a last-minute news item, Mother finished reading the last galley proof, and Junius made a correction on the general store's advertisement so that it would say that coats, not goats, were on sale at $14.95. Daddy took his news item out to Mr. Wooliver, who was wearing camphor that day, even though it was very spring-like outside.

"Leave a place on the front page for the Press Club report," said Daddy. "I'll write it when I get home. You're the boss while I'm gone."

Mr. Wooliver winked at Malinda. "In that case, I'll ask the young miss to help me today," he said. "I'll have my hands full, seeing tomorrow's press day."

"Anything you like," said Daddy. "Good-by, Baby."

Malinda did wish that Daddy wouldn't call her Baby, but Mr. Wooliver seemed not to hear.

"Now, young miss," he said, settling the little rolls of camphor-cotton more securely behind his ears, "I have a feeling in my bones that it's going to rain. I favor your hurrying home for your boots and raincoat."

"Yes, sir," said Malinda.

"Oh, yes, and tell your Great-aunt Essie that you won't be home until after supper. The day before press day is a pretty busy day, but I think we can manage—that is, with the two of us."

"It's pouring down rain," said Malinda when she came back, puffing from the climb up the hill. "You were right. Camphor was just right for today."

"I very seldom miss," said Mr. Wooliver. "Let me see, now! Would you like to take these handbills over to the auctioneer? He's in a hurry for them."

Malinda scampered off. It was raining harder than ever now. The low place on the corner where the rain collected during every storm already looked like a small lake.

"Now you may put some of these leads between each line on this front-page story," said Mr. Wooliver, when she returned. "The leads, you know, are what make the fresh air between the rows of type."

Why, even the boys weren't allowed to touch Mr. Wooliver's type!

"You're so nice," said Malinda. "I'm having the best time!"

"I have to have help," said Mr. Wooliver gruffly. "Can't get this paper out all by myself. Now, then, will you answer the telephone?"

It was somebody from out in the country wanting to know if Malinda knew anything about a flood.

"No," said Malinda politely, "we don't. But it's raining quite hard."

"We Get the News"

It must have been raining harder than Malinda imagined, because pretty soon Great-aunt Essie called up to tell Malinda to stay on the hill.

"Been trying to get you for an hour," said Great-aunt Essie, who sounded like a sputtering firecracker when she was excited. "Radio says everybody get out of the valley on account of the flood. Water's already halfway up the basement steps. It put the furnace fire out. I'll be at the Methodist Church. The Ladies' Aid's going to serve supper for everybody."

"Wh-what about Mother and D-daddy?" asked Malinda, but Great-aunt Essie had already hung up.

"They'll be all right," said Mr. Wooliver, who had been listening over her shoulder. "They're at Highlands, safe and sound. It's a lucky thing you're here and not there, busy as I am! Now, then, people will be calling up here to see where to go and where to sleep and all. Better call up the Mayor and see what to tell them."

Malinda put in a very busy afternoon. The telephone rang every five minutes, and people came in to ask questions. And all the time it kept on raining.

"Radio says the road from Highlands is closed," Mr. Wooliver reported. "Looks as though we'll have to get this paper out by ourselves." Both Malinda and Mr. Wooliver knew very well that the *Argus* couldn't miss its publication day, flood or no flood.

"Lucky thing they wrote everything before they left, for writing is not my line," said Mr. Wooliver, counting page forms. "One, two, three, four, five, six, seven—oh, bless my stars! There's that big gap in the front page."

Malinda looked at the streamer at the top of Page One. "*Riverdale Argus,*" it said. "We Get the News."

"I think we should telephone Daddy," Malinda decided. "It says we get the news, and the flood is news, and Daddy won't like it if it's not in the paper."

"Long-distance telephone lines are out," said Mr. Wooliver gloomily.

There was a long pause while Malinda thought very hard. "Daddy won't let me write for the paper," she said, "on account of being too young."

There was another long pause. "But I guess I'll have to," she decided, "since I'm the only one in the family that's home."

"Quite right, too, young miss," said Mr. Wooliver. "And you'd better start now."

Malinda nibbled her pencil and tried to remember all the things that she had heard about the flood and also all the things that Daddy had told the boys about how to write stories for the *Argus*.

"Put the most important things first," Daddy always said, "in case you might not have room for the rest."

"Everybody in Riverdale is up on the Hill," wrote Malinda, "on account of the big flood. People are eating at the Methodist Church and sleeping in the city hall and the library. It looks very queer, but it is not so wet as it is at home.

"Mrs. Eustace said her clothes basket was floating around in her basement like a boat. Annabelle Douglas's cat, Mee-Yow, led her six kittens up the Hill to the fire house. Spotty, the fire department dog, does not like so many cats there.

"The Mayor says he thinks that people can go home in another day. Mrs. Ransome said she hoped so, because she wanted to take down her wash, which was hanging in the basement. It is under water now, but Mrs. Ransome says for once her wash got plenty of rinsing in fresh rain water."

Before Malinda knew it, it was time to go to the Methodist Church for supper.

"You sleep on the couch in Daddy's office," Malinda told Great-aunt Essie. "I can sleep on his desk."

"I know a better place than that," said Mr. Wooliver. "Sleep on the press. More room to turn over."

As she fell asleep, Malinda could hear Mr. Wooliver setting the type for her story about the flood. And then she didn't remember a thing until Mr. Wooliver was shaking her to wake her up.

"Big Eph's here, young miss," he said, "and we can't print the paper with little girls asleep on the press. Rain's settled down to a drizzle, and the water's starting to go down. You go to the church and get your breakfast, and then scoot along to school."

When Malinda came back from school in the afternoon, Daddy and Mother and Junius and Jeremy and David were all there. There was a neat stack of new papers on the counter. Malinda gave everybody a big hug.

"Did you have a good time?" she asked. "I slept on the press. And I helped Mr. Wooliver. And I—"

Suddenly she caught sight of the paper and the big headline which said, "Flood Routs Riverdale Residents." Right at the beginning of her story were the words, "By Malinda Rebel."

Malinda gasped. Why, even the boys had never had a by-line! She did hope that Daddy wouldn't be cross with Mr. Wooliver. "Daddy," she said, "did we do right? We couldn't get you and—"

"Hush, Malinda," said Mother. "Daddy's writing an editorial."

"You come and sit beside me while I write it," said Daddy. "It's about you."

Malinda leaned her chin against Daddy's shoulder. Beside Daddy's typewriter lay a proof of the masthead. A new name had been added: "Malinda Rebel, Reporter."

"Oh, Daddy!" said Malinda.

But Daddy's typewriter was going clickety-clack.

"A Chip Off the Old Block," wrote Daddy. Then, "I'm a proud man today, and for once I am going to brag about one of my children. My daughter, Malinda—"

"Oh, Daddy!" said Malinda again.

Why, even the boys had never had an editorial written about them! Mother and Junius and Jeremy and David all stood around and watched Daddy while he wrote. Even Mr. Wooliver came in and peered over his glasses. In spite of the drizzle outside, Malinda knew that it was going to be a lovely day, because Mr. Wooliver smelled like an extra-large bottle of citronella.

The Middle Bear

Eleanor Estes

When a play was given at the Town Hall, Sylvie was usually the only one of the four Moffats who was in it. However, once in a while the others were in a play. For instance, Rufus had been the smallest of the seven dwarfs. And once Janey had been a butterfly. She had not been an altogether successful butterfly, though, for she had tripped on the sole of her stocking, turning a somersault all across the stage. And whereas Joey was rarely in a play, he was often in charge of switching the lights on and off.

Jane liked the plays at the Town Hall. In fact she liked them better than the moving pictures. In the moving pictures Jane always found it difficult to tell the good man from the bad man. Especially if they both wore black mustaches. Of course the pianist usually played ominous music just before the bad man came on the scene, and that helped. Even so, Jane preferred the plays at the Town Hall. There she had no trouble at all telling the good from the bad.

Now there was to be a play at the Town Hall, "The Three Bears," and all four of the Moffats were going to be in it. Miss Chichester, the dancing school teacher, was putting it on. But the money for the tickets was not going into her pocket or into the Moffats' pocket, even though they were all in the play. The money was to help pay for the new parish house. The old one had burned down last May and now a new one was being built. "The Three Bears" was to help raise the money to finish it. A benefit performance, it was called.

In this benefit performance, Sylvie was to play the part of Goldilocks. Joey was to be the big bear, Rufus the little bear, and Janey the middle bear. Jane had not asked to be the middle bear. It just naturally came out that way. The middle Moffat was going to be the middle bear.

As a rule, Joey did not enjoy the idea of acting in a play any more than he liked going to dancing school. However, he felt this play would be different. He felt it would be like having a disguise on, to be inside of a bear costume. And Jane felt the same way. She thought the people in the audience would not recognize her as the butterfly who turned a somersault across the stage, because she would be comfortably hidden inside her brown bear costume. As for Rufus, he hoped that Sylvie, the Goldilocks of this game, would not sit down too hard on that nice little chair of his and really break it to bits. It was such a good chair, and he wished he had it at home.

Mama was making all the costumes, even the bear heads. A big one for Joey, a little one for Rufus, and a middle-sized one for Jane. Of course, she wasn't making them out of bear fur; she was using brown outing flannel.

Now Jane was trying on her middle bear costume. She stepped into the body of the costume and then Mama put the head on her.

"Make the holes for the eyes big enough," Jane begged. "So I'll see where I'm going and won't turn somersaults."

"Well," said Mama, "if I cut the eyes any larger, you will look like a deep sea diver instead of a bear."

"Oh, well . . ." said Jane hastily. "A bear's got to look like a bear. Never mind making them bigger, then."

Besides being in the play, each of the Moffats also had ten tickets to sell. And since Rufus really was too little to go from house to house and street to street selling tickets, the other three Moffats had even more to dispose of. Forty tickets!

At first Jane wondered if a girl should sell tickets to a play she was going to be in. Was that being conceited? Well, since the money was for the new parish house and not for the Moffats, she finally decided it was all right to sell the tickets. Besides, she thought, who would recognize her as the girl who sold tickets once she was inside her bear costume?

Sylvie sold most of her tickets like lightning to the ladies in the choir. But Joey's and Janey's tickets became grimier and grimier, they had such trouble disposing of them. Nancy Stokes said she would help even though she went to a different parish house. She and Joey and Jane went quietly and politely up on people's verandas and rang the bell.

"Buy a ticket for the benefit of the new parish house?" was all they meant to say. But very often no one at all answered the bell.

"They can't all be away," said Nancy. "Do you think they hide behind the curtains when they see us coming?"

"Oh no," said Jane. "You see it'd be different if the money was for us. But it isn't. It's a benefit. Why should they hide?"

One lady said she was very sorry but she was making mincemeat. "See?" she said, holding up her hands. They were all covered with mincemeat. So she could not buy a ticket. Not possibly, and she closed the door in their faces.

"She could wash her hands," said Nancy angrily. The children called this lady "mincemeat," ever after. Of course, she never knew it.

Yes, the tickets were very hard to sell. But little by little the pile did dwindle. If only everybody were like Mrs. Stokes, they would go very fast. She bought four tickets! Jane was embarrassed.

"Tell your mother she doesn't have to buy all those tickets just 'cause all of us are in the play," she instructed Nancy.

But all the Stokes insisted they really wanted to go. And even if none of the Moffats were in it, they would still want to go, for the play would help to build a new parish house. What nice people! thought Jane. Here they were, a family who went to the white church, buying tickets to help build a parish house for Janey's church. She hoped she would be a good middle bear, so they would be proud they knew her.

At last, it was the night of the play. The four Moffats knew their lines perfectly. This was not surprising, considering they all lived in the same house and could practice their lines any time they wanted to. And, besides this, they had had two rehearsals, one in regular clothes and one in their bear costumes.

When Jane reached the Town Hall, she was surprised to find there were many features on the program besides "The Three Bears." The Gillespie twins were going to give a piano duet. "By the Brook," it was called. A boy was going to play the violin. Someone else was going to toe dance. And Miss Beale was going to sing a song. A big program. And the Moffats, all of them except Mama, were going to watch this whole performance from behind the scenes. They could not sit in the audience with the regular people with their bear costumes on, for that would give the whole show away.

Jane fastened her eye to a hole in the curtain. Mama had not yet come. Of course Mama would have to sit out front there with the regular people, even though she had made the costumes. The only people who had arrived so far were Clara Pringle and Brud. They were sitting in the front row and Jane wondered how they had gotten in because the front door that all the regular people were supposed to use wasn't even open yet.

When Jane wasn't peering through a hole in the curtain, Joey or Rufus was. Each one hoped he would be the first to see Mama when she came in. Or now and then, they tried to squeeze through the opening at the side of the asbestos curtain. But the gnarled little janitor shook his head at them. So they stayed inside.

Sylvie was busy putting make-up on herself and on the dancers' faces. Jane watched them enviously. The only trouble with wearing a bear costume, she thought, was that she couldn't have her face painted. Well, she quickly consoled herself, she certainly would not have stage fright inside her bear head. Whereas she might if there were just paint on her face. "Somebody has been sitting in my chair," she rehearsed her lines. She stepped into her bear costume. But before putting on her head, she helped Rufus into *his* bear uniform. He didn't call it a costume. A uniform. A bear uniform. Jane set his head on his shoulders, found his two eyes for him so he could see out, and the little bear was ready.

Joey had no difficulty stepping into his costume and in finding his own two eyes. Now the big bear and the little bear were ready. Jane looked around for her head, to put it on. Where was it?

"Where's my head?" she asked. "My bear head."

Nobody paid any attention to her. Miss Chichester was running back and forth and all around, giving an order here and an order there. Once, as she rushed by, causing a great breeze, Jane yelled to make herself heard, "How can we act 'The Three Bears' unless I find my middle bear head?"

"Not just now. I'm too busy," was all Miss Chichester said.

Everybody was too busy to help Jane find her head. Sylvie was busy helping the toe dancer dress. Joey was busy running around doing this and doing that for Miss Chichester. And the little old janitor was busy tightening ropes and making sure the lights were working. Rufus could not be torn from a hole in the curtain. He was looking for Mama.

Jane sighed. Everybody is busy, she thought. She rummaged around in a big box of costumes. Maybe her bear head had been stuck into it. She found a dragon head and tried it on. How would that be? She looked in the mirror. The effect was interesting. But, no, she could not wear this, for a bear cannot be a dragon.

A Headless Bear

Goodness, thought Jane. The curtain will go up, and the middle bear won't be a whole bear. This was worse than tripping over her stocking the time she was a butterfly. Maybe Joey and Rufus somehow or another had two heads on. They didn't, though, just their own. Phew, it was warm inside these bear costumes. Jane stood beside Rufus and looked through another small hole in the curtain. Oh! The big door was open! People were beginning to arrive. And what kind of a bear would she be without a head? Maybe she wouldn't be allowed to be a bear at all. But there certainly could not be three bears without a middle one.

"Don't worry," said Rufus, not moving an inch from his spot. "Lend you mine for half the play . . ."

"Thanks," said Jane. "But we all have to have our heads on all through the whole thing."

The Stokes were coming in! Jane felt worried. The only person who might be able to fix a new bear head for her in a hurry was Mama. Oh, if she had only made a couple of spare heads. But Mama wasn't coming yet. Jane resolved to go and meet her. She put on her tam and her chinchilla coat over her bear costume. Then she ran down the three narrow steps into the Hall. She crouched low in her coat in order not to give away the fact that she was clad in a bear costume. Nobody on this side of the curtain was supposed to know what people on her side of the curtain had on until the curtain rolled up. Surprise. That's what was important in a play.

Mr. Buckle was coming in now, walking towards the front row. Jane stooped low, with her knees bent beneath her. In front her coat nearly reached the ground. From the way she looked from the front, few would guess that she was the middle bear. Of course, her feet showed. They were encased in the brown costume. But she might be a brownie or even a squirrel.

"Hello, Mr. Buckle," said Jane. "I'm in a hurry . . ."

"Where are you going, middle Moffat?" he asked. "Aren't you the prima donna?"

"No, just the middle bear."

"Well, that's fine. The middle Moffat is the middle bear."

"Yes. Or I was until I lost my head."

"Oh, my," said Mr. Buckle. "This, then, is not your head?" he asked, pointing to her tam.

"Yes, but not my bear head. I don't mean bare head. Bear head! B-e-a-r. That kind of head."

"Mystifying. Very mystifying," said Mr. Buckle, settling himself slowly in a seat in the front row.

"You'll see later," said Jane, running down the aisle.

She ran all the way home. But the house was dark. Mama had already left. And she must have gone around the other way, or Jane would have passed her. Jane raced back to the Town Hall. There! Now! The lights were dim. The entertainment had begun. Jane tried to open the side door. Chief Mulligan was guarding this entrance. He did not want to let her in at first. He thought she was just a person. But when she showed him her costume, he opened the door just wide enough for her. The bear costume was as good as a password.

The toe dancer was doing the split. Jane tiptoed up the three steps and went backstage, wondering what would happen now. The show always goes on. There was some comfort in that thought. Somehow, someone would fix her head. Or possibly, while she was gone, her middle bear head had been found. She hoped she would not have to act with her head bare.

Miss Chichester snatched her.

"Oh, there you are, Jane! Hop into your costume, dear."

"I'm in it," said Jane. "But I can't find my middle bear head."

"Heavens!" said Miss Chichester, grasping her own head. "What else will go wrong?"

Jane looked at her in surprise. What else *had* gone wrong? Had others lost worse than their heads?

"Where's the janitor?" Miss Chichester asked. "Maybe he let his grandchildren borrow it."

Jane knew he hadn't, but she couldn't tell Miss Chichester, for she had already flown off. And then Janey had an idea.

"I know what," she said to Joey. "Pin me together." And she pulled the neck part of her costume up over her head. Joey pinned it with two safety pins, and he cut two holes for her eyes. This costume was not comfortable now. Pulling it up and pinning it this way lifted Jane's arms so she had trouble making them hang down the way she thought a bear's should. However, at any rate, she now had a bear head of sorts.

"Do I look like a bear?" she asked Rufus.

"You look like a brown ghost," Rufus replied.

"Don't you worry," said Sylvie, coming up. "You look like a very nice little animal."

"But I'm supposed to be a bear, not a nice little animal," said Jane.

"Well," said Sylvie, "people will know you are supposed to be a bear because Rufus and Joey both have their bear heads on."

So Jane resigned herself to not being a perfect bear. She tried to comfort herself with the thought that she would still be in disguise. She hoped her acting would be so good it would counterbalance her bad head. "Somebody has been eating my porridge," she practiced.

Miss Chichester appeared. "The janitor said 'No,'" she said. She thoughtfully surveyed Jane a moment. "Hm-m-m, a makeshift," she observed. "Well, it's better than nothing," she agreed with Jane. But she decided to switch the order of the program around in order to give everybody one last chance to find the middle bear's head. She sent Miss Beale out onto the stage. Everybody hoped that while Miss Beale was singing, "In an Old-fashioned Garden," the head would appear. But it didn't.

"Keep a little in the background," said Miss Chichester to Jane. "Perhaps people will not notice."

"If I can only see where the background is," thought Jane. For she found it even harder to keep her eyes close to the holes cut in her costume than it had been to the real ones in her regular bear head.

Now the heavy curtain rolled up. It didn't stick halfway up as it sometimes did, and Sylvie, Goldilocks, in a blue pinafore and socks, ran out onto the stage amidst loud applause. The play had begun! Sylvie had a great deal of acting to do all by herself before the three bears came home. But she wasn't scared. She was used to being on the stage alone.

The Show Must Go On

Jane's heart pounded as she and Joey and Rufus waited for their cue to come home. If only she didn't trip and turn a somersault!—for she really could not see very well. Somehow she managed to see out of only one eye at a time. These eyeholes must have been cut crooked. One hole kept getting hooked on her nose.

"Now!" Miss Chichester whispered. "Cue! Out with you three bears."

Joe, Jane, and Rufus, the three bears, lumbered out onto the stage. They were never supposed to just walk, always lumber and lope.

The applause was tremendous. It startled the three bears. The Town Hall was packed. Somebody must have sold a lot of tickets.

"There's Mama," said Rufus. He said it out loud.

He wasn't supposed to say anything out loud except about his porridge, his chair, and his bed. But anyway he said, "There's Mama." Jane could not see Mama. Lumbering out onto the stage had dislocated her costume, so that now she could not see at all. Fortunately, the footlights shone through the brown flannel of her costume so she could keep away from the edge of the stage.

The Moffats all knew their lines so well they did not forget them once. The only trouble was they did not have much chance to say them because the applause was so great every time they opened their mouths. At last, however, they reached the act about the three beds. An extra platform had been set up on the stage to look like the upstairs of a three bears' house. The three bears lumbered slowly up the steps.

Suddenly, shouts arose all over the Hall:

"Her head! Her head! The middle bear's head!"

"Sh-sh-sh," said others. "See what's going to happen."

As Jane could not see very well, she had no idea what these shouts referred to. She had the same head on now that she had had on all during this play so far. Why then all these shouts? Or had she really stayed in the background the way Miss Chichester had asked her to, and the audience had only just discovered the makeshift?

"Oh," whispered Joey to Jane. "I see it. It's your real bear head and it's on the top of my bed post."

"O-o-o-h!" said Jane. "Get it down."

"How can I?" said Joe. "With all these people watching me?"

"Try and get it when you punch your bed," urged Jane.

Joey was examining his big bear's bed now. "Hm-m-m," he said fiercely. "Somebody has been lying on my bed . . ." But he couldn't reach the middle bear's head. He did try. But he couldn't quite reach it, and there was more laughter from the audience.

Jane pulled her costume about until she could see through the eyehole. Ah, there was her head! On the post of the big bear's bed. No wonder people were laughing. What a place for the middle bear's head. Here she was, without it. And there it was, without her. Jane resolved to get it. Somehow or other she would rescue her head before this play was completely over. Now was her chance. It was her turn to talk about her bed. Instead, Jane said:

"Somebody has been trying on my head, and there it is!"

Jane hopped up on Joey's bed. She grabbed her middle bear head.

"Yes," she repeated. "Somebody has been trying on my head," but as she added, "and here it is!" the safety pins that held her makeshift head together popped open. The audience burst into roars of laughter as Janey's own real head emerged. Only for a second, though. For she clapped her middle bear head right on as fast as she could, and hopped off the bed. Goodness, she thought, I showed my real face and I didn't have any paint on it.

Unfortunately, Jane still could not see, for she had stuck her bear head on backwards. But the audience loved it. They clapped and they stamped. Bravo! Bravo! Bravo, middle bear! Big boys at the back of the hall put their fingers in their mouths and whistled. And it was a long time before Jane could say:

"Somebody has been sleeping in my bed," and the play could go on. At last, Rufus discovered Goldilocks in his little bed, and she leaped out of the window. That was the end of the play and the curtain rolled down.

When the bowing began, Miss Chichester tried to send Jane in backwards, thinking the back of her was the front of her. Fortunately, Rufus held Jane by one paw, and Joey held the other. So she didn't get lost. And the three bears lumbered dizzily on and off many times, sometimes with Sylvie, and sometimes alone. And somebody yelled for "The mysterious middle bear!" It must have been the oldest inhabitant.

Miss Chichester turned Jane's head around for this bow, and at last Jane really did look like a perfect middle bear. Furthermore, she could see out. There was Mama, laughing so hard the tears were rolling down her cheeks. And there was Nancy Stokes with all the Stokes, and Olga was there. And there was Mr. Buckle, beaming up at the stage. Jane bowed and lumbered off the stage. She felt good now. Acting was fun, she thought, especially if you could be disguised in a bear uniform. And this time she had not turned a somersault across the stage as she had the time she was a butterfly. True, she had lost her head. But she had found it. And the show had gone on, the way people always say shows do.

Moreover, the Moffats had nice warm bear pajamas to sleep in for the rest of the winter. Of course, they didn't go to bed with the bear heads on. But the rest of the costumes were nice and warm.

Locked In

Elizabeth Enright

"And then what?" asked Garnet.

"That's all," said Citronella. "They lived happy ever after."

Garnet sighed. "You always tell stories about people that are grown up and fall in love. I like stories about children and wild animals and explorers." She sat up suddenly. "I know what. Let's go to town to the library and read. It's going to rain anyway."

Citronella said she didn't feel like walking all that way just to read a book. But Garnet was sure they could get a ride with someone.

As luck would have it, the moment they went out of the gate they saw Mr. Freebody's truck clattering down the road towards them. They waved and called. Mr. Freebody stopped and opened the door to let them in.

"We'd rather ride outside, if you don't mind," said Garnet. The two girls scrambled into the back of the truck and stood up holding onto the roof over the driver's seat.

It was fun to ride like that. As soon as he got on the highway, Mr. Freebody drove very fast, and the wind blew so hard against them that Garnet's pigtails stuck straight out behind. Citronella's bangs stood up on end like a hedge.

"I feel like a thing on the front of a boat," shouted Garnet. "A figurehead, I think it's called."

Citronella had never heard of figureheads and it was hard to explain, because you had to yell so. The wind roared and Mr. Freebody's truck was a very loud one. Also, if you opened your mouth too wide, lazy beetles on the wing were apt to be swept into it.

The little gray town of Blaiseville flew towards them. There it was, all just as usual: the courthouse with its tower and gilded dome, the gasoline station, and Mrs. Elson's yellow house with clothes leaping on the line. There was Opal Clyde, the doctor's daughter, bouncing a ball on the walk in front of her house. There was Junior Gertz pulling his dog along in a little express wagon. Garnet and Citronella waved as they rode grandly by. Mr. Freebody drew up in front of the Farm Bureau. The girls jumped down.

"How you two little girls going to git home?" asked Mr. Freebody.

"Oh, we'll walk maybe," answered Garnet. "Or get a ride with someone," added Citronella hopefully.

They thanked him and walked up Main Street, past the drugstore and the post office. There was a bulletin in the post office window that said: "Big Hollow Ladies Annual Picnic Next Sunday. Come One, Come All!" Garnet giggled at this notice, seeing in her mind a group of huge, balloon-like creatures in dresses eating sandwiches under a tree. Of course, she knew that the Big Hollow Ladies were simply ladies that lived in Big Hollow, but it had a funny sound all the same.

Finally, on the outskirts of the town, they came to the library, an old-fashioned frame building set back from the road among thick-foliaged maple trees.

Garnet loved the library. It smelled of old books and was full of stories that she had never read. Miss Pentland, the librarian, was a nice little fat lady who sat behind a desk facing the door.

"Good afternoon, Citronella," she said, smiling. "Good afternoon, Garnet."

Garnet and Citronella poked about until each found the book she wanted. Then they settled down on a broad window seat between two tall cases of large old volumes. Garnet had *The Jungle Book*. Citronella, with a sigh of pleasure, began to read a wonderful story called *Duchess Olga; or The Sapphire Signet*.

The screen door of the library closed many times with a dull bang. People came and went. For a while, rain splintered against the window beside the two girls. But they scarcely heard it. Garnet was thousands of miles away with Kotick, the white seal, swimming the wide seas. Citronella was in a ballroom lighted by a hundred

chandeliers and crowded with beautiful ladies and gentlemen in full evening dress.

Once, Garnet looked up and stretched. "My, it's quiet,"
she whispered. "I wonder if it's late."

"Oh, we haven't been here long," said Citronella impatiently. Duchess Olga was being lowered on a rope down
the face of a huge cliff. The trouble was that the man who
held the rope didn't like Duchess Olga. He was planning
to let her drop at any minute. Citronella thought everything would turn out all right, but she wasn't sure.

By the time that Garnet had re-read "Rikki-Tikki-
Tavi," and Duchess Olga had been rescued and safely
returned to the ballroom, the light began to fade.

"What does the word 'insidious' mean?" asked Citronella. But Garnet didn't know.

"My, it is kind of still here," Citronella went on. "I'll
ask Miss Pentland what time it is." She disappeared behind
the bookcases.

"Garnet!" she called loudly the next moment. "Miss
Pentland's gone! Everyone's gone!"

Too Much Adventure

Garnet leaped from the window seat. It was true; there
was no one there. They ran to the door. It was firmly
locked. The back door was locked, too. The heavy glass
windows had not been opened in years.

"Good night!" moaned Citronella. "We're locked in!"
She was on the verge of tears.

"But Citronella," Garnet said solemnly, "this is an adventure. We'll be able to tell our children and grandchildren about it. I hope we stay here all night!"

"Oh, gee," sobbed Citronella. She wished with all her heart that she hadn't read *Duchess Olga.* It was too scary. If only she had picked out a good peaceful book about boarding school girls or something! Suddenly, she had such a terrible thought that she stopped crying.

"Garnet!" she cried. "Do you know what day it is? Saturday! That means we'll be here till day after tomorrow. We'll starve!"

Garnet's excitement went flat. It would be awful to stay in here as long as that.

"Let's bang on the window," she suggested. "Maybe someone will come."

They banged on the glass and shouted at the tops of their lungs. But the library was some distance from the street. Blaiseville people were peacefully eating their suppers and never heard a sound.

Slowly the dusk sifted into the room. The bookcases looked tall and solemn. The pictures on the wall were solemn too! Napoleon at Elba, and Washington Crossing the Delaware.

There was no telephone in the library and no electric light. There were gas fixtures, but Garnet and Citronella could not find any matches. Miss Pentland's desk was full of useless things like filing cards, rubber stamps, elastic bands, and neat little rolls of string.

Citronella pounced upon a chocolate bar in a pigeon-hole. "We won't starve right away anyhow," she said, brightening a little. "I don't think Miss Pentland would mind if we ate it, do you?"

"We'll buy her another when we get out," said Garnet. So they divided it and stood, sadly munching, at the window nearest the street. The twilight deepened.

"Who is that!" cried Garnet suddenly. They saw a dim, small figure slowly approaching on the cement walk that led to the library door. The person seemed to be bowing.

Citronella began thumping on the window joyously. "It's Opal Clyde, bouncing her ball," she said. "Yell, Garnet. Yell and bang."

They both yelled and banged. Opal, after a scared glance at the dark window, scurried down the path.

"Do you think she'll tell someone?" asked Citronella anxiously.

"Oh, she thought it was a spook," said Garnet in disgust. "No one will believe her if she does."

All over Blaiseville, the street lamps blossomed suddenly with light. The two girls heard cars coming and going and faint shouts of children playing in back yards. They pounded and called till they were hoarse. But nobody came. After a while, they gave it up as a bad job and returned to the window seat.

The room was very dark now—strange, unknown, and filled with shadows. There were tiny creaking sounds and rustlings, and airy scamperings of mouse feet.

"I don't like it," whispered Citronella. "My own voice scares me. I don't dare talk out loud."

"Neither do I," murmured Garnet. "I feel as if all those books were alive and listening."

"I wonder why our folks don't come after us," said Citronella.

"They don't know where we are," answered Garnet. "They don't even know we came to town. We didn't tell Mr. Freebody that we were going to the library."

"I wish I'd never learned to read," sighed Citronella. "I wish I was some kind of animal and didn't have to be educated."

"It might be fun to be a panther," agreed Garnet, "or a kangaroo, or a monkey."

"Or a pig, even," said Citronella. "A safe, happy pig, asleep in its own pen with its own family!"

They heard the courthouse clock strike eight, then nine. But when it struck ten they were both asleep.

At a little before midnight, they were wakened by a tremendous pounding and shouting.

"Who? What's that? Where am I?" shrieked Citronella. Garnet, her heart thumping, said, "In the library, remember? Someone's at the door."

She ran forward in the dark, barking her shins and whacking her elbows on unfamiliar surfaces.

"Who's there?" she called.

Two Genu-wine Bookworms

"That you, Garnet? Thank the Lord we've found you at last," said a voice that was unmistakably Mr. Freebody's. "Is Citronella with you? Fine! Both your dads are scouring the town. Open the door!"

"But we're locked *in*, Mr. Freebody," called Garnet. "Miss Pentland has the key."

"I'll get it, I'll get it," shouted Mr. Freebody excitedly. "You wait there."

"We can't do anything *but* wait," said Citronella crossly. She was always cross when she first woke up.

In a little while, they heard rapid footsteps on the front walk, and voices, and then the lovely sound of a key turning in the lock. Miss Pentland, with her hat on sideways, rushed in and embraced them.

"You poor little things!" she cried. "Such a thing has *never* happened before. I always make sure everyone's gone before I lock up. I can't understand how I missed you!"

"That's all right, Miss Pentland," said Garnet. "It was an adventure. And we ate your chocolate!"

Garnet's father and Mr. Freebody and Mr. Hauser came in too, all talking and exclaiming.

"Are you both sure you're all right?" asked Mr. Hauser anxiously.

"We're all right, Papa," said Citronella. "But we're awfully hungry."

"I'll go telephone the folks at home," volunteered Mr. Freebody. "So's they won't have to worry no longer. You better take the little girls down to the lunch wagon for a bite. Only place that's open at this hour."

The lunch wagon was full of bright yellow light and powerful food smells. It was wonderful to go there so late at night and eat fried egg sandwiches and apple pie and tell everybody what had happened to them.

"Yes, sir!" said Mr. Freebody, coming in the door. "Don't you be fooled! Those ain't two little girls. Those are two genu-wine bookworms. Couldn't stop reading long enough to come home. Planning to take up residence in the library from now on, ain'tcha?"

Everyone laughed.

"Just the same," whispered Garnet to Citronella. "I sort of wish they hadn't found us until morning. Then we could have told our grandchildren that once we stayed in the public library all night long!"

Winner Take a Mule

E. H. Lansing

Eleven-year-old Jeb Tillson and mean Sam Cotter had a dispute about a mule. It might have meant blood, but Jeb's Uncle Raff proposed a shooting match instead, winner to take the mule. Uncle Raff and Sam were both known in the mountains as crack shots. Mr. Olmstead agreed to judge the contest.

"You men are to shoot at the two targets on the fence," shouted Mr. Olmstead so everyone could hear. "Ten shots each, turn and turn about. Raff take the target to the right. Sam the one to the left. The man who gets the most shots nearest his bull's-eye wins."

Every head turned toward the two targets on the fence. Each one was a square of white paper with a red circle in its center. Jeb thought the red circles looked very small. He stood close to the mule and held tight to the halter rope. He watched Uncle Raff as he stepped forward to take the first shot. Jeb heard the report of the gun, but he couldn't see whether the shot had hit. Then it was Sam's turn.

Jeb counted the shots. Three for Uncle Raff, three for Sam. Mr. Olmstead wasn't to look at the targets until each man had ten shots.

From SHOOT FOR A MULE by Elisabeth H. Lansing, copyright 1951 by E. H. Lansing; reprinted by permission of the publisher, Thomas Y. Crowell Company.

Jeb's hands were stiff from holding the mule's rope. His eyes ached from trying to see the red circles. The shots rang in his ears like the crash of thunder. He lost count of them.

At last Mr. Olmstead raised his hand. "Ten each," he called. "That's all."

A rustle of talk ran through the crowd as Mr. Olmstead went toward the targets. Jeb closed his eyes and leaned against the mule. But he couldn't keep them closed. He had to know that Uncle Raff had won.

Mr. Olmstead looked from one target to the other. He studied each one so long the crowd grew impatient. Cries of "Who won?" came from every side.

Mr. Olmstead turned to the crowd. "Every one of those shots hit the red circles," he shouted. "The contest's a draw."

A great shout came from the people. Both Uncle Raff and Sam looked very pleased with themselves. But Jeb did not shout. The question of who was to have the mule was still unsettled.

Mr. Olmstead raised his hand for silence. He held up a shining half dollar. "I'll toss this in the air twice. Raff gets first shot at it. Sam second. The one who hits nearest the center wins."

Uncle Raff and Sam nodded agreement. They watched Mr. Olmstead as he stood by the fence with the coin in his hand. Uncle Raff limped forward down the slope of the meadow to take his stand for his shot.

Then Jeb caught his breath with a sharp sound. Uncle Raff had slipped and fallen. He landed with a thud on his shooting arm. When he sat up, his arm hung at his side. Jeb dropped the rope and raced to kneel down by Uncle Raff.

"Wrenched bad," said Uncle Raff. His face was tight with pain.

"I win," said Sam in a loud voice. "I win 'cause he can't shoot no more and I kin."

Uncle Raff did not answer Sam in words. He looked at Jeb and handed him his gun. Jeb knew what he must do. He got to his feet with the gun in his hands.

"I ain't shooting against no boy!" Sam's harsh voice made Jeb jump.

"Don't mind him, Jeb," said Uncle Raff in his easy way. "You got a right to shoot. You're a Tillson."

"I won already!" bellowed Sam.

Mr. Olmstead opened his mouth to speak, but someone got ahead of him. A shrill voice came from the crowd.

"Don't you pay him no never mind, Jeb Tillson! You kin shoot as good as him any day in the mornin'."

Jeb suddenly felt better. Granny hadn't been able to keep away from the shooting match after all. Now she pushed her way forward through the crowd. Her sharp face was bright with anger.

A loud murmur of approval came from the listening people. Everyone agreed with Granny that Jeb had a right to shoot in Uncle Raff's place.

Mr. Olmstead nodded at Jeb. "Go ahead," he said.

But Sam Cotter was not going to let the crowd have everything its own way. "Iffen I'm to shoot agin a mere boy I claim the right to shoot first," he said fiercely. "I got some say-so in this shootin' match."

Mr. Olmstead shrugged his shoulders. "I guess Jeb doesn't mind who goes first. Do you, Jeb?"

Jeb shook his head. "I don't mind." He was glad to let Sam shoot first. It would give him time to steady his nerve.

Mr. Olmstead held the coin in his hand, waiting for Sam to give him the signal. Sam lifted his gun to his shoulder, then nodded at Mr. Olmstead. The coin flew high into the air, a bright flash of silver in the sunshine. Jeb watched the coin, waiting for the sound of Sam's shot. But no sound came.

Sam was holding his gun in both hands, staring angrily at the trigger. "Jammed," muttered Sam, "jammed tighter'n sausage meat."

Uncle Raff chuckled. "Mebbe Jeb wins. He kin shoot and you can't."

Sam glared at Uncle Raff. His own words were coming back to him and he could think of nothing to say.

Then Jeb moved forward with Uncle Raff's gun in his hands. He did not think what he was doing. But deep in

his heart, he wanted to win the mule fairly. He held out
Uncle Raff's gun toward Sam.

"Use this gun," said Jeb quietly.

For a long minute, Sam looked at Jeb without moving.
Then the hard lines of his jaw softened. "Thanks, boy,"
said Sam. His voice was as quiet as Jeb's had been. He took
the gun and stepped into shooting position.

Once again Sam nodded at Mr. Olmstead. Once again
the coin rose in a whirling flash toward the sky. This time,
Sam's shot rang out loud and clear. The coin jerked and
fell to the ground.

Jeb watched Mr. Olmstead walk toward the place where
the coin had fallen. Mr. Olmstead picked up the coin and
studied it carefully. Then he held it up to the people.
"Nicked off the edge," he cried.

The watching crowd murmured its applause. No one
liked Sam well enough to cheer him loudly. But everyone
was polite enough to acknowledge a good shot.

Sam did not look at Jeb as he handed back the gun. Jeb
clutched the smooth barrel with both hands and walked
to the shooting stand. He did not think or feel anything.
For a moment his eyes blurred, and he had a horrible fear
that he would not even see the coin, much less hit it.

Then he heard a sharp familiar voice. "Stand up to hit,
Jeb. Act like you was glad-proud to be a Tillson."

Granny's brisk words were like a dash of cold water in

Jeb's face. His muscles stiffened and he could think clearly. He turned and grinned at Granny.

Then he lifted the gun and looked at Mr. Olmstead. He saw the tiny coin in Mr. Olmstead's hands. When he gave the signal, it would fly into the air.

Jeb's hands shook. He lowered his gun and looked toward the mule. The mule was watching Jeb. One long ear flapped forward in a friendly greeting.

"Go it, Jeb!" Ben Larkin's high excited voice sounded very loud to Jeb.

Then another voice spoke. "What you waitin' fer, Jeb?" Uncle Raff's calm, sure words steadied the boy.

He took a firm grip on the rifle. He lifted it to his shoulder and nodded at Mr. Olmstead. The sun caught at the silver coin. Jeb saw its brightness right at the end of the gun barrel. His finger pressed the trigger. Then Jeb shut his eyes.

He didn't open them until he heard a shout from the people. Then he saw Mr. Olmstead holding the coin high.

"Right plunk in the middle!" shouted Mr. Olmstead.

The crowd surged forward and pushed around Jeb. People thumped him on the back. Ben jumped up and down like a jack-in-the-box, yelling with joy. Granny's thin face was stiff with pride.

Jeb scarcely felt the thumps on his back. He didn't hear what anyone said. He just stood still and knew the mule was his for keeps.

Glossary

This glossary, or small dictionary, contains the more unusual words from the stories in this book. Usually, only the meaning is given which fits the word the first time it is used. The "key" at the bottom of the pages helps to show how each word is pronounced. The regular dictionary should be used to find meanings of other words you find difficult, or other meanings for the words given here.

A

a·ban'doned (*a*·băn'dŭnd). Deserted, no longer lived in.

a·bound' (*a*·bound'). To be numerous or plentiful.

ab'so·lute (ăb'sô·lūt). Complete, perfect.

ac·com'mo·dat'ing (*a*·kŏm'ô·dāt'ĭng). Obliging, eager to please.

a·chieve'ment (*a*·chēv'mĕnt). Accomplishment, performance of an act deserving praise.

ac·knowl'edg·ment (ăk·nŏl'ĕj·mĕnt). Act of admitting the truth about any matter.

ac·quire' (*a*·kwīr'). To get or obtain, usually by one's own work.

a·loft' (*a*·lôft'). In the air.

am·bi'tious (ăm·bĭsh'ŭs). Eager to win fame, power, or superiority.

an'ces'tor (ăn'sĕs'tēr). Forefather, person who lived long ago and from whom one is descended.

a·nem'o·ne (*a*·nĕm'ô·nĕ). Spring-flowering plant with white or bright-colored blossoms.

an'te·lope (ăn'tĕ·lōp). Graceful, swift-footed animal of the goat family.

ap·par'ent (*a*·păr'ĕnt). Clear to the mind, easily understood.

ap·peal' (*a*·pēl'). To beg for help.

ap·proach' (*a*·prōch'). To come or to go near.

as·bes'tos (ăs·bĕs'tŏs). Grayish, fireproof mineral used especially for shingles.

as·sure' (*a*·shoor'). To make one sure or certain of something.

at·tend' (*a*·tĕnd'). To pay attention, listen.

auc'tion·eer' (ôk'shŭn·ēr'). Person who runs a sale of goods to whoever offers the highest prices.

auk (ôk). Diving sea bird of the Northern Hemisphere.

au·thor'i·ty (ô·thŏr'ĭ·tĭ). Power to rule or govern.

a·void' (*a*·void'). To keep away from, shun.

awk'ward (ôk'wērd). Not skillful, clumsy.

B

bag (băg). To kill on a hunt.

ban'is·ters (băn'ĭs·tērz). The railing beside a staircase.

ban'quet (băng'kwĕt). Feast.

ban'ter (băn'tēr). Good-natured joking.

bat'ter (băt'ēr). To wear down through long, hard use.

bay (bā). Reddish-brown.

be·hold' (bė·hōld'). To see, gaze upon.

ā, āte; *a*, furnåce; ă, ăt; *a*, ăppear; â, câre; ä, cär; *a*, påss; *a*, sofå; ē, bē; ė, bėgin; ĕ, lĕt; ẽ, silẽnt; ē, wātēr; ē, hēre; ī, hīde; ĭ, hĭd; *i*, cabĭn; ō, hōpe; ô, ômit; ŏ, hŏp; ǒ, cǒntain; ô, ôr; ô, sôft; ōo, fōod; ŏo, fŏot; oi, oil; ou, out; ū, ūse; û, ûnite; ŭ, ŭs; *u*, circŭs; û, fûr; t*u*, nāt*u*re; d*u*, verd*u*re; th, thin; t̶h̶, t̶h̶an.

ben'e·fit (bĕn'ĕ·fĭt). Advantage.

be·ware' (bĕ·wâr'). To be cautious, careful, or on guard.

bick'er (bĭk'ẽr). To quarrel.

bliss (blĭs). Great happiness.

blown (blōn). Out of breath, tired and panting.

bore (bōr). To weary or tire someone by dullness.

box (bŏks). Small section or compartment in a theater or sports arena. It contains several seats with a very good view of the stage or field.

bran'dish (brăn'dĭsh). To wave something threateningly.

bri'dle (brī'd'l). Straps around a horse's head by which the rider controls the animal.

brood (brōōd). Young birds having the same mother.

buc'ca·neer' (bŭk'ȧ·nẽr'). Pirate.

bun'ting (bŭn'tĭng). Cloth printed in the colors of the flag and used for decorations on patriotic occasions.

bur'dock' (bûr'dŏk'). Coarse weed with burlike flower heads.

bur'row (bûr'ō). Hole in the ground dug by some kinds of animals for a home.

by'—line' (bī'·lĭn'). Line at the head of a newspaper article telling who wrote it.

C

cache (kăsh). To hide treasure.

cal'cu·late (kăl'kṻ·lāt). To measure by using either actual figures or careful thought and estimate.

ca'liph (kā'lĭf). Title formerly given to rulers of the Mohammedan countries of Asia.

cam'phor (kăm'fẽr). Sap of an Asiatic tree used for medicine.

can'ter (kăn'tẽr). Slow gallop.

ca·reer' (kȧ·rẽr'). Course of one's life.

cask (kȧsk). Barrel.

cast (kȧst). To throw.

cav'ern (kăv'ẽrn). Large cave.

cen'tu·ry (sĕn'tṻ·rĭ). Period of 100 years.

chan'de·lier' (shăn'dĕ·lẽr'). Branched, glittering light fixture hanging from the ceiling.

chest'nut (chĕs'nŭt). Orange-brown—used in describing a horse.

chil'blain' (chĭl'blān'). Itching sore caused by cold weather.

chin·chil'la (chĭn·chĭl'ȧ). Small South American animal. Its soft gray fur is used in expensive coats.

chis'el (chĭz''l). To chip with a sharp-edged tool.

cir'cu·la'tion (sûr'kṻ·lā'shŭn). Movement of blood through the body.

clus'ter (klŭs'tẽr). Bunch.

clutch (klŭch). To grip or hold tightly.

coil (koil). To wind in a circle.

col·lapse' (kŏ·lăps'). To fall in a heap.

col·lect' (kŏ·lĕkt'). To gather in one place.

com·bine' (kŏm·bīn'). To unite, make into one.

con'cha (kŏng'kȧ). Flat, round, metal trimming.

Con'es·to'ga wag'on (kŏn'ĕs·tō'gȧ wăg'ŭn). Covered wagon.

ā, āte; ȧ, furnȧce; ă, ăt; ȧ, ȧppear; â, câre; ä, cär; ȧ, pȧss; ȧ, sofȧ; ē, bē; ĕ, bĕgin; ĕ, lĕt; ĕ, silĕnt; ē, watẽr; ẹ, hẹre; ī, hīde; ĭ, hĭd; ĭ, cabĭn; ō, hōpe;

con'scious (kŏn'shŭs). Aware, able to notice.

con·sid'er·a·ble (kŏn·sĭd'ẽr·a·b'l). Large.

con·sole' (kŏn·sōl'). To comfort.

con·sult' (kŏn·sŭlt'). To seek someone's advice or opinion.

con'trast (kŏn'trăst). Very great difference.

con·ven'ient (kŏn·vēn'yĕnt). Easy and satisfactory.

copse (kŏps). Thicket.

coun'ter·bal'ance (koun'tẽr·băl'ăns). To offset, make up for.

cou'pling (kŭp'lĭng). Connector.

cove (kōv). Small bay.

coy (koi). Bashful or shy in an impish way.

crafts'man (krȧfts'măn). Person who works at a skilled trade.

crane (krān). To stretch out one's neck as a crane does.

crave (krāv). To long for.

crea'ture (krē'tụr). Any kind of animal.

crim'son (krĭm'z'n). Blood-red.

cus·to'di·an (kŭs·tō'dĭ·ăn). Person who takes care of a building. Some of his duties are like those of a janitor.

cut'lass (kŭt'lȧs). Short, heavy sword with a curved blade.

D

dain'ty (dān'tĭ). Pretty but also frail or weak.

dam'ask (dăm'ȧsk). Cloth used in covering chairs, sofas, etc.

daze (dāz). To confuse, bewilder.

de·lib'er·ate (dė·lĭb'ẽr·ĭt). Carefully planned.

del'i·cate (dĕl'ĭ·kĭt). Frail, easily injured.

de·pend'a·ble (dė·pĕn'dȧ·b'l). Trustworthy, reliable.

di·late' (dī·lāt'). To grow larger.

dis·cuss' (dĭs·kŭs'). To talk about.

dis·dain' (dĭs·dān'). Scorn.

dis·lo·cate (dĭs'lô·kāt). To disarrange, put out of order or out of place.

dis·tinc'tion (dĭs·tĭngk'shŭn). Honor, special recognition.

dis·tin'guish (dĭs·tĭng'gwĭsh). To set apart, make noticeable.

dis·tin'guished (dĭs·tĭng'gwĭsht). Famous.

dis·tract' (dĭs·trăkt'). To confuse, perplex.

doff (dŏf). To lift or take off, as a hat.

dome (dōm). Roof shaped like half a ball.

dor'sal (dôr'săl). Back fin.

dou'ble [back] (dŭb''l). To make a sharp turn and almost retrace one's steps as a way of throwing a pursuer off the track.

dour (do͞or). Stern, severe.

drake (drāk). Male duck.

drawl (drôl). Slow manner of speaking.

driz'zle (drĭz''l). To rain in very small drops, to sprinkle.

E

ed'i·to'ri·al (ĕd'ĭ·tō'rĭ·ăl). Newspaper article giving the editor's or publisher's opinion.

ee'rie (ē'rĭ). Weird, causing fear.

ei'der down (ī'dẽr doun). Very soft feathers growing under the outer feathers of the eider or sea duck.

ô, ȯmit; ŏ, hŏp; ǒ, cŏntain; ô, ôr; ộ, sộft; o͞o, fo͞od; o͝o, fo͝ot; oi, oil; ou, out; ū, ūse; ů, ůnite; ŭ, ŭs; ụ, circụs; û, fûr; tụ, natụre; dụ, verdụre; th, thin; th, than.

e·lab'o·rate (ė·lăb'ō·rĭt). Carefully planned in all details.

e·merge' (ė·mûrj'). To come out into view.

en·gage' (ĕn·gāj'). To hire, employ.

en·gulf' (ĕn·gŭlf'). To swallow up.

en·thu'si·as'tic (ĕn·thū'zĭ·ăs'tĭk). Eager.

en'vi·ous (ĕn'vĭ·ŭs). Feeling discontent at someone else's good fortune.

ev'i·dent (ĕv'ĭ·dĕnt). Clearly seen and understood.

ex·cel' (ĕk·sĕl'). To do something better than other people do.

ex'e·cute (ĕk'sė·kūt). To perform, to do.

ex·pose' (ĕks·pōz'). To leave unprotected.

ex'quis·ite (ĕks'kwĭ·zĭt). Very beautiful.

F

fag'got (făg'ŭt). Bundle of sticks to be used as firewood.

fal'con (fôl'kŭn). Small, swift hawk.

fa·mil'iar (fȧ·mĭl'yẽr). Friendly.

fes'ti·val (fĕs'tĭ·vȧl). Time of feasting and joy.

fidg'et·y (fĭj'ĕ·tĭ). Moving restlessly.

fig'ure·head' (fĭg'ûr·hĕd'). Carved wooden head or statue formerly used to decorate the bow of a sailing vessel.

fil'i·al (fĭl'ĭ·ȧl). Like a son.

flick (flĭk). To move something jerkily.

flick'er (flĭk'ẽr). To flap or flutter; to glow brightly and dimly by turns.

flush (flŭsh). To blush, turn red.

foal (fōl). Colt, young horse.

ford (fōrd). Place where one can wade across a river.

fra'grant (frā'grȧnt). Sweet-smelling.

frank (frăngk). Free in expressing one's opinions, outspoken, not reserved.

fran'tic (frăn'tĭk). Wild, deeply troubled.

frisk (frĭsk). To frolic, to leap about in joy.

frond (frŏnd). Leaf of a palm or a fern.

fur'nish (fûr'nĭsh). To equip, supply.

G

gal'lant (găl'ȧnt). Noble, stately.

gal'ley proof (găl'ĭ pro͞of). Sheet of paper printed from type set in a tray but not arranged in page form.

gan'der (găn'dẽr). Male goose.

gar'ment (gär'mĕnt). Any article of clothing.

gaunt (gônt). Very thin or lean, as if from illness.

glimpse (glĭmps). Short, quick view.

gloom (glō͞om). Thick shade.

gnu (nō͞o). Large antelope or goat-like animal of Africa.

gor'geous (gôr'jŭs). Beautiful, magnificent.

gruff (grŭf). Harsh.

grum'ble (grŭm'b'l). To show displeasure or complaint by making a low rumbling sound; to growl.

gul'let (gŭl'ĕt). Throat.

gust (gŭst). Sudden, strong blast, particularly of wind.

H

haugh'ty (hô'tĭ). Scornfully proud.

heath'er (hĕth'ẽr). British bush with lavender flowers.

ā, āte; ȧ, furnȧce; ă, ăt; ȧ, ȧppear; â, câre; ä, cär; ȧ, pȧss; ȧ, sofȧ; ē, bē; ė, bėgin; ĕ, lĕt; ė, silėnt; ẽ, watẽr; ę, hęre; ī, hīde; ĭ, hĭd; ĭ, cabĭn; ō, hōpe;

her′ring (hĕr′ĭng). A kind of food fish, usually smoked or salted. Young herring are called sardines.

hes′i·tate (hĕz′ĭ·tāt). To pause while making up one's mind.

high′boy′ (hī′boi′). Narrow chest of drawers mounted on a wider base.

hi·lar′i·ty (hĭ·lăr′ĭ·tĭ). Noisy gaiety.

hind (hīnd). Female red deer.

hith′er (hĭth′ẽr). To this place, here.

hob′ble (hŏb″l). To limp.

home′stead·er (hōm′stĕd·ẽr). Person who lives on land bought from our national government.

I

ig′no·rance (ĭg′nô·răns). Lack of knowledge.

ig·nore′ (ĭg·nōr′). To pay no attention to.

i·gua′na (ĭ·gwä′nà). Large lizard of tropical America.

il·le′gal (ĭl·lē′găl). Not lawful.

im·mense′ (ĭ·mĕns′). Very great, vast.

im′pact (ĭm′păkt). Hard bump or blow.

im·pres′sion (ĭm·prĕsh′ŭn). Idea, opinion.

in·dig′nant (ĭn·dĭg′nănt). Angry.

in·fer′nal (ĭn·fûr′năl). Devilish.

in·quire′ (ĭn·kwīr′). To ask about.

in·sid′i·ous (ĭn·sĭd′ĭ·ŭs). Sly, deceitful.

in·sist′ (ĭn·sĭst′). To take a stand or a point of view and refuse to give it up.

in·stinc′tive (ĭn·stĭngk′tĭv). Natural, unthinking, impulsive.

in·ten′tion (ĭn·tĕn′shŭn). Determination to do something, purpose.

in′ter·rupt′ (ĭn′tẽ·rŭpt′). To break in with words of one's own when someone else is speaking.

in′tro·duce′ (ĭn′trô·dūs′). To cause someone to meet other people.

in·vig′o·rate (ĭn·vĭg′ô·rāt). To refresh, enliven.

in·vis′i·ble (ĭn·vĭz′ĭ·b'l). Not able to be seen.

irk′some (ûrk′sŭm). Tiresome.

K

kilt (kĭlt). Short, pleated skirt worn by men in Scotland.

ki·mo′no (kĭ·mō′nŭ). Loose robe worn by Japanese people.

knap′sack′ (năp′săk′). Canvas bag for carrying clothing, etc., on one's back.

L

lag (lăg). To move slowly.

land′scape (lănd′skāp). Total area of land that one can see at a glance.

lard′er (lär′dẽr). Storeroom for meats and other foods.

lathe (lāth). Machine for cutting and shaping wood or metal to a desired form.

lay′out′ (lā′out′). Arrangement, plan.

leash (lēsh). Strap for controlling an animal when one is walking with him.

li′cense (lī′sĕns). Paper giving one legal permission to do something, such as own a dog, drive a car, etc.

lim′ber (lĭm′bẽr). Bending easily.

lim′pid (lĭm′pĭd). Very clear.

lope (lōp). To bound along easily.

lore (lōr). Knowledge, learning.

ȯ, ȯmit; ŏ, hŏp; ǒ, cǒntain; ô, ôr; ô, sôft; ōō, fōōd; ŏŏ, fŏŏt; oi, oil; ou, out; ū, ūse; ů, ůnite; ŭ, ŭs; ů, circŭs; û, fûr; tů, natůre; dů, verdůre; th, thin; th, than.

lunge (lŭnj). To plunge, move forward in headlong fashion.

M

mag'is·trate (măj'ĭs·trāt). City official or officer.

ma·hog'a·ny (ma·hŏg'a·nĭ). Valuable tropical wood, reddish-brown in color, used for furniture.

man'go (măng'gō). A tropical fruit.

man'sion (măn'shŭn). Large, expensive house.

marsh (märsh). Swamp.

mast'head' (mast'hĕd'). Statement printed in every newspaper giving title of paper, name of owner and editor, advertising rates, etc.

meg'a·phone (mĕg'a·fōn). Speaking trumpet; funnel-shaped device to make one's voice sound louder and carry farther.

men'tion (mĕn'shŭn). To name or refer to briefly.

mer'chant (mûr'chănt). Trader, storekeeper.

mer'maid' (mûr'mād'). Imaginary inhabitant of the ocean, half woman and half fish.

me'te·or (mē'tē·ẽr). Shooting star.

mil'let (mĭl'ĕt). Kind of grain, cereal.

mis'sion·ar'y (mĭsh'ŭn·ẽr'ĭ). Person sent out by a church to teach religion, usually in a foreign land.

moat (mōt). Deep, wide ditch, usually full of water, around a castle.

mod'est (mŏd'ĕst). Not boastful.

mon'grel (mŭng'grĕl). Animal, especially a dog, of mixed breed.

moor (mōor). Area of waste land.

mould (mōld). Furry, often greenish growth on anything damp or rotten.

muf'fler (mŭf'lẽr). Scarf, usually of thick wool.

mu·se'um (mû·zē'ŭm). Building where one may see articles valuable from a historical point of view.

mys'ti·fy (mĭs'tĭ·fī). To puzzle.

N

nos'tril (nŏs'trĭl). One of the two holes in a nose.

nour'ish·ing (nûr'ĭsh·ĭng). Helping the growth of one's body, nutritious.

numb (nŭm). Without feeling.

O

oc·ca'sion (ŏ·kā'zhŭn). Time.

oc'to·pus (ŏk'tô·pŭs). Sea creature with eight arms.

o·ka'pi (ô·kä'pĭ). Rare African animal like the giraffe, but with a much shorter neck.

om'ni·bus (ŏm'nĭ·bŭs). Bus, public vehicle which carries many people.

or'a·tor (ŏr'a·tẽr). Public speaker.

or'di·nar'y (ôr'dĭ·nẽr'ĭ). Usual, common, normal.

out'rage (out'rāj). To insult or offend very much.

out'skirts' (out'skûrts'). Edges or outlying parts of a town or city.

o'ver·whelm' (ō'vẽr·hwĕlm'). To cover over completely, submerge.

P

pal'try (pôl'trĭ). Worthless, trifling.

pan'el (păn'ĕl). Sliding section of a wall.

ā, āte;　à, furnâce;　ă, ăt;　ă, ăppear;　â, câre;　ä, cär;　a, pàss;　a, sofa;　ē, bē;
ê, bêgin;　ĕ, lĕt;　ê, silĕnt;　ē, watẽr;　ē, hẽre;　ī, hīde;　ĭ, hĭd;　ĭ, cabĭn;　ō, hōpe;

356

par'ti·cle (pär'tĭ·k'l). Tiny piece.

peas'ant (pĕz'ănt). A poor farmer of Europe.

peb'ble (pĕb''l). Small stone.

pen'al·ty (pĕn'ăl·tĭ). A fine.

per·cale' (pĕr·kāl'). Closely woven cotton cloth, often printed on one side.

per'ma·nent (pûr'mȧ·nĕnt). Lasting, unchanging.

per·suade' (pĕr·swād'). To talk someone into doing something.

pert (pûrt). Mildly saucy.

pest (pĕst). Destructive, troublesome insect or animal.

pheas'ant (fĕz'ănt). Long-tailed, brilliantly colored game bird.

phlox (flŏks). A garden flower of various colors.

pi·az'za (pĭ·ăz'ȧ). Porch, veranda.

pick'et (pĭk'ĕt). To tie to a stake.

pi'geon·hole' (pĭj'ŭn·hōl'). One of several sections in a desk in which letters and papers are kept.

pin'a·fore' (pĭn'ȧ·fōr'). Girl's apron.

plas'ter (plàs'tēr). To coat or cover with a thin layer.

plight (plīt). Unpleasant state or condition.

plod'der (plŏd'ẽr). One who moves slowly but steadily.

plume (plo͞om). Long feather, or anything which looks like one.

por'ter (pōr'tẽr). Person who carries heavy loads to earn his living.

pos'se (pŏs'ė). Group of men forming a search party.

pre·cise' (prė·sīs'). Exact.

pri'ma don'na (prē'mȧ dŏn'ȧ). Female star of a play.

pro·test' (prô·tĕst'). To object, argue against.

prowl (proul). To move quietly about as if in search of something to eat or to steal.

Q

quail (kwāl). To lose courage; to tremble in fear.

quaint (kwānt). Strange but pleasing.

quer'u·lous (kwĕr'ů·lŭs). Complaining, fretful.

R

raft'er (ràf'tēr). One of many slanting beams or timbers in a roof.

rak'ish (rāk'ĭsh). Sporty, spirited.

ram'shack'le (răm'shăk''l). Tumbledown, rickety.

rash (răsh). Too hasty, not cautious.

reck'less (rĕk'lĕs). Careless, not cautious.

reef (rēf). Rocky or sandy ridge at or near the surface of the sea.

re·flec'tion (rė·flĕk'shŭn). Image seen in a mirror.

re·form' (rė·fôrm'). To correct or improve one's behavior.

re·frain' (rė·frān'). Repeated verse in a song or a poem.

re·late' (rė·lāt'). To tell or to narrate.

re·lieve' (rė·lēv'). To free from strain or worry.

re·proach' (rė·prōch'). To find fault with, blame.

rep'u·ta'tion (rĕp'ů·tā'shŭn). Fame.

ȯ, ȯmit; ŏ, hŏp; ǒ, cǒntain; ô, ôr; o̥, sȯft; o͞o, fo͞od; o͝o, fo͝ot; oi, oil; ou, out; ū, ūse; ů, ůnite; ŭ, ŭs; ů, circŭs; û, fûr; t̯ů, nat̯ůre; d̯ů, verd̯ůre; th, thin; t̶h̶, t̶h̶an.

357

re·quest′ (rē·kwĕst′). Something asked for.

re·solve′ (rē·zŏlv′). To decide or determine.

re·tired′ (rē·tīrd′). No longer working at one's chosen career—usually because of old age.

re·tir′ing (rē·tīr′ĭng). Shy.

re·tort′ (rē·tôrt′). To answer back, reply sharply.

rind (rīnd). Thick skin of fruit.

roach (rōch). A kind of fresh-water fish.

rogue (rōg). Rascal, good-for-nothing fellow.

rol′lick·ing (rŏl′ĭk·ĭng). Loud and gay, boisterous.

ro·sette′ (rô·zĕt′). Likeness of a rose, as made of ribbon or carved in wood.

rue (rōō). To regret very much.

ruff (rŭf). Fur which grows on the neck of an animal and looks like a collar.

rus′tle (rŭs″l). To make a series of small sounds like swishing silk, leaves, etc.

S

sag (săg). To droop, hang limply.

scald (skôld). To burn with a hot liquid.

scam′per (skăm′pēr). To run lightly and hurriedly.

sched′ule (skĕd′ūl). Timetable, list of events in the order in which they should happen.

scroll (skrōl). Pretty design drawn on paper.

se·cure′ (sê·kūr′). Firm, safe.

se·date′ (sê·dāt′). Quiet, calm.

sel′dom (sĕl′dŭm). Not often, rarely.

ser′geant (sär′jĕnt). An officer in a police force, usually next below a captain in rank.

se′ri·ous (sēr′ĭ·ŭs). Important.

ser′pent (sûr′pĕnt). Large snake.

sheep′ish (shēp′ĭsh). Stupid or timid as a sheep.

shel′ter (shĕl′tēr). To protect, give refuge to.

shuf′fle (shŭf″l). To move about in a clumsy way, dragging one's feet.

slight (slīt). Small.

smoth′er (smŭth′ēr). To be choked from lack of air.

sooth′ing (sōōth′ĭng). Calming, comforting.

splen′dor (splĕn′dēr). Brilliance, magnificence, glory.

sprout (sprout). To grow rapidly.

spruce (sprōōs). A kind of evergreen tree with a pointed top.

spry (sprī). Brisk, lively.

star′tle (stär′t′l). To frighten suddenly but briefly.

stern (stûrn). Harsh.

sti′fle (stī′f′l). To smother, to cause to gasp for air.

stile (stīl). Steps going over a fence or a wall.

stir′rup (stĭr′ŭp). One of two supports for the feet of a horseback rider.

stow (stō). To pack.

strain (strān). To use to the utmost or as much as possible.

stub′born (stŭb′ērn). Determined, willful.

sug·ges′tion (sŭg·jĕs′chŭn). Idea presented in the hope that someone else will accept it and act accordingly.

ā, āte; å, furnåce; ă, ăt; ȧ, ȧppear; â, câre; ä, cär; ȧ, pȧss; ȧ, sofȧ; ē, bē; ê, bêgin; ĕ, lĕt; ẽ, silẽnt; ē, watēr; ê, hêre; ī, hīde; ĭ, hĭd; ĭ, cabĭn; ō, hōpe;

su′per·sti′tious (sū′pēr·stǐsh′ŭs). Believing in magic.

surge (sûrj). To move forward like a great wave.

sur·vey′ (sēr·vā′). To look at closely.

swath (swôth). Strip of grass, grain, etc., cut by a mowing machine.

sway (swā). To swing from side to side.

sway′—backed (swā′·bǎkt). Having a sagging back.

swift (swǐft). Bird which looks like a swallow but is related to the hummingbird.

T

tal′ent (tǎl′ĕnt). Skill and ability.

tan′ta·lize (tǎn′ta·līz). To tease.

tar′tan (tär′tǎn). Woolen cloth with a Scotch plaid or crisscross pattern of various colors.

tem′po·rar′y (tĕm′pô·rĕr′ǐ). Lasting only a short time; not permanent.

tend′en·cy (tĕn′dĕn·sǐ). Natural liking for or leaning toward.

ten′sion (tĕn′shŭn). Straining, pulling.

ter′race (tĕr′ǐs). Flat stretch of ground higher than the surrounding lawn or garden.

thigh (thī). Part of the leg above the knee.

thim′ble·ber′ry (thǐm′b'l·bĕr′ǐ). A kind of raspberry.

thor′ough (thûr′ô). Complete.

tilt (tǐlt). To tip; to lean to one side or the other.

tim′ber (tǐm′bēr). Woods, forest.

tim′id (tǐm′ǐd). Fearful, not brave.

tingo (tǐnj). To color slightly, to tint.

ton′ic (tŏn′ǐk). Medicine.

trin′ket (trǐng′kĕt). Inexpensive ring, pin, or other bit of jewelry.

trudge (trŭj). To walk steadily but wearily.

tur′ban (tûr′bǎn). Hat like a cap with a scarf wound about it.

U

un·do′ing (ŭn·dōō′ǐng). Ruin, downfall.

u′ni·corn (ū′nǐ·kôrn). Imaginary animal like a horse with one horn.

up′wind′ (ŭp′wǐnd′). Into or against the wind.

ut′most (ŭt′mōst). Greatest.

V

vague (vāg). Not clear, indefinite.

van′ish (vǎn′ǐsh). To disappear.

var′i·ous (vâr′ǐ·ŭs). Several, different.

ve′hi·cle (vē′ǐ·k'l). Wagon, carriage.

ven′er·a·ble (vĕn′ēr·a·b'l). Deserving honor and respect because of great age.

vex (vĕks). To annoy or irritate.

vol′un·teer′ (vŏl′ŭn·tēr′). To offer freely.

W

wal′low (wŏl′ō). Place where animals roll in mud.

wane (wān). To grow smaller or fewer; to decrease.

ware′house′ (wâr′hous′). Storehouse.

wheeze (hwēz). To breathe hard and with a sort of whistling sound.

whith′er (hwǐth′ēr). To which place.

wran′gler (răng′glēr). Cowboy.

ô, ômit; ŏ, hŏp; ǒ, cŏntain; ô, ôr; ộ, sŏft; ōō, fōōd; ǒǒ, fǒǒt; oi, oil; ou, out; ū, ūse;
û, ûnite; ŭ, ŭs; ŭ, circŭs; û, fûr; tụ, natụre; dụ, verdụre; th, thin; ~~th, than~~.

359

ACKNOWLEDGMENTS

For their courteous permission to use the following selections, we wish to express our gratitude and appreciation to the following authors, agents, publishers, and periodicals:

Abingdon-Cokesbury Press: "The Shindig" from COWBOY BOOTS by Shannon Garst, copyright 1946 by Doris Shannon Garst. — Brandt & Brandt: "Peregrine White and Virginia Dare" by Rosemary and Stephen Vincent Benét, from A BOOK OF AMERICANS, published by Rinehart & Company, Inc., copyright 1933 by Rosemary and Stephen Vincent Benét; "Jimmy Takes Vanishing Lessons" by Walter Brooks, copyright 1950 by Walter Brooks; and "The Horseshoe" by Edna St. Vincent Millay, from Part VII of "From a Very Little Sphinx" in SELECTED POEMS FOR YOUNG PEOPLE, published by Harper & Brothers, copyright 1923, 1951 by Edna St. Vincent Millay. — Thomas Y. Crowell Company: "Winner Take a Mule" from SHOOT FOR A MULE by Elisabeth H. Lansing, copyright 1951 by E. H. Lansing. — Mary Carolyn Davies: "The Day Before April" from THE DRUMS IN OUR STREET. — Doubleday & Company, Inc.: "Frosty's Surprise" from HOBBY HORSE HILL by Lavinia R. Davis, copyright 1939 by Lavinia R. Davis; "Papa Takes Over" from KILDEE HOUSE by Rutherford Montgomery, copyright 1949 by Rutherford Montgomery; and "The President's Whiskers" from LINCOLN'S LITTLE CORRESPONDENT by Hertha Pauli, copyright 1951, 1952, by Hertha Pauli. — Mrs. Linka Friedman and Louis Loveman: "April Rain" from MY POETRY BOOK by Robert Loveman. — Harcourt, Brace and Company, Inc.: "The Middle Bear" from THE MIDDLE MOFFAT by Eleanor Estes, copyright 1942 by Harcourt, Brace and Company, Inc. — Harper & Brothers: "The Blizzard" from THE LONG WINTER by Laura Ingalls Wilder, copyright 1940 by Harper & Brothers. — Henry Holt and Company, Inc.: "Tillie" from COLLECTED POEMS by Walter de la Mare, copyright 1920 by Henry Holt and Company, Inc., 1948 by Walter de la Mare; "Dust of Snow" and "Stopping by Woods on a Snowy Evening" from NEW HAMPSHIRE by Robert Frost, copyright 1923 by Henry Holt and Company, Inc., 1951 by Robert Frost. — Houghton Mifflin Company: "The Apple and the Arrow" by Mary and Conrad Buff, copyright 1951 by Houghton Mifflin Company; and "Texas Trains and Trails" from THE CHILDREN SING IN THE FAR WEST by Mary Austin. — Little, Brown & Company: "Troubles With a Penguin" from MR. POPPER'S PENGUINS by Richard and Florence Atwater, copyright 1938 by Richard and Florence Atwater; "Old Quin Queeribus" from ZODIAC TOWN by Nancy Byrd Turner; and "Autumn" from POEMS BY EMILY DICKINSON, edited by Martha Dickinson and Alfred Leete Hampson, Little, Brown & Co., 1939. — David Lloyd: "Jiya Makes a Choice" from THE BIG WAVE by Pearl S. Buck, copyright 1947 by The Curtis Publishing Company, 1948 by Pearl S. Buck, published by The John Day Company. — Mrs. Ruby Terrill Lomax: "The Cowboy's Life" and "Whoopee Ti Yi Yo" from COWBOY SONGS, collected by John A. Lomax. — Longmans, Green & Co.: "Duff Strikes Back" from DUFF, THE STORY OF A BEAR by William Marshall Rush, copyright 1950 by William Marshall Rush. — The Macmillan Company: "An Iceland Christmas" from SMOKY BAY by Steingrimur Arason, copyright 1942; "Swift Things Are Beautiful" and "The Cat and the Bear" from AWAY GOES SALLY by Elizabeth Coatsworth, copyright 1943; "The Lion" from JOHNNY APPLESEED AND OTHER POEMS by Vachel Lindsay, copyright 1928; "Faith, I Wish I Were a Leprechaun" from MIRRORS by Margaret Ritter, copyright 1925; and "The Shark" from CALL IT COURAGE by Armstrong Sperry, copyright 1940. —Clifford H. Meigs: "The Pirate Don Durk of Dowdee," "Silver Ships" and "Abraham Lincoln," from Child Life, by Mildred Plew Meigs. — G. P. Putnam's Sons: "Master of All Masters" from ENGLISH FAIRY TALES by Joseph Jacobs, copyright 1902. — Rinehart & Company, Inc.: "Locked In" from THIMBLE SUMMER by Elizabeth Enright, copyright 1938 by Elizabeth Enright Gillham; and "Andy Stands Guard" from YOUNG HICKORY by Stanley Young, copyright 1940 by Stanley Young. — Charles Scribner's Sons: "Duck's Ditty" from THE WIND IN THE WILLOWS by Kenneth Grahame, copyright 1908, 1935 by Charles Scribner's Sons. — Story Parade, Inc., for the following stories, copyright in the years indicated by Story Parade, Inc.: "Riding the Pony Express" by Marion Garthwaite (1949); "The Old Woman and the Tiger" by Mary Hemingway (1946); "Citronella Weather" by Mildred Lawrence (1949); "Knute, the Giant Bullsnake" and "Whitey and Jinglebob" by Glen Rounds (1937, 1946). — The Viking Press, Inc.: "The Boy Who Loved Tools" from CHILDREN OF THE HANDCRAFTS by Carolyn Sherwin Bailey, copyright 1935 by Carolyn Sherwin Bailey; "Little Georgie Sings a Song" from RABBIT HILL by Robert Lawson, copyright 1944 by Robert Lawson; adapted from the original texts by permission of The Viking Press, Inc., and "Water Noises" from UNDER THE TREE by Elizabeth Madox Roberts, copyright 1922 by B. W. Huebsch, Inc.; 1950 by Ivor S. Roberts. — James W. Shearer: "Dogs and Weather" from SKIPPING ALONG ALONE by Winifred Welles, copyright 1931 by The Macmillan Company. — Dixie Willson: "The Mist and All" from Child Life. — Yale University Press: "Comparison" from SONGS FOR PARENTS by John Farrar, copyright 1921 by Yale University Press.